September Wind
Book One

Kathleen Janz-Anderson

ISBN: 979-8-9872130-0-1

Mary Wright ~ Graphic Designer
www.fiverr.com/mary_k_wright

~ To my son Chad ~
"I hope you're working on your awesome piano song Chaddieboy, so I can hear it first thing after I give you a great big hug. I love you and miss you with all of my heart and soul. This world will never be the same without you. I can't wait to see you again."

"To sweet Tesslynn O'Cull, Jessica Maria Lunsford, & Orla Fay Fipps (a girl I knew since age five) and all those who were savagely murdered. ~ May God soon put an end to evil."

"To those who have lived through tragedies and yet found a way to keep going – – Never give up. To those who couldn't… I'm sorry."

Weaver of Fate

'Sometimes'
the greatest tragedy is not the dying
but for the weaver of fate
who stills the call to release chains
that bind
from cherub-cushioned beds,
through the determination of youth
sewing
stubbornly fighting against the innocence
sweet and crimson with love.
And so
while vengeance like thorns of hate
pierce dreams filled
with treasures of hope and honor
the winner is called
The Weaver, the Reaper, the Sower,
the Destroyer

By Kathleen Janz-Anderson

Prologue

Rachael & Emily
1942, Illinois

Long ago, someone said when two souls who share a tragedy have a supernatural connection, it can't be broken by human limits. This is such a time....

September wind carried the scent of wheat through the upstairs window, where Rachael lay across her bed, angry and in tears. Six months ago, she leaped from her bed each morning with so much joy that she would sing out the window in high octaves and playful yodels, greeting anyone within earshot.

But as the long hot summer turned to fall, and with the bustle of harvest coming to an end, her dreams were pushed to the side like dying leaves crumbling beneath feet of ruin.

Her suitcase was packed and ready to go. The only thing keeping her from leaving was Timothy, her freckle-faced, bushy-haired brother who was sitting in a chair at the bottom of the stairs whittling on a pipe.

Blinking away tears, she fixed her eyes on the door.

"You're a rotten traitor, Timothy! And I *hate* you for it!"

Infuriated by his silence, she pulled herself out of bed, trundled across the room, and yanked the door open.

"The train leaves at five, and I'm going no matter what you say."

Timothy glanced up at her, groaned, and turned back to his whittling.

"I… I need to use the john."

"Liar. You went no more'n fifteen minutes ago."

She blew a wisp of blonde hair from her face, stooped for her suitcase, and headed down the steps.

"I'll be eighteen soon, and you've got no *right* to keep me here." She caught his gaze, hesitating for a moment before continuing down. "You'd better let me *go…*you… You *creep*!"

He calmly set his whittling aside. And as she moved past, he flew out of his chair, grabbed the suitcase, and marched her back up to her room, firmly putting her inside.

"You know there's a windstorm coming in," he said, sliding her luggage in behind her. He poked his head in the doorway.

"Come on, Rachael, give up. Lay low for a while."

"I'll never give up. Not ever!"

She reached into a pot of acorns—meant for games and planting oak trees—and hurled a handful at him. He covered his head, taking the steps two at a time as another round whizzed by. One of the acorns snagged an empty tin can at the far end of the hallway and rolled back down. Timothy took the last step and scooped it up. When he turned, ready to fire, she ducked inside and slammed the door.

He sighed and dropped to the chair. "Take it *easy*, Sis."

Rachael went to the back window and looked down where a ladder had been sitting for repairs. It was gone.

She moaned and turned back across the room towards the two front windows. Halfway there, a kick to her ribcage took her breath. She stepped in front of the dresser mirror, opened her blouse, and moved a hand over her swollen belly. Although there was gain around her middle, she was tall but slight, even with a nearly full-grown baby inside.

Tears rolled down her cheeks as she lifted her gaze to eyes filled with pain, to a brow lined with worry, and lips that hadn't smiled for months. She knew if she didn't leave now, she never would.

Shadows from an oak tree, with branches nearly bursting through the left window pane, caught her eye. She buttoned her blouse, went over, and slipped on a sweater lying across the back of a rocking chair. This was where her mother had lulled her to sleep and where she had hoped to do the same for her own baby. She tapped her fingers on the armrest and watched the rocker move back and forth just long enough to widen the ache in her heart. Turning away, she went to the door, released the hooks on her suitcase, and laid it open.

Reaching for a sapphire birthstone ring, she slipped it on, hefted her purse over a shoulder, and went to the left window where her parent's bedroom extended several feet and where branches from an oak tree grew parallel to the roof, making an easy exit to the ground.

She hoisted the window open, sat on the sill, and heaved a leg outside. Looking back into her room, she felt nothing but the grief that waited if she stayed. Her father's anger ruined their once beautiful relationship and made life unbearable. Now the tree that had been a playground of happier days would be her escape.

Ducking her head out the window, she climbed onto the roof, catching a blast of wind as she used a limb to guide her way down. When she neared the edge, she tightened her grip and stepped onto a branch as she had done a hundred times before. One foot after the other, she moved along the branch with confidence that did not wane, did not wane for a moment—until the wind picked up with an abrupt gust and put her off balance.

Her eyes shot up to the curtains flapping out the window, realizing it was too late to turn back. Seconds later, a squalling wind barreled in, ripping leaves from

—

vines and snapping twigs like toothpicks. In a rush to get down, she lost her footing, and her arms jolted from the sudden weight of her body. Her fingernails sliced into her palms as she gripped a branch with all her might. But it was no use. Her hands slipped...eight fingers, four fingers... And she dropped to the ground with a thud.

Silence.

Footsteps approached across gravel, stepping along the wooden sidewalk, over the grass, to the dirt mound where she lay. Rachael opened her eyes when she saw Claude standing above her, wondering if, by chance, he had come to help.

Timothy stuck his head out the veranda door, and two dogs rushed past him and down the steps. He hopped off the porch and went to look around the corner.

"What in the name of...?"

"Think we're about to witness a birth, right here in the front yard," Claude declared, squatting beside Rachael.

Timothy froze to the spot as the pickup, carrying his parents and his brother Steven pulled into the yard. Steven slammed on the brakes, and they leaped from the vehicle—Rupert before the wheels stopped turning, and Steven not far behind, hollering to his brother.

"Don't just stand there gawking, Timothy. Get a doctor!"

When they reached the scene, Steven dropped to his knees. Once he found Rachael's pulse, he glared at Claude.

"What the hell happened?"

Claude stood, lit a cigarette, and tossed the match aside. "Don't look at me. I didn't tell her to climb out the window."

Rupert lifted Rachael into his arms and carried her to the house with his wife lamenting at his heels.

—

"You've gone too far this time, Rupert. You've gone *way* too far."

Rupert took his daughter up to her bedroom and laid her on the bed, weeping, "Oh, Rachael! Rachael! What've I done? What've I done?"

Outside, the wind had died and left a gentle breeze. But within the walls of the old farmhouse, the wail of labor pains had just begun. When the doctor and Rupert's sister Francine arrived, the men escaped to the basement with a bottle of whiskey. Francine gathered supplies and kept pots of water on the stove in preparation for the birth while Martha sat by Rachael's side, comforting her through contractions that continued to come and go.

In the wee hours of the morning, cries of pain sent hair-raising chills through the house and out into the night. Doctor Grant's voice called through the painful fog.

"Come on, push, Rachael, push. You're almost there. That's it! You've done it. You've done it, Rachael."

The room became still. And there was a snap as the doctor slapped the baby's bottom. Finally, wails broke through the silence.

"It's a girl, everyone! It's a girl!"

Francine came with warm water and towels, helping attend to mother and baby. Before long, it was clear that something was terribly wrong with Rachael. When doctor Grant could do no more for her, he took Martha aside.

"I think you should prepare for the worst. I'm very sorry."

Martha went to stand beside her daughter and placed the bundle on her chest. Rachael opened her eyes, and her hand trembled as she reached over and stroked the soft dark ringlets in her baby's hair.

"Oh, Emily, my beautiful little girl. I love you."

Holding back tears, she turned to her mother.

"Ma. Please, Ma. Don't cry when I'm gone. I'll be okay. Just not here."

"No, honey. No. Don't... Don't say that."

"Ma, please... Just promise you'll keep her safe."

Tears poured down Martha's cheeks as she looked down at her granddaughter.

"I will... I will, but..." She moaned and pressed a hand over Rachael's. "Yes, of course. I'll keep her safe."

"And Ma? Tell Timothy I'm sorry."

"Whatever for?"

"Ma...please."

A sob shook Martha's shoulders as she strained to hold back her grief. "Yes, honey, yes. I'll tell him."

"And... Tell Pa I forgive him."

Rachael turned to her baby daughter once again and cupped a hand around her tiny cheek. She smiled, and her hand fell to the side, her face filling with peace as she closed her eyes and surrendered to the waiting light.

Martha brushed back Rachael's hair, and with sobs of heartbreak, she gently kissed her daughter's forehead as the doctor came to her side. She lifted Emily into her arms, took a bottle Francine had prepared, and went to sit in the corner rocking chair.

Tears streamed down Martha's cheeks as she sang *You Are My Sunshine* to her baby granddaughter, sang as the attendants took her precious Rachael away, and sang until exhaustion finally brought her sleep.

Dawn came with gusts of wind that sent Martha to a window with the child cradled against her bosom. She pulled the curtain aside and watched shadows move across the yard and settle over a barn that was old and weathered from the brush of winds. The front door squeaked on its hinges. And on top, a rusty weathervane spun out of control, making the building seem eerie under darkening skies. Martha dropped the curtain and pulled Emily closer.

"A storm is headed our way, my little Bambina. I can feel it in my bones."

~

You have a row of dominoes set up, you knock over the first one, and what will happen to the last one is the certainty that it will go over very quickly. So you could have a beginning of a disintegration that would have the most profound influences.

President Dwight D Eisenhower

Chapter One

Emily age 9
1950

*E*mily tiptoed down the steps, up the hallway, and into the kitchen, scooting past the table to the door. Her hand was on the knob when Grandfather looked in from the hallway.

"Where're you off to?"

"Just checking the veranda, seeing if the dogs are out, that's all."

"The coffee's not on," the old man grumbled, pulling a towel from a shelf and turning back up the hallway.

Emily let the dogs out of the veranda and made sure they had water. In a hurry to make coffee, she fired up the wood stove and put the coffee pot over the heat.

Grabbing a basket, she sped to the barn, to the far corner, and looked down at the baby kittens snuggled against their mamma. They looked so content it was heartwarming. But she knew this perfect little scene would never play out the way nature intended.

Not with Claude around it wouldn't. Everyone knew that he had no compassion for such beings. His motto was that one or two of those hairy beasts were more than enough for any household to keep the mice population down. She didn't understand why he had any say at all about what went on around the farm. She wasn't even sure why he was there. Except, from what she heard, he was the son of a deceased couple who were good friends with her grandfather. Since then, he had been living in a small cabin amongst a grove of trees just beyond the barn.

She knelt and gave the mamma cat a good rubbing. Kidders, a stray cat who wandered into the yard, was barely an adult herself, although she purred and yawned, at peace with her new role.

"Sorry," Emily said, scratching the area around her whiskers. "I wish they could stay. But it's for their own good."

To be sure the baby kittens would be safe, Emily talked her uncle Steven into taking them to town on his way to the market.

Familiar footsteps came alongside the barn. Emily held her breath and watched Claude's shadow pass between cracks in the wall. When he was gone, she set out water for Kidders and went to put on breakfast before the men started fussing.

*A*fter cleaning the kitchen, Emily sat on the front steps stripping peas and dumping pods into a bowl as she watched Grandfather and Timothy crank up the tractors. When they left for the fields, she kept an eye out for Steven, waiting for him to prepare for his trip into town. As soon as he started loading eggs and vegetables into the bed of his truck, she rushed to the barn and placed the kittens into a basket. He was already in the driver's seat when she hurried over.

"What's this?"

"Remember? You're taking the kittens to a shelter."

He groaned and turned up his eyes.

"You promised."

"Oh, all right."

He reached for the basket, set it on the seat, and drove off.

When Steven disappeared into the stretch of trees separating the old farmhouse from Aunt Francine's, Emily returned to the steps to finish shucking peas. It had taken some persuasion to talk her uncle into taking the kittens, and she was pleased with herself for pulling it off. For the first time, she felt grownup. *And why not... I'm about to turn nine, after all.*

With everything that had happened in the last few days, it was a treat not having to put braids in her hair to keep it properly tamed. Emily was seven when her grandmother died. She had been in deep shock and grief, walking around with her hair in such disarray that Aunt Francine threatened it with the scissors. To keep her aunt from cutting off her beautiful locks, she put in her first set of braids that night. But now that she had the right kind of shampoo and conditioner, braids were an option.

The week before, she convinced her uncle Steven to buy a shampoo and conditioner she saw in a newspaper advertisement. This morning, while making breakfast, she dunked her head under the kitchen tap and washed her hair. In between stirring scrambled eggs and turning the bacon, she worked the conditioner in and tamed her hair into some real nice curls. Her aunt didn't complain when she showed up. She merely stopped in the doorway, gawked for a moment, and went about her business preparing for a day of canning.

Not that her aunt had a say in how she wore her hair any longer. It was Emily taking care of the house, taking care of the men as well, except for the times like today when her aunt came over to help can vegetables.

The new pups, Angel and Tokee, began to bark. And Emily popped a pod into her mouth and watched a black car come up the driveway and stop between the barn and the house. The engine knocked several times before it died, and a woman in a red and white print dress stepped out. Her blonde hair was held back off her face with barrettes. And loose curls hung about her shoulders. Emily couldn't take her eyes off the woman she thought might just as well be her mother. It was no secret that Grandfather was so pained by Rachael's death that he did near anything to block it from his memory. Not only his memory but everyone else's. Yet, Emily didn't see any harm in imagining.

Aunt Francine came around from the backyard with a pail of tomatoes they were about to blanch and peel.

"I'm Miss O'Reilly from the school board," the woman called as she made her way towards the house.

Francine stopped next to the arbor, shielding her eyes with a free hand. "You're who?"

"Miss O'Reilly. Miss Mary Jane O'Reilly. I'm from the school board."

Emily stuck another pod into her mouth, wondering what the school board, whatever that was, wanted with them.

"We're told there's a young girl here that should be in school."

"That would be, Emily. My great-niece," Francine said, tipping her head towards the house.

"And how old is Emily?"

"She'll be nine in September."

"You realize school is mandatory."

Aunt Francine scoffed and headed through the arbor and up the sidewalk. "Might as well save your breath. I told my brother long ago that Emily should be in school."

She stopped next to her great-niece, glancing back. "I'll tell 'em you came by.

"But that's not saying it'll do any good," she added as she marched up the steps.

"Tell your brother I'll be back Tuesday afternoon at three," Miss O'Reilly called after her.

She waited until the veranda door slammed.

"Hi, Emily," she said as she walked over. "How would you like to go to school?"

"I would, very much."

"So, um. Do you know why your grandfather keeps you home?"

"Too much work to do."

"Too much work?"

"Yep." Emily raised the bowl. "Want one?"

Miss O'Reilly reached for a pea. "Thanks."

"My grandmother taught me to read, you know."

"Oh, that'll help once you start school."

"I can write as well and do arithmetic…a little."

Emily set the bowl of peas next to her as she talked about her grandmother.

"She even taught me to make cookies when I was three."

"I'll bet they're delicious, too."

"No one complains until they're gone."

She moved the bowl next to her feet. "Wanna sit?"

Miss O'Reilly took a seat and reached for another pea as Emily continued.

"Sometimes Grandmother and I would sit right here with a bowl of porridge." Emily patted the space between her and Miss O'Reilly. "We'd watch the sunrise as we ate. Oh, and see that tree over yonder?"

She pointed towards the west of the property. "That's a sycamore. Sometimes, at night, we'd take a blanket, lean up against the trunk and watch the sunset. Other times we'd lay on the grass and study the stars."

Emily looked up at Miss O'Reilly thinking how nice it was to have someone listen to her again. "I still study the stars. And I watch sunsets too. Only now I watch from one of the tree branches. You can't see them from here. But I nailed pieces of wood up the trunk for steps and cut some branches for a better view."

"You know… It's good that you're creative and have such nice memories."

Miss O'Reilly gazed at the Sycamore. "Sunsets are so romantic. Well…you're kind of young for that." She

—

18

laughed and patted the top of Emily's head. "Anyway… Um… What about your mother?"

"Oh, she died back when I was born. I keep a picture of her hid up in my room, though."

"Why's that? Why would you hide it?"

"Grandfather wants to forget that my mom died. We try not to remind him."

Emily reached into a pocket, pulled out an acorn, and tossed it into a tin can sitting on the lawn.

"My grandmother told me about her."

"I'm sure that was to keep her memory alive and give you something to hold onto when you're alone."

"I do. I hold onto all kinds of memories. Like grandmother's chocolate cake for my birthday. And at Christmas, we baked for days and made all kinds of cookies, candies, and pies. And guess what. I helped her knit socks and scarves for presents, and she made me dolls and stuffed animals."

Emily pulled out another acorn and tossed it into the can. "My aunt Francine comes over on Christmas day and we make dinner."

She pointed to a line of trees at the end of the driveway. "She lives at the end of those maple and pine trees."

"Do you help chop down the Christmas tree?"

"My Uncle Steven picks one up on the way back from town.

"But I get to decorate it. And after, I bake cookies."

Emily wrapped her arms around her knees, nodding towards the side of the house. "If you look out back when you leave, you'll see some oak trees. My mother planted them."

"Oh really," Miss O'Reilly said, glancing at the can of acorns. "And now you're doing the same?"

"I've tried. But I think the squirrels eat the acorns before they get a chance to grow."

"You might want to plant them in an area without trees. Maybe that'll help."

Miss O'Reilly watched her for a few moments before standing. "Why don't you walk me to my car? I have a book I'd like to give you. It's called *Down Our Street*. It has some lovely stories I think you'll enjoy."

After she left, Emily went up to her room. She was about to place her new book on a shelf next to the others when she changed her mind and set it on the nightstand beside her bed. She treasured the books her mother left behind. Book one of the Nancy Drew series *The Secret of the Old Clock*, and book one of the Mark Twain series *The Adventures of Tom Sawyer*, were her favorites. She had read them many times and would do so many more times.

Her wish was to one day have the entire series.

She looked over her treasures again before skipping down the stairs to help her aunt with the canning, thinking what a lovely day it had turned out to be. Aunt Francine was bound to mention that Miss O'Reilly stopped by.

They canned green beans, and boiled, peeled, and packed tomatoes. When they finished, they hauled the jars down to the basement, and still not a word from her great-aunt about the visitor. As they were preparing dinner, Emily found enough courage to bring it up herself. She stood on a stool stirring butter into a mixture of peas and carrots.

"Looks like they want me in school, huh?"

"Sounds that way," was all her aunt said. Emily didn't expect more. Her aunt was moody more times than not and didn't speak unless she felt like it. In many ways, she was like the men in the house. Her hair looked like sprouts of corn stock, gray, and cut to ear-length as far back as Emily could remember. Mood-wise, she was like her brother, Rupert, with a tongue sharp as nails, especially early mornings. The only difference was that Grandfather stood like a mountain next to his sister, and his once-red hair had turned white as snow.

Steven, the mild-mannered uncle, was slightly taller than his brother Timothy, and heavier around the shoulders, with hair brown like bread crust out of the oven and straight as a cutting board against his pear-shaped face. Timothy, who had his silent days, and times of sudden outbursts, was known for his tousled hair and months without a cut. His long nose and high check-bones, much like his Italian mother's had been, gave him a hollowed look. Claude was hefty and solid as an ox with darting blue eyes and hair the color of rust one might find at the bottom of a pail. He worked like a mule for months. Then out of the blue, he pulled the shades in his cabin and stayed for days. Sometimes he gave Emily a look that made her feel like she had just swallowed a glass of dishwater. At times, she wondered why her grandfather kept him around.

Miss O'Reilly's great news prompted Emily to bring out her grandmother's white linen tablecloth. The yellow trim matched the linoleum floors and flowered wallpaper. Even though everything had faded, the extra touch brightened the room and made for a perfect celebration.

Aunt Francine stayed for dinner, and Emily kept waiting for her to mention the exciting news. The men didn't have much to say besides pass that over or go get this or that. It usually took bad or good news to get them talking. A little drink helped, but too much of that brought out the worst in all of them. That didn't happen much when Francine was around. But when it did, she would eye the whiskey, bottles of beer, or whatever they were drinking, telling them they ought to be ashamed for carrying on in such a disgraceful way.

"You're nothing but a bunch of nincompoops," she would say before traipsing home. Once in a while

Emily saw her snatch up a bottle of whiskey on her way out the door, guessing her aunt hoped that would keep the men in line for a few days or a week at least.

Finally, just as Emily brought dessert to the table, Aunt Francine clicked her tongue and sucked in her breath like she did when something important occurred.

"Oh... I almost forgot. The school board sent a young lady over today."

There it is. The big news. Emily positioned herself for a good look at Grandfather as his brows met in a furry line.

"What in tarnation did they want?"

"Emily's supposed to be in school, that's what. She should've gone several years ago, just like I warned you."

"I mentioned it myself," Steven piped in.

Emily dished Grandfather the first piece of apple pie. *School is mandatory*, she wanted to tell him.

He picked up a fork and tapped his plate. "Where's the ice cream?"

"Oh, yeah. I was just about to get it."

Emily set the spatula in the pie dish and hurried to the refrigerator keeping her ears set on what they were saying.

"I suppose someone's coming to pick her up each morning," Grandfather bellowed. "Maybe they'll send someone over to do her chores." He jabbed a fork into his pie, pulling off a chunk. "What the devil does she need schooling for, anyway?"

"Timothy and I went up to the eighth grade," Steven reminded him.

"Seventh for me," Timothy grunted. "I dropped out mid-spring. Remember? Tilling started early that year."

Emily brought the container of homemade ice cream to the table and placed a scoop next to Grandfather's pie. Francine had dished up the men's pie and they held out their plates.

—

"I can walk to school," Emily said as she scooped more ice cream. "It's not that far past Aunt Francine's.

"I know... I'll ride Star!"

Timothy threw his head back and laughed. "Listen here, bright eyes. You take that horse, and they'll send you right back home."

"You are *not* taking Star to school!" Grandfather bellowed.

His jaw was pulsing which meant he was seething inside. But, for once, Emily didn't feel threatened by his mood. Instead, she felt empowered by the knowledge that he had no say in her going to school.

Star had been her mother's horse—a filly at the time—and the only thing Grandfather allowed in his site that would remind him of his beloved daughter. Emily wondered if he thought the breath inside that horse kept Rachael alive, in some way, and why he controlled when, where, and who rode her. That seemed a contradiction to how he silenced any reference to her mother, be it her death or otherwise. But from all that Emily knew and heard from her grandmother, putting reason behind his grief wasn't possible.

*F*ollowing dinner, Emily turned on the radio, cleaned the kitchen, and washed and waxed the floors. If it wasn't for Grandfather's dislike of music—most likely anything her mother might've listened to—she would have the radio on the entire day.

Her appreciation for music came early on while listening to records by Nat King Cole, Bing Crosby, Glenn Miller, and Gershwin on the Victrola. Her grandmother reminded her many a time that, even before Emily could walk, she would sit on the kitchen floor, bouncing and waving her hands to the beat of music. As soon as she could walk, she would whirl and dance around the kitchen and living rooms, stopping to tap a foot and wiggle her shoulders and hips when the music swelled to a heightened state. Her grandmother would laugh and clap her hands, telling her she had natural rhythm.

The Victrola finally broke. But even then, the radio played in the background as they went about their chores. When her grandmother saw that Grandfather was on his way in, more times than not, she would turn the music off.

Recently, Emily had been taken aback by flashes of herself as a toddler peeking from behind the sink curtains in the kitchen. What brought those flashes on she didn't know, and the meaning of the image was blurred. But, what was clear, was Grandfather's troubled soul and that her grandmother appeased him out of love, not fear.

In the Mood began to play on the radio just as Emily was putting the supplies away. Turning up the volume, she whirled around, flinging her arms and hips, adding foot moves on the slick floor, and ending the song in the splits. She rolled onto her back, wishing the song would play again. Oh, how she wished her grandmother was still around to enjoy this with her.

"Glen's a hero," Martha said to Emily one day. *"He put his career on hold to entertain troops. Sadly, his plane disappeared over the English Channel."*

She had looked into Emily's eyes and lovingly brushed a wisp of curls off her face.

"Just imagine all the music we're going to miss out on, Bambina."

He wasn't the only entertainer that touched her grandmother's tender heart. Billie Holiday's *God Bless the Child* was one of her favorite songs. Emily figured she wasn't yet two the first time she heard it. One day while making a quilt, her grandmother was listening to that song with tears streaming down her cheeks.

"What's the matter, Grandmother?" she asked.

"Oh, my Bella Bambina, that song, that came out the same year you were born. It reminds me of your mother and you."

From then on, each time it came on, they would sit in silence until it finished. Emily fumbled with the dial, hoping to find the song again. When her search became futile, she pulled the plug and took the radio up the stairs that was always lit up by a wall lamp in the hallway.

They still hadn't gotten around to putting electricity up in her bedroom. But she had talked Steven into rigging an extension cord up through the wall into her closet, where she would take a pillow, lay on the floor, and listen to the radio to her heart's content. Sometimes she plugged it into the bathroom outlet while she bathed, but her favorite spot was in her closet. The only drawback of taking it up to her room for the night was that Grandfather listened to the farm report most mornings, and she had to make sure it was back down before he got up.

She loved being in her mother's old bedroom—with wallpaper of cerise roses—tucked away like a secret haven in the only upstairs room in the house. A rocking chair sat in the corner piled with rag dolls and animals that her grandmother made. Each night before sunset, Emily would go upstairs and light a lantern. A vent in the corner let the heat up from the wood stove and fireplace during the cold months. It was comforting up there—until a thunderstorm hit. When that happened, she would hide under the covers. If it got too bad, she would wrap herself in a blanket and lay on her closet floor with the door closed.

On the other hand, she was mesmerized when she heard a gentle breeze through the trees, a steady tapping of raindrops on the roof, or a train rumbling through the night. She wondered if her mother had enjoyed these pleasures as much as she did.

There were four windows in her bedroom. Two windows faced the front yard and driveway, making it easy to see who was coming or going. Her grandparent's bedroom extension outside the left window, with a view of a crabapple tree, was a temptation that Emily succumbed to at the age of seven. The day she was caught sitting on the rooftop with the wind whipping her hair about, enjoying herself immensely, was the only scolding she ever received from her grandmother. So unlike her, it left Emily bewildered. But it was the terror in the woman's eyes that kept her from going out on the roof again.

She learned, from a conversation between her uncles—cut short when they realize she was within earshot—that once another tree took the place of the apple tree. Why there was secrecy regarding the tree, she couldn't say. But she had an idea it had something to do with her mother.

Each of her bedroom views were like an adventure to Emily. But the most exciting was the window high above her bed that looked out over the yard and distant fields. It was where lightening crossed the skies, and where she gazed at the moon and stars at night. The window that faced the backyard was where she could watch the growth of the oak trees her mother planted.

Once again, as she brought up the radio, there was a sense of delight and risk in the secret she shared with Steven. She plugged it in, took a pillow and blankets from a shelf, and curled up on the closet floor. From that point of view, with the door open, and if the skies were clear, she could see stars out the window above her bed. At just the right time of the year, she could see the moon.

Morning brought the clamor of Grandfather hollering from the kitchen. She scrambled to her feet, unplugged the radio, and hurried down.

"There it is," he growled as she rounded the corner and returned the radio to its spot on the counter.

"I was hoping to hear a song Grandmother and I used to—"

"You can just as well listen in here."

Yes, until you make me turn it off, she wanted to say.

He pushed the plug into the wall socket and turned to the farm report.

"I'm making bacon grits and eggs," she said, hoping to appease him.

*W*hen Tuesday arrived, Emily kept an eye out the window for Miss O'Reilly. She was up in her bedroom reading *Down Our Street* for the seventh time when a car pulled up. Seeing that it was Miss O'Reilly, she rushed downstairs and peeked around the doorway as Grandfather let her into the kitchen.

"I'm here to discuss your granddaughter," she said, introducing herself.

"I'm aware of why you're here. And I don't know what the rush is. Some people are busy, you know."

"Don't you think Emily's education is important, Mr. Rezell? Reading and arithmetic will come in handy one day."

"Phooey. Her grandmother taught her all she needs to know.

"And there's a radio over there," he snapped, nodding towards the counter. "Besides, we pick up a newspaper every week or so."

"The law says she should be in school unless there's a hardship.

"Listen, Mr. Rezell. She's already set to be in the room with first through seventh graders. You should be excited for her."

Miss O'Reilly unfolded a piece of paper, handing it to him. "These are dates and hours of school, as well as supplies she'll need."

"Supplies?"

"Yes, sir. She'll need paper, pencils, crayons...."

Her voice trailed as Grandfather clenched his jaw and glared at the list.

Emily strained to catch every word. She leaned a bit too far, lost her balance, and stumbled into the kitchen.

Miss O'Reilly chuckled. "Why, hello, Emily. It's nice to see you again."

"Hi, Miss O'Reilly."

Emily clutched her book, watching her grandfather drop the list onto the table and stomp out through the veranda.

The two females exchanged smiles.

Miss O'Reilly went to stand beside Emily, placing an arm around her shoulders. "You're all set now," she said, bending to give her a squeeze. "And please, don't be afraid to let the teacher know if there're any problems."

"I won't."

Emily stood at the kitchen window and watched Miss O'Reilly disappear up the road. She could still feel her arm around her shoulders. The last time she felt something like that was when her grandmother died, and Aunt Francine stood with her at the graveside and slipped a hand on her left shoulder.

*F*or the rest of the summer, Emily tried to imagine what school would be like. She had only seen the building from afar whenever she rode to Watseka with Steven. With less than a week to go, she stopped at her aunt's house for a visit before walking to the schoolhouse to see how long it would take her to make the trip. She yearned to try one of the swings and check out the playground in back, but there wasn't time. Even hurrying as she did, when she returned home, it was lunchtime and the men had come home to eat.

Her uncles were heading down the steps eating sandwiches as she walked up.

"You're late," Steven barked, letting her pass.

"Where in the heck have you been?" Grandfather grumbled the moment she walked into the house. He looked out of place making a sandwich.

"I'll do that," she said, rushing over. She took the bread out of his hands, and he went to sit at the table.

"If you think going to school's gonna change things around here, you'd better think again."

"No, I don't. I... I don't. I was over at Aunt Francine's, and I walked to the schoolhouse to see how long it would take me. I need to know what time I have to be up."

"Before dawn, I'm sure.

"And stay away from Francine's"

"Why? I don't go over that much."

"How many times have I told you that Sundays are enough? I let you go one time, and you start marching over whenever you please. Remember the night you were two hours late making dinner?"

"But Grandfather—"

"Sundays, and that's final!"

He sat stone-faced as she finished making his roast beef sandwich. Emily didn't mind that Grandfather liked everything, just so. Even the yard had to be perfect. Whenever he walked into the barn or the tool shed and found something out of place, he would throw a fit. But he seldom noticed if she did something extra, like paint a picture with watercolors to hang on the wall or fix her hair differently. Recently, she started wearing it in a ponytail. Sometimes, she walked so it would swing. She made ribbons out of scraps to put in her hair, but even the brightest prints and colors didn't make him notice her. On occasion, she wore one of her mother's ribbons. She wondered what he would say if she told him.

Francine wasn't the most pleasant person to visit, either. But even she noticed something different now and then—like just that very morning when she stopped by to visit her aunt.

"Your knees are beginning to look knobby, Emily. Ever notice how bony chicken legs are? Well, that's what yours'll look like if you don't put some meat on."

Her aunt had been in good spirits, considering her usual moods. Although Emily noticed she was acting peculiar, something that had been happening more often. She thought about that as she left, closing the door—deciding it didn't matter now that she would be going to school.

Emily was shocked later that day when the old woman ventured over to lay into her brother.

"You're a damn fool sometimes, Rupert. You'd better stop being so ornery about Emily going to school. It's time you resign yourself to the idea."

Chapter Two

If Grandfather resigned himself to Emily going to school, he certainly had an odd way of showing it. He hadn't said a word at breakfast. Although when the other men left, he lingered in the doorway. Emily was at the sink when she heard him shuffle around.

"Mark my word, young lady. If you fall behind in your chores... Dang it, I'll sure as hell find a way to take you out of school."

She wasn't so sure he could do that. But she worked tirelessly for a week and a half catching up on the washing and ironing. She planned meals as her aunt taught her, and prepared dinner ahead of time, just like her grandmother used to do before heading into town for the day.

Steven bought her school supplies, and she carefully lined them up on her dresser. Several times a day, she checked on them moving them around as if they were pieces of gold. Whenever she felt nervous about going, she reminded herself that Miss O'Reilly would be there.

She tried to imagine what it would be like to be around other children. And the most delightful thought formed into an image of a girl who would be her best friend. She would have long blond pigtails like her mother used to have, pretty ribbons, flowery dresses, and a pleasant laugh like her grandmother's. They would be inseparable. She would invite her over and they would talk and giggle late into the night. These thoughts consumed Emily and made it near impossible to concentrate on anything else.

When the big day arrived, Emily rose before the sun. She dressed and made her bed. Then, kneeling by

---

her window, she thanked God for the special day. After laying out her school clothes, she hurried downstairs.

It was Timothy's turn to milk the cows and her turn to feed the animals and gather eggs. She flew through her chores and hurried back across the yard with a pail of milk in one hand while balancing a heaping basket of eggs in the other.

Breakfast was on the table when the men came in. She poured them each a cup of coffee and went upstairs to dress for school. Twenty minutes later, she came back down toting her supplies in a gunnysack.

"Well... I'm ready for my first day of school," she announced.

She went over and set her bag next to the kitchen door, smoothing out her calf-length, blue and white checkered dress with pockets and trim around the hem.

"Aunt Francine and I made it a little big so I could grow into it."

She checked her left pocket for the two acorns she placed for comfort—if need be. Slipping a hand into her right pocket, she felt the acorns she prepared for planting, with sprouting roots, and wrapped in gunnysack material. Once she got to school, she would plant them just beyond the playground. There were several trees on either side of the school and a row of trees in front. Otherwise, the land was bare, which meant less chance of squirrels messing with the acorns before they took root. She couldn't wait to share her plans with Miss O'Reilly.

Steven nodded his approval, and Grandfather grunted and shoved his cup at Emily. She filled it with coffee and pulled up a chair.

"Miss O'Reilly said I'd be able to bring plenty of books home. Of course, I can't keep them like the one she gave me."

Emily didn't mind that her grandfather and uncles weren't really listening. She didn't expect them to be excited when they weren't the ones going on this big adventure. Steven bought her school supplies. And that was good enough for her.

The men left for work, and Emily washed the dishes and prepared everyone's lunches. She stored the men's in the refrigerator, wrapped hers in a dish towel, and placed it inside her gunnysack.

Once the beds were made, she tossed laundry into the washing machine. She considered that a privilege as she had never forgotten her grandmother having to handwash everything in a deep tub that sat in the back entryway. Not long after she died, the Maytag washer was put in its place. The room was so small they had to block the door to the outside. But the setup was well worth the fuss of having to go around through the front door to hang wet clothes in the backyard. To make things easier during the winter months, Timothy had put up a pulley drying rack above the washer.

When everything was in order, Emily picked up her gunnysack, hefted it over a shoulder, and headed out the door, running most of the way to Aunt Francine's. Twenty minutes later, she reached the white schoolhouse with windows running up the side along two classrooms and a long wooden porch in front. No one else had arrived, so Emily left her sack on the front porch and walked alongside the building, checking out the row of swings. Further down, at the back of the school, was a merry-go-round, a slide, and other equipment she couldn't name. She continued to the end of the building and looked around the corner, surprised to see a basketball court. Steven had put up a hoop against the barn, but here instead of dirt, there was cement.

She walked back to the front of the building and up the steps. As she took a seat, a car pulled up and parked at the side of the building. A minute later, a woman came around and up to where she sat.

—

"Hello, young lady. I'm Mrs. Lupin. I teach eighth through twelve grades. And what is your name?"

"Emily."

"Well, it's nice to meet you, Emily."

The teacher went to unlock the door as children began to wander towards the schoolhouse from both directions carrying notebooks and lunches in paper bags and tin buckets. They were so caught up in chatter that most didn't notice Emily.

She stood and moved to the railing where she had left her gunny sack as several older boys came up the steps. One of them caught her eye and smiled before following the others inside.

When a black car approached, Emily watched intently, sure that it was Miss O'Reilly. But the woman who got out wore dark-rimmed glasses and had brown hair rolled into tight curls.

"I'll bet you're Emily, the new girl," the woman said as she came up the steps. "I'm Miss Tucker."

"Is the other teacher on her way?"

"You mean Miss O'Reilly, the young lady from the school board?"

Emily nodded.

"No, I'm sorry. She worked for the school board in Watseka. But she recently married and moved to Chicago."

"Oh."

Miss Tucker placed a hand on Emily's shoulder and went to the door, holding it open as she gazed back.

"I'll wait out here," Emily said as several children came up the steps and hurried to the waiting door.

A car stopped in front, and two girls hopped out and headed up. Emily smiled at the one with big blue eyes and shiny ringlets the color of maple syrup. The girl next to her, wearing a large pink bow at the crown, screwed up her mouth and nudged her friend as they approached.

"Look, she's got a potato sack."

They set their eyes on Emily's bag when they passed, giggling as if she had dropped it in cow poop.

One of the boys who had gone in earlier came back out and blew a whistle. Emily rolled up her sack to make it smaller and cradled it close to her chest, waiting for everyone to pass before going inside.

Miss Tucker cleared her throat. "Children. Find yourselves a desk. You can sit wherever you like. And I'll separate you into classes at the end of the week."

Emily was about to take a seat when the girl with the pink bow cut her off.

"Connie," the teacher said. "We know you and Sally are in the fifth grade. Why don't you girls move towards the back."

Connie lifted her chin, which only put her eye-to-nose with Emily, gave a "humph," and marched off.

Emily placed her sack under her desk, sat, and watched several more classmates wander in. She perked up when she saw an Indian girl named Haity St Clair, who had visited the farm with her father the summer before. She would never forget those smoky deep-set eyes. The girls had spent most of the afternoon in the treehouse Emily was building while Mr. St Clair did business with the men.

Haity headed straight for Emily. "Hey, I remember you."

"You've grown," Emily said, meaning up. Although it was apparent she had not only grown several inches taller in the last two years but sideways too.

Haity squeezed into the seat next to her. "I'm sure glad you're here."

Emily glanced towards the back, sure she had found her friend.

"Not as glad as I am to see you."

Two girls joined Connie and Sally in the back. They huddled together, whispered, and giggled as they turned their eyes up front.

"They always cackle like that?" Emily asked.

Haity looked back and pinched her eyes into slits. "They're nothing but snobs.

"You Indian?" she asked, giving Emily a closer look. "They don't care much for Indians. 'Course, they might hate you more because you've got more going for you than any of them do."

Emily couldn't believe what she was hearing. It made her chest grow warm to know she had a friend. And with several smiles and hellos from other classmates, aside from the group of hens in back, things were looking up.

Not more than a minute later, a group of boys sitting behind them began to joke around. One of them whispered a little too loud. "Fatty, fatty two-by-four."

Haity's face turned deep red, and her eyes widened. She pulled herself out of her seat, marched over to the boy, grabbed a chunk of his hair, and slammed his head on his desk.

There were howls of laughter as the boy sank down in his seat rubbing his forehead. Haity wiggled back into her chair grinning like a Cheshire cat.

"I'm sure glad you're here, Emily."

After dismissing the children for recess, Miss Tucker stood with her arms folded.

"Haity Louise. I'd like you to stay seated."

Emily wondered if she should stay too—until Miss Tucker nodded for her to leave. When Haity smiled comically, it was obvious she was in good hands.

Deciding it was a perfect time to plant the acorns, Emily went out past the playground, dug holes with a stick, and laid the acorns inside. Just an inch or two of dirt on top was all that was needed. She dusted her hands off, looking around with satisfaction before she headed to the swings and pumped herself up as high as safety allowed. Her stomach lifted into her chest as she careened through the air and pretended that if she let go, she would fly to the stars or maybe right into the sunset. She became so carried away that she didn't hear the whistle and suddenly found herself alone.

Mortified, she turned to see through the windows that everyone was already seated inside. All eyes were on her. Miss Tucker came to the window and waved her in.

Emily tried to ignore the taunts as she walked in. But when she caught the look on Haity's face, a rush of willful defiance made her giddy.

"Just waiting for two *rabid coyotes* to leave," she said, making her voice quiver along with her shoulders.

A number of the girls squealed. Others wondered how they would ever get home. One of the boys pulled out a slingshot and a rock and aimed it at the window.

"I'm not afraid of no stupid coyote, rabid or not."

The class was in an uproar.

"Quiet, everyone!" Miss Tucker said as she marched over to the boy's desk and held her hand out.

"Sheldon, give me the rock."

He stuck out his lower lip, crossed his eyes, and handed it over.

"All right, class," Miss Tucker said as she headed to the blackboard. She exchanged the rock for chalk and scribbled out numbers.

"I want you to work through these problems. When you're done, put your work on my desk."

She replaced the chalk and brushed off her hands. "Emily, would you please step outside?"

Emily glanced at Haity, knowing she had gone too far.

"So, Emily," Miss Tucker said when they stood in the hallway, "did you really see coyotes? They don't normally hang out in these parts."

"Well, no. Not today. But I saw one on the way to Watseka one time."

"Emileee," the teacher said sternly, "I don't tolerate lying from my students."

"I hardly ever lie. But some of the kids are mean to Haity. Besides, they giggle like... Ninnies."

Miss Tucker smiled. "Yes, I've noticed."

She folded her arms and straightened her shoulders. "I see now that you've come, Haity has more confidence. That's fine, but you're still going to have to learn to get along with the others."

"I will."

Miss Tucker placed a hand beneath her chin. "You know, Emily, I had a talk with Miss O'Reilly. She mentioned that you have a great imagination. And, well, I've been thinking maybe you should do something constructive like, well...maybe write stories or draw pictures. What do you think?"

Emily shivered with delight, feeling her dark eyes widen, imagining them as two drops of ink swelling across sheets of paper.

"I've thought of it. I've even tried...some. Once, I wrote about our dogs when they got into a pot of stew."

She pushed a hand into her left pocket in search of the acorns.

"Well, that wasn't anything much, but...."

"Listen, Emily. That's exactly what you're supposed to do. Begin with your thoughts and dreams, or even what you've done that day, like with the dogs. I'm certain it'll come to you. If that's what you really want."

"I'll try, Miss Tucker."

That night, Emily hurried with her chores. She put a meatloaf into the oven, prepared potatoes and gravy, and made a garden salad with walnuts and a side of homemade cottage cheese. When everyone was sitting at the table eating, she waited for the right moment.

—

"I have a friend. Her name's Haity. Remember the Indian girl that was here a while back with her father? So, am I Indian?"

Grandfather jabbed his fork into a fresh piece of meatloaf and dropped it onto his plate.

"What in tarnation kinda question is that?"

He had no answer for her, but her curiosity was awakened. The next day, she stopped by Aunt Francine's on her way home from school. When Francine didn't answer the door, Emily went around to the back of the house and found her piling wood into the wood bin.

"Hi, Aunt Francine."

Her aunt looked around, tugged at her leather gloves, and went back to pitching wood.

"How's school?"

"Good."

Emily went to stand next to Francine. "I have a friend now. She's Indian. Her name's Haity."

"I see."

Emily stepped closer, shielding her eyes from the sun.

"Am I Indian?"

Francine heaved a piece of wood into the bin, took off her gloves, and marched up the steps.

"You know good and well that your grandmother was Italian. Your grandfather is French. And whatever else blood you may or may not have, who knows. At this point, what does it matter?"

"Some of the kids don't like her because she's Indian."

Francine stopped at the door and looked down at her.

"Then tell 'em you're French-Italian."

"But...."

Francine pushed the door open and walked inside, leaving it cracked open.

Emily watched her wander off, set her gunnysack on the porch, and started tossing wood into the bin. When she had thrown in the last piece, she walked up the steps and hollered to her aunt.

"I'm heading home!"

She peeked through the doorway into the dimly lit living room. Even when her aunt wasn't in a talking mood, Emily enjoyed going over and reading in the cozy area with stacked pillows between the wood stove and a bookshelf her aunt remodeled from an old fireplace. She longed to go in and read awhile. But remembering her grandfather's senseless demands, she called out again. When there was no answer, she closed the door, picked up her gunnysack, and left.

*T*he following week, Miss Tucker called Emily up to her desk.

"Beginning this week, I'm giving an arithmetic quiz every Friday morning, although you won't be taking one quite yet."

She handed her two sheets of paper. "Work through these and hand them in by Friday. This will help me decide which class I'll put you in."

Friday morning, Emily turned in both sheets of problems. On Monday morning, Miss Tucker handed them back to her. There was a '*100*' written across the top of each page. Emily didn't know what to think.

"What do these mean?"

"That means you got them all correct. I'm impressed. And I've decided to put you in the third grade."

Emily looked to where Haity sat. "Can I move now?"

"Sure, go on over."

While Emily settled next to Haity, she heard Connie and her friends whispering. She didn't understand what they were saying, but she knew something was up. And when she and Haity went out for morning recess, the girls followed them to where they were about to sit on the merry-go-round.

"Hey, fatso," one of them called out.

They all giggled as Connie put a hand on the holding post and turned to Haity.

"You'd better stop riding on this or it's gonna break."

The group of girls laughed as if that was the funniest thing they ever heard. Emily was so angry she stepped around Haity and glared down at the girls.

"Don't talk to my *best friend* that way! Just leave her be!"

They were in the midst of an all-out fight when Mrs. Lupin stormed over.

"Alright guys. Whatever this's about, stops... Right now!"

She looked at Emily and Haity and turned to the group of girls.

"Connie and Sally. And you," she said to the others. "There'd better not be another complaint about any of you! You Hear?"

Mrs. Lupin was a big woman herself with a voice that carried well. And by the looks on Connie and her friends' faces, they knew she meant business.

It was confirmed, Emily and Haity were best friend. And as the girls' friendship grew, Emily never took a moment of her time with Haity for granted.

Haity was as excited as Emily to watch the growth of the four oak trees she planted beyond the playground. Several times a month, they went to check on their progress. The girls did everything together. And their loyalty to each other gained respect from many of the others. Swings were turned over, and lines were opened. No one enjoyed this more than Haity.

One day as they walked by a group of boys playing basketball, the ball rolled in front of the girls. Emily picked it up and shot a long one through the hoop. She had used Steven and Timothy's basketball hoop enough to know she could do another. But when one of the boys threw it to her, she tossed it back and walked off.

Haity caught up with her. "Go back and show them. You've got to go back and shoot another basket."

Emily just smiled and kept walking.

There were a few cackles once in a while, but it didn't seem to bother Haity much anymore. She would just grin and take Emily's hand. They were like two peas in a pod, and it seemed that nearly everyone accepted that as something good.

"You want to spend the weekend with me?" Haity asked one day. "Maybe we'll hike out over the ridge and shoot some coyotes."

She said this loud enough for Connie and her friends to hear.

Emily was so excited she blurted it out the minute she saw Grandfather. "Haity wants me to go home with her for the weekend. We're gonna shoot some coyotes."

"What the hell has gotten into you?" Grandfather bellowed as if they were planning to burn the house down.

"You don't shoot coyotes for fun. You trap them for fur."

"Can I go?"

"No!"

Emily shuffled upstairs to change her clothes. This was her first invite to anyone's house, and she was frustrated to tears. If only she hadn't been so excited and mentioned the coyotes. Next time, she would know better. She would wait until Grandfather was sitting at his favorite meal or had *just* enough drinks under his belt.

◇◇◇

*S*ome weeks later, on a Saturday afternoon, Haity stopped by with her father. As Emily stood at her bedroom window, she could see that the men had put out chairs and were drinking beer and gabbing. She called Haity up, and they gazed out the window watching the men carry on.

"Now's the time to ask Grandfather."

"Okay. What're we asking?"

"For me to spend the night, of course."

Grandfather had started on whiskey and was at that in-between state as Emily thought of it. During this period, his spirits were high—the same with the other men. That's until they had too much. By their dress that afternoon, razored faces, and combed hair, something big was happening wherever they were going.

When the girls went down to ask if Emily could spend the night, Grandfather was in such a good mood he said *yes* before they knew what happened.

"Long as you make it home for your chores."

Steven, who'd had more than one or two drinks himself, offered his support. "It's Timothy's turn to milk the cows. Just be home to gather eggs and put on breakfast."

Emily was grateful that each Sunday night, Grandfather dished out the chores. Since harvest was winding down, that meant she would have sixteen straight hours to spend with Haity.

As for the men, it was obvious they were looking forward to a night out. Emily wondered if a woman or two had something to do with the way they were dressed and how happy they were acting.

Timothy had never had a serious girlfriend, as far as Emily knew. And more than likely none since she

—

43

couldn't imagine someone putting up with his stubborn side. Still, even with his moodiness, he wasn't so bad most of the time. There was a gentle side to him—like when she caught him staring at the trees his sister planted with tears in his eyes. When Emily was much younger, he taught her games Rachael used to play. One of her favorite had been where she sat at the head of the staircase rolling acorns down the steps trying to land one in the tin can laying on its side at the far end of the hallway. Timothy never mentioned his sister by name, but from everything Emily heard, they were close as they grew up. Sometimes she wondered if losing her had given him an edge.

Now and then, a woman might wander from Claude's cabin. He never invited them to the house and usually took them home early morning—except for one. She had beautiful red hair and freckles, quite pretty, Emily thought. He acted differently around her––until the day the young woman's father stopped by in a rage. After a screaming match with Claude, he grabbed his daughter and left. And that was the last Emily saw of her.

Steven had shown up with a few different women. The last one was a divorcee named Bernadette. She was tall and slender with long black hair, slim jeans, and shiny cowboy boots. It was quite a shock to Emily the night she caught them lying in front of the fireplace, entangled in a passionate embrace. She had gone downstairs for some water. And there, in the kitchen doorway, she witnessed the most tender moment she had ever seen as Steven kissed Bernadette.

When Emily was able to pull her eyes away, she tiptoed back up the stairs to bed, still thirsty, but filled with a longing she couldn't explain. Each time she thought of her uncle kissing Bernadette, she tried to imagine how it would feel when it happened to her. She promised herself that when it did happen, it would be the best moment of her life.

Emily was sorry when Bernadette stopped coming over. Not only for Steven's sake but because she seemed to have a way with all four of the men. The most surprising thing of all was that she wouldn't let Grandfather get by without a laugh. Although, Emily could tell she almost pushed it too far at times. Whatever happened with their relationship, Steven was in the pits for some time. After that, he never brought another woman into the house.

Wherever the men were heading that night, Emily hoped it was all about a woman—one for each of them. Everyone was much happier that way.

With permission for a sleepover, the girls ran up to Emily's room so she could pack an overnight bag. When they walked downstairs, she half expected her grandfather had already changed his mind. She nudged Haity as they walked outside.

"Tell your father we're ready, okay?"

They rushed down the steps and towards the pickup, Haity calling over a shoulder.

"We've got to get home, Pa!"

Mr. St Clair stood right up, and they were driving down the road within minutes.

Haity's mother, Anaya, was a full-blooded Indian. It was clear that she and her daughter shared many of the same physical features. The most remarkable was their smoky deep-set eyes. Anaya was at least half a foot taller than Haity, and Emily expected that as Haity grew taller, she would have her wish to grow out of her baby fat—as her mother called it when Haity spoke of being teased about her weight.

Anaya was confident in her role as wife and mother. She was more animated than her husband, content cooking meals, taking care of the house, and after, sitting in her rocker, crocheting. Mr. St Clair was tall

—

and thin. He had short dark brown hair, a quiet and kind man, tanned and weathered from his work as a farmer who did his job without complaint.

Emily would never forget the excitement of those hours spent with Haity. It was hard to leave the next morning, but she made it home before the men woke. They seemed pleased when they came into the kitchen as she was putting breakfast on the table.

Several times a month, she caught her grandfather in just the right mood, and she was allowed to spend the night with Haity. Each time was a new adventure. The girls were free to roam the property and do almost anything they pleased. During the summer months, they swam, took the horses out, and slept in the backyard. They made cookies, listened to music, and talked until all hours.

Emily woke up at Haity's one Sunday morning remembering she didn't have to rush home. The men had gone out early to fish and planned to stop at the grange hall for a yearly fishermen's breakfast. The St Clairs were going to church that day, planning to drop Emily at home. As they got ready to leave, Anaya asked her if she wanted to go with them.

"I can? I can go with you?"

"Church? I don't see why not."

Emily had gone to church with her grandmother numerous times. And she longed to go again, never forgetting the peace and joy it brought as they sat in the pews singing hymns and listening to the minister talk about God and Jesus. And a beautiful place called heaven. Once in a while he talked of hell too, which could have been frightening, but he made it clear it was by choice—something Emily knew she would never choose.

As she walked into church with the St Clairs, she was overcome with excitement. She noticed several children from school. The older boy she exchanged smiles with now and then, whose name she learned was Daniel Burchett, was there with his family. Sally sat with her parents. She glanced at Emily and Haity with a grin that may have included a hint of embarrassment.

Haity nudged Emily every so often and smiled as they sang hymns along with the congregation. Emily kept thinking that if only her grandfather would come to church, that everything would be different, praying silently that one day he would.

When they pulled into the yard at twelve-thirty, Grandfather stormed to the pickup. The girls were sitting in the back, and Haity crouched down waving goodbye with an impish smile. Emily said goodbye and stuck out her tongue as she swung her legs over the rail and hopped down.

"Sorry, Grandfather," she said as she passed him and headed towards the house. She could hear Haity's parents apologize, saying it was their fault and it would never happen again. Grandfather calmed down in a hurry and came close to admitting he shouldn't have gotten so upset. At times like that, Emily saw hope in him.

Planning for the future, never had a real purpose for Emily and Haity until one day when they sat at the edge of a ravine that looked out over the plains. A geography class got them to thinking about places they would like to visit and where they would eventually live after graduation. They decided the best way to see historical sites would be to ride a train across country. After that, they would settle down in New York City.

Emily jumped up and imitated dance moves she envisioned from an advertisement she saw for *Three Little Words*, and from the movie *Singing in the Rain* that Steven had taken her to see.

"Maybe I'll be in a Broadway production."

"I'll bet you could," Haity said, lying back on the grass and resting her head in her hands. "And I'll open a restaurant and serve cornbread and buffalo stew."

Emily did a pirouette and sank to the grass. "Yes. That's where we'll hang out after the shows."

She lay beside Haity and watched a couple of birds flittering about. "I want to be a teacher too.

"When I'm done dancing," she added, smiling at Haity.

"Then that's what you should do."

Chapter Three

Emily's friendship with Haity began nearly four years ago. Even after all this time, whenever Mr. St Clair dropped her off at home, with Haity waving and hollering that she would see her soon, Emily longed to call her back to spend the night. Her reluctance to ask Grandfather's permission was that it would ruin what they already had.

As much as she wanted to protect their friendship, she made a careless decision during summer break when Haity stopped by with her father. Seeing that the men had left for the evening, Haity asked if she could stay the night. Emily was so excited that she agreed before thinking it through.

The girls made Kool-Aid and hotdogs. For dessert, they baked cookies. Later, they made a pan of popcorn and played *Uncle Wiggily* and *Stop Thief.*

Eventually, they tired of games, and Emily turned on the radio. She had just perfected the cartwheel a few days earlier and now spun across the kitchen and living room floors. Haity tried her turn but gave up in a heap. When Emily did the splits, Haity said that it looked like a piece of cake. She didn't get halfway down before her pants ripped down the middle. They rolled on the floor laughing so hard they cried.

With all the excitement, Emily forgot to keep track of time. When the men pulled into the yard at two in the morning, the girls panicked and ran upstairs, leaving the kitchen in shambles. She thought of the mess as they kicked off their shoes and crawled under the covers, although she counted on her grandfather's inebriated condition to blind him as he headed to bed. Her intent was to sleep a few hours and clean before the men got up.

Emily woke to the sound of Timothy banging on her bedroom door. "Get out of bed, Emily! And hurry it up!"

"I'm coming!"

She hopped out of bed with Haity right behind her.

"No...stay here. I'm just going down to do my chores. Once I'm finish, we'll sneak up the road and wait for your father."

"I'm hungry."

"Can't you wait? Grandfather doesn't know you're here."

Emily looked at the door and sighed. "After that mess we left, I'm already in trouble."

Haity pulled on her shoes, went to a window and looked outside. She noticed several acorns sitting on the windowsill. "Mind if I eat these?"

"Don't be silly. I'm gonna plant those."

"How about some toast, then." Haity turned to Emily mischievously, rubbing her stomach.

"Oh, all right," Emily said with a grin, "but you gotta be quiet."

Downstairs, Emily was relieved no one was in the kitchen. The dishes were under the sink in less than five minutes, the food was put away, popcorn and cookie crumbs swept off the floor, and the games and everything else crammed into a storage trunk. Once that was taken care of, she opened the firebox on the wood stove, added small pieces of dried oak, and opened the damper for a quick fire. She made coffee, glancing out the window every once in a while, hoping, by chance, someone was bringing eggs in for breakfast.

Grandfather walked in from the hallway as she was placing two slices of bread into the oven.

"What in tarnation were you doing last night?"

"Just playing."

His eyes darted about the room. Emily was tickled he didn't guess she had stored the dirty dishes under the sink.

"Where's the eggs?" he asked, scanning the length of the counters. "Some of us are hungry."

"I was just about to go out."

Haity would just have to wait.

Grandfather poured a cup of coffee while Emily pulled the half-done pieces of toast from the oven. Setting them on the stove, she left for the barn.

She was still gathering eggs when the dogs began to bark. Someone was coming up the driveway. She set the basket of eggs aside and rushed outside as Haity's father pulled up to the house.

Grandfather was sitting on the front steps drinking coffee when Mr. St Clair leaned out the window and called to him.

"Just here to pick up my girl."

"Haity? She's not here," Grandfather bellowed as he came from under the arbor.

"Well, I sure as heck hope she is. This is where I left her yesterday afternoon."

Haity came down the steps and up the walk, eating a cookie.

"Bye, Mr. Rezell," she said as she passed him.

She waved at Emily. "Bye, Emily. See you soon."

If things weren't so serious, Emily would have laughed at Haity's confident smile, with her ripped pants and underwear showing through, as she hopped into the pickup and drove off with her father, waving like she always did.

Emily noticed the wild look in Grandfather's eyes and made a turn back to the barn.

"Wait right there, young lady," he said coming up behind her.

She stopped and turned to face him.

He took one last step and swung, catching her alongside the jaw with the back of his hand.

"Don't ever ask to spend the night again."

The next few weeks were grueling for Emily. She was angry with herself for allowing Haity to spend the night without Grandfather's permission. She should have known better. If only they hadn't left the kitchen in such a mess.

Chapter Four

Journaling
A shoulder of comfort when we hurt
A pounding-board for our anger
A vest of strength when we have none
A bridge that leads to healing.

By Kathleen Janz-Anderson

*S*ummer vacation was over and school was finally back in session. Emily was so excited that she left the house early. Once she reached the schoolhouse, she went to check on the oak trees. They had grown at least ten inches, the tallest one coming to her shoulders. Eager to tell Haity, she went back around to the front porch to wait for her.

When the whistle blew, and she still hadn't arrived, Emily went inside feeling uneasy about Haity's absence. The teacher was usually preparing for the day, but that morning she stood in front of the classroom waiting for everyone to settle in.

"I have some sad news to report."

She looked at Emily for a moment before continuing.

"You probably notice that Haity isn't here. Well... That's because yesterday afternoon, she drowned."

There were gasps, and everyone turned and gazed at Emily. She wanted to lash out, throw books, and scream into the faces of those who had taunted her friend. Her jaw tightened until she thought it would break. She looked to where Haity should be sitting. It was true. Her friend was gone and never coming back. She clenched her arms across her chest as tears flowed down her cheeks onto her desk.

———

Miss Tucker brought Emily a tissue, helped her from her seat, and led her out of the classroom.

"I'm sorry, Emily. I thought you already knew. Would you like to go home?"

Emily nodded, and started to leave, but turned back.

"You see... It's all my fault."

"Oh, Emily, how could you say that? That's just not so."

"But it is. If I hadn't let Haity spend the night without Grandfather's permission, I would've been with her."

Miss Tucker sank to a knee. "Look at me."

Emily looked at her teacher, her shoulder's shaking as she wept and wiped away tears.

"This is not your fault. You hear? It's not your fault. You don't know that you would have been with her. Or that you could have saved her even if you had been there."

"But it hurts."

"I know. And I'm so sorry."

"Listen... I want you to know that I'm here if you ever want to talk. Ok?"

"Okay.

"Why don't you let me drive you home."

Emily shook her head. "I want to walk."

"Are you, sure?"

"Mhmm."

Miss Tucker gave Emily a hug as she stood.

"Go on home then and take it easy for a few days."

Emily left but didn't go home. Instead, she walked to Haity's nearly blinded by tears as she picked flowers. Once she turned into the driveway, she couldn't bring herself to go up and knock on the door. The St Clair house was over a mile beyond the school. And she was so exhausted from the walk, and the crying, that when she sat against a tree for a rest, she fell asleep.

When she opened her eyes, Haity's father was standing above her.

"Emily. How'd you get here?"

"I walked."

She sat up, brushing dead leaves and twigs off her clothes as she picked up the flowers and stood.

"Here," she said, handing them over. "I picked them for Haity. For her grave."

"Thank you, Emily. I know that…."

Overcome, he stopped to gather his composure. "I know that Haity would appreciate these."

He brushed tears away, looking around the yard, up the road, and back at Emily. "You were the only real friend she ever had."

Emily nodded, fresh tears streaming down her cheeks. "I know. Me too."

They stood facing each other—he shaking his head, brushing away tears with the back of his hand, and she sniffling and wiping tears on her sleeves.

He looked up at the sky. "I believe my girl's in heaven. I do. I really do."

Emily gazed up, searching the sky for clues. "I bet so."

"Listen, Emily… We're taking Haity up north to family. I'll make sure these flowers are with her."

"Thank you."

Emily picked up her gunnysack. "I should be on my way."

She gazed into his eyes, seeing the deep pain. "I'm sorry."

He put a hand on her back and started walking with her. "Come on. I'll drive you home."

They rode in silence, Emily sitting where Haity should've been, wishing she could comfort him. He parked next to the arbor and she got out and stood with the door open.

"I'll never forget Haity. She was great... Just great."

She closed the door and watched him drive away, understanding what her grandfather must have gone through.

When she walked into the house, the men stopped talking. And unlike them, they didn't say a word as she passed through the kitchen and trudged upstairs.

Her bedroom felt strange with the presence of Haity still there. Dropping her school supplies on the floor, she kicked off her shoes, and crawled into bed, weeping until she fell asleep.

That evening, when the men were asleep, she went downstairs, cleaned the kitchen, and went back to bed. The next morning, she took care of the men's needs, cleaned up after them, and returned to bed. She hadn't slept like that since her grandmother died, but she was grateful for the relief it gave her.

On Thursday morning, she returned to school, ready to defend Haity if need be—or at least honor her memory. Tears flooded her eyes as she walked in and saw Haity's empty desk. Several of her classmates came over and told her they were sorry.

When she sat, she found a notebook made from cardboard, covered with construction paper and bound with ribbons. On the inside cover was a pocket holding a pen, a pencil, and a note. Emily pulled out the note, unfolding it as she gazed around the room, stunned when she saw that many of her classmates had tears in their eyes. Sally was weeping into a hanky.

Tears streamed down Emily's cheeks as she read in silence.

Dear Emily

Your natural talent in the art of imagination is a gift. If you take care of it, as you did your friend, it will take care of you. Use this to create whatever you want. I have a feeling if

---

you use this as a journal, one day,
you will cherish it.

Everyone saw how close you and
Haity were. We are all very sorry for
your loss.

Sincerely,
Miss Tucker and the class

At recess, Emily sat with her notebook on a grassy area
next to the school building, feeling as if the world
would never be good again. She turned to the first page,
pulled out the pen and wrote — *I miss Haity so much. But*
I'm too sad to write about her just yet. She exchanged the
pen for the pencil, closed the journal, and on the cover,
she began a sketch.

Sally came over with Connie and the other girls in
their group. They sat with her, gave their condolences
and said they wished things had turned out differently.
Emily wished they had been nicer to Haity when she
was alive, and it angered her to think about how they
treated her. But she could see that they really were
sorry and were grieving too. Something told her that
Haity had already forgiven them. And it would be a
slow process, but because of their sincere gesture, she
knew that's what she needed to do as well.

That night Grandfather and her uncles still seemed
to be in shock and didn't grumble when she hurried
with dinner and went up to her room. She turned her
lamp on dim and curled up, wanting only to fall into a
deep sleep. But instead of sleeping, she wept, tossed
and turned, and wept some more, waiting for sleep to
overtake her.

Finally, she sat up and picked up her journal and
wrote — *When others grieve for the loss of someone we*
love, there is comfort in their grief. Oh, how I love Haity and
wish to bring her back. As that is not impossible, I want to
remember all that we shared. I'll treasure every moment.

But I can't dwell on any of it, not yet. I miss her too much. My heart is broken.

That Friday, as everyone left for lunch, Emily asked Miss Tucker if she could be dismissed for the rest of the day so she could visit Haity's parents. She explained that going over any other time would be a problem for her grandfather. Miss Tucker told her she understood. And after making sure Emily had lunch, she urged her to go.

Anaya wept when she saw her daughter's friend at the door. She thanked her for coming and continued to weep throughout the visit. Emily did her best to become the comforter. But the woman's grief was too great for her to be comforted. Emily began to wonder how Anaya would ever make it through such a loss. Finally, Mr. St Claire walked in. He was pale and shaken, but with Emily's help, they found the strength to speak of happy memories they shared with Haity. And it was relieved to see that, even through tears, Anaya found enough solace to smile.

Emily went back to visit the St Clairs every few weeks for over six months. By then it was clear that Mr. St Claire had fallen ill. They brought in more help to work the farm. And Anaya spent much of her time cooking for the men and taking care of her sick husband. After he died and Anaya became focused on her new life, it seemed to Emily that she would be okay. Gradually her visits slowed and eventually stopped.

Visiting Haity's parents helped Emily with her grief, even though she still missed her friend every day. Sometimes it hurt so much, that during recess, she would visit the four oak trees where she could have a breakdown without being seen. There was something refreshing about weeping for her friend. It not only brought Haity closer, but it brought relief. Although, she knew from the experience of her grandmother's death that the heart never forgets and that time doesn't always heal all wounds, but the loss becomes easier.

Emily continued to sit in the grassy area next to the school building and work on her assignments. It was more convenient that way instead of taking her work home where it would interfere with her chores. When she needed a break from her studies, she worked on the drawing she started on the cover of her journal. At first, her sketch was a distraction from her pain. She had erased and redrawn it several times until she began to use the colored pencils she received as a Christmas gift—that's when the picture took form.

Sally began to join Emily beside the school several times a week. They talked during lunch and recess, shared rides on the swings, and played tic-tac-toe or tetherball. Emily was glad she had someone to talk with, but she didn't expect anyone could ever take Haity's place.

Chapter Five

1955
Age 14

*The most beautiful love story
ever told is in my heart. It's how
I feel about you....*

*E*mily was sitting against the building when Daniel, the boy several grades ahead of her, ran over from the basketball court. She had become more aware of him lately, that slow smile she noticed from way back, how his hair fell over his right eye, and how he flung it back off his face.

He looked down at her, and she watched a golden wave slide across his right cheek. She hadn't noticed until then how green his eyes were.

"Excuse me," he said, "but us guys," He motioned to the court. "we're looking for another player. If you're interested."

From what she had seen, he excelled in sports and was always the one to calm his teammates whenever there was trouble. She glanced over to the other boys, who looked on hesitantly, smiling and joking to themselves.

"Yes," she said, looking up at Daniel, "I think I am interested."

She became one of them on the court. When the boys needed an extra person to fill a team, they would ask her. Usually, Daniel did the asking.

If the boys weren't playing basketball, Daniel sat with her from time to time. One day, he walked her part way home from school. When they reached his corner, she turned to say goodbye, and he gave her a peck on the cheek. Seeming as surprised as she was, he said a quick goodbye and headed home. She slipped a hand over the spot where he kissed her and watched him disappear up the road.

Her cheek burned all the way home and even more so as she lingered on the steps before tiptoeing into the kitchen, hoping no one noticed her flush. Steven turned from where he was filling a thermos bottle with Kool-Aid. His eyebrows lifted curiously as if he could see right through her. She zipped past him, blurting something about how she was about to bring it out…if he had only waited.

She smiled on her way upstairs, realizing the episode Steven had with Bernadette made more sense now that she had something to compare it to. Once in her room, she went to the mirror and leaned forward until her lips touched the cold glass. Closing her eyes, she tried to recreate the scene she had witnessed from the kitchen doorway, although it was Daniel she thought of.

The next day she couldn't wait to see him. But he wouldn't even look at her. She was heartbroken and confused. If she asked him what was wrong and he turned away, that would even be worse. So, she ignored him and pretended that riding on the swings and the merry-go-round and playing tetherball was what she wanted to do. But all she really wanted was to be close to Daniel.

Eventually, she tired of the act and returned to her spot against the building, doing homework, journaling, and working on the cover drawing. It wasn't long before Daniel came over and sat next to her.

"How've you been?" he asked as if nothing had come between them.

Basketball was her game again. Daniel always made sure she was on his team. Although his personality was more subdued than most of the others, he cheered her on, giving her one of those slow sweet smiles whenever she made a difficult shot.

On the last day of school, they were heading back inside after recess when he walked up beside her. "Makin' it over to play basketball this summer?"

"Well... I *could*." She didn't know how she would manage, but she had to find a way.

"My father sold our farm, so any day's good for me. How about you?"

"Um...a week from Friday. Anyway, I'll try my best."

"I'll be here every afternoon. So whenever you can make it, that'll be cool."

She wanted to meet Daniel at the school more than anything. The thing was, if her grandfather found out, he would stop her from going. It was hard enough to even visit her aunt several times a month. But whatever it took, she wouldn't allow her grandfather or anything else to ruin this for her.

Friday morning, Emily hurried about the house making sure it was spotless. That way, if Grandfather happened to come in from the field when she was with Daniel, it was less likely he would come looking for her.

On her way to meet him, light-footed and happier than she had ever been, she walked around the corner of the schoolhouse just in time to see Daniel make a basket. When he saw her he stopped in his tracks and gave her one of his memorable smiles. She waved and smiled back as she walked towards him.

"Hey," Daniel said, scooping up the ball as it rolled in front of him. He pitched it to her, she caught the ball, and they were off playing as if not a day had gone by since their last game. Emily had seen that he was more reserved than the other boys at school. Now she saw his fun-loving side and that they shared the same kind of

---

competitiveness. There had always been other kids nearby when they were together, and their time alone brought them closer as they began to joke around with each other.

Everything was perfect that day and it was hard to leave him. But when they reached his corner, something about the way he squeezed her hand and said goodbye, she knew this was just the beginning of their friendship.

*T*hroughout the week, Emily thought about Daniel, day and night. His face was blazed in her memory. She thought of the kiss that still warmed her insides and the sound of his voice and smile that lingered long after he was gone. Each night she hurried with the dinner dishes so she could go to bed and dream about him. And each morning she awoke with a smile, knowing she would see him again.

When she returned to school the next Friday, two of Daniel's friends, Joseph and Martin, were playing basketball with him. As she walked around the corner, they smiled knowingly when Daniel went to meet her.

"You're just in time. We're about to play a game of horse."

He nodded at the boys. "They're spending their last free weekend with me before their fathers put them to work."

Thinking about Daniel during the past week had planted seeds of expectation, wondering if he would kiss her on the cheek again and tell her how much he cared about her. With this hope on her mind, she couldn't help but wish they could be alone. Although with the fierce competition, and Daniel's green eyes smiling at her each time he passed by, her disappointment soon faded away.

As they all headed home, Daniel put an arm around her shoulders and held her back so they would trail behind Joseph and Martin.

"Say. I was wondering if I could stop by your house and visit sometime."

"Um… To be honest... If I ask my grandfather, he'll be sure to say no. Then I'll never be able to see you. He's odd that way. I'm pretty sure he doesn't believe life is meant to enjoy."

"Gee, that's too bad."

As they continued up the road, she was afraid that her grandfather's strict rules would dissuade Daniel. But then he dropped his arm from her shoulders and leaped into a ditch. He climbed up the other side and picked a handful of yellow sundrops that grew alongside a fence. Hopping back over, he arranged the flowers as they walked. When they neared his turnoff, he handed them to her.

"They're beautiful, Daniel. Thank you."

His hand lingered on hers. She thought he was going to kiss her, but he pulled back and glanced to where Joseph and Martin were throwing rocks at a fence post.

"You know," he said, turning back to her. "I could walk you partway home, if you like."

Emily pointed to the grove of trees where Francine lived. "See over there? That's my aunt's house."

"Really? That's your aunt?"

"You know her?"

"No. But I see her out hunting now and then."

"She does that…traps too.

"And I'm positive she would say I'm too young for this sort of thing."

Emily considered her next words. "You see... My mother… She, um… She got herself into trouble. And I don't know if you realize this, but she died right after I was born."

———

"I had no idea. That's sad. That's really sad."

"Yeah. Sure wish I'd known her."

"I wish you had too." Daniel squeezed her hand. "I'm sorry."

He glanced at his friends and back to Emily.

"When will I see you again?"

"Fridays are about the only day I can get away."

"So...next Friday then?"

"I'll try, Daniel. I'll really try."

She was determined to make it back the following Friday. But she didn't want to promise and not show up.

When she arrived home, she placed the flowers in a cup of water and took them up to her room. In about ten days, she would hang them upside down to start the drying process.

To Emily's delight, she was able to see Daniel several weeks in a row. At times their basketball games got out of hand and they laughed and carried on like two boys. But after, as they walked to his turnoff, their goodbyes lingered a little longer each time. She began to wonder why he hadn't kissed her again.

No one had warned her about the change that would take place as she neared womanhood. Her aunt attempted something of an explanation, but it left Emily wanting to know more. Especially about her changing emotions. The first time was when she caught her uncle Steven and Bernadette in a passionate embrace. The second time was when Daniel came to her as she sat beside the schoolhouse, his hair falling across his right cheek, and his green eyes gazing down at her. Although it was the kiss on her cheek that sparked a flame she could not subdue.

Just when Emily was about to enter the eighth grade, her grandfather surprised her with a bombshell.

"Don't get all excited about going back to school, because you're not going."

"What?"

"You heard me."

"But you can't do this, remember? I *have* to go to school."

"Well, you did, but you don't no more. I already talked to the school board.

"If your grandmother were here it would be a different story. But as it is, we've got more cows coming in, and someone's building a chicken coop for us. There'll be more chickens to take care of and more eggs to sell. Not only that, but we're expanding our crops."

"How could you do this? You know how much—"

He came at her, and she backed against the wall, both of them glaring at each other. All at once, she wasn't so fearless. She was grateful when someone entered the veranda. Grandfather heard it too and backed off as Steven walked into the kitchen.

She slipped around the old man and went to fix lunch, wishing she had the nerve to tell him how she felt. If only he would sit and hash things out with her. That would never happen, though. He would just resent her for saying the truth.

Now that Emily wouldn't be going back to school, she wanted it more than ever. She would miss English and reading, math, science, geography, and history, anything to do with space or the study of flowers and birds. She would miss basketball during lunch and recess. But most of all, she would miss seeing Daniel five whole days a week.

She thought of him nearly every moment of the day and relived the kiss on her cheek a hundred times or more. She thought of him whenever she was allowed to take Star out for an evening ride, each time, tempted to take off up the road to see him. She thought of him as she looked out the window above her bed and gazed at the moon. And she thought of him when she sat in the sycamore tree and watched the sun set over the ridge as colors changed from yellow to orange and red. It was near as beautiful as he was. She thought of being with him in their spot against the schoolhouse. He didn't always say a lot—just sat there with that woodsy, orange, and vanilla scent he always carried. Her blood stirred when she imagined the *real kiss* that was bound to happen one day—the one she was sure would be with him.

Each day she pondered all these things, deciding not to tell Daniel she wouldn't be returning to school. There was talk of hiring someone, and she still hoped her grandfather would change his mind.

Emily waited patiently to see Daniel. But her grandfather was right. They were busier than ever. The chicken coop was being built, and a truck load of cows showed up the day before. Emily found out that an old farmer had died and his family sold everything at a price her grandfather couldn't pass up. She understood the why, but she didn't like how it kept her from seeing Daniel.

"What's gotten into you, young lady?" Grandfather said when he caught her looking out the window. "The damn stew's about to burn."

She rushed over and pulled the pot off the stove. "Sorry. Thought I heard something."

No one understood why she sulked around as if she were dying one minute and stood dreamy-eyed the next. The truth was that nothing got her out of a rut faster than to think about Daniel.

*W*ithout warning, there was a break in the madness. Emily was so excited she nearly spilled a container of hot gravy she was carrying to the table when she heard Grandfather say that the men were all driving up to Kankakee with two loads of hay the next morning. They wouldn't be back until at least five or six.

After tossing and turning much of the night, Emily leaped from her bed before dawn, hurried through chores, and put on breakfast. Once they finished eating and the dishes were washed, dried, and put away, she filled a basket with a hearty lunch and took it out to the men as they were about to leave.

With them on the road, she turned on the radio and baked a chicken and vegetable casserole for dinner. After storing it in the refrigerator, she headed wistfully up the road to the schoolhouse.

The warm breeze and whiffs of daffodils reminded her of the days when she romped through the fields with Haity. She missed her and always would, although thoughts of her didn't hurt like when the loss was new. And unlike those days, it felt good to be reminded of their happy times together. Tears would flow now and then when she thought of her, but she had finally come to terms with the loss of her best friend.

Nearing Francine's house, Emily saw her aunt in the backyard. And she took extra care not to be seen. In another fourth of a mile, she stood at Daniel's turnoff in the very spot where he had kissed her. The thought stirred her memory and burned her face red straight down to the middle of her chest where it sat like a warm fire. She loved that feeling and let it sit unquenched as she searched the road for him before heading off again.

When she reached the schoolhouse, she walked around the building to the basketball court, expecting he would be there, and disappointed when he wasn't. She looked up at the hoop, wondering how many times

—

he had been there while she was home thinking about him. Continuing across the court, her eyes turned to the four oaks that had started out to be about her mother and became a reminder of Haity too. The trees were at least fifteen feet tall now and had become a natural part of the scenery. Recently, she noticed that some of the students were starting to sit beneath them.

Her gaze drifted back to the schoolyard where the tetherball hung dirty and slightly moving with the wind. She went over, picked it up, and swung a fist, winding the rope around the pole with one good punch. It felt good to be there, knowing she would see Daniel soon.

She went to the swings to wait for him and pumped herself up so high her spirits soared right through to the roots of her hair. When she saw someone come up the road, she held her breath until she knew it was Daniel by his slow, steady saunter.

He called to her as he came across the lawn carrying his basketball.

"Hey," she said as she slid from the swing and went to him.

He smiled and nodded towards the basketball court. "Glad you finally made it."

"Me too."

They reached the court, and he swished the basketball through the hoop. She caught the rebound and hooked one over a shoulder. He was impressed and suggested a game with no straight-on shots allowed— three points gained for a completed shot and one point lost for a miss. She knew his aim was to bring out her strong points. And as much as she enjoyed the game, the butterflies and the longing that had become part of her life made it difficult to focus on anything but him.

When they finished their last game and headed back across the schoolyard, Emily's gaze wandered to the swings. And on the spur of the moment, she asked him if he wanted to take a ride with her. Most of the older boys wouldn't be caught dead doing such girlish things, and she thought he might laugh at her for even asking. She was surprised when he said yes.

They raced to the swings and hopped on, each trying to reach the height of the trees across the road before the other, then seeing who could jump-land the furthest out. They were having so much fun that Emily didn't realize how late it was until she noticed the position of the sun. She hollered to Daniel as she bailed out, telling him it was time to go.

He landed beside her, and they headed up the road slower than they probably should have, slowing even more as they approached his turnoff.

They were close enough to kiss, almost toe to toe, with the warm sun off her back and his green eyes glistening in the rays. Her pulse raced, and the familiar flush burned her cheeks with pleasure.

Just when she thought the real kiss was about to happen, his eyes dropped. The moment was lost. And he flipped the ball from under his arm, twirling it on the tips of his fingers until it flew off into the ditch.

"Oops," he said, jumping in after it.

As he climbed back up, he gave her one of those smiles that always warmed her heart and stayed with her long after he was gone.

They were about to part ways when they heard vehicles approaching. Knowing it was the men returning from Kankakee, Emily ducked behind Daniel and waited for the trucks to disappear into the trees.

"That's my family," she groaned, peeking around his shoulder. "I'd better get going."

They said their goodbyes and Emily left in a hurry realizing she had become careless. When she arrived home, she crossed the driveway and squeezed in-between loose boards in the fence. The men were carrying supplies into the barn and toolshed. And she was thankful the dogs were distracted by their activity as she slipped into the house.

By the time the men rumbled into the kitchen, dinner was on the table, and she was pulling a cake out of the oven. Steven gave her a look that said he saw her scurrying across the yard. Whether it was the sweet smell of dessert that kept his tongue or just a good day for him, she was grateful.

Chapter Six

*T*here was nothing Emily wanted more than to be with Daniel. Each time they met, her feelings for him deepened. Whether she was gardening, canning, washing clothes, or cooking—or whether she was feeding animals or bringing in eggs from the barn, thoughts of him made life easier. Not much got her down for long except the thought of something stopping her from seeing him.

Now that she had someone in her life again, even the men's quarrels didn't upset her quite as much as they used to—not even Tuesday morning's doozy of a brawl. It started during breakfast.

"That damn tractor's ticking like an old washing machine," Timothy grumbled as he pushed his plate aside.

Grandfather had already eaten and was on his third toothpick when he freshened his coffee and wandered outside. Steven was leaning against the counter where he usually had his first and last cup of coffee each morning.

"I dropped the oil pan last night. Looks like the bearings are out."

Timothy was hunched over, tying his shoelaces. "Damn you, Steven, you shudda told me."

"Didn't know till last night, ya ninny."

Timothy yanked his pants over his shoes and snapped his fingers. "I asked you about it a week ago. Now what do I do?"

"Oh, crap. Take the John Deere. There's plenty else I can do."

Emily tried to keep her mind elsewhere, although it wasn't easy to ignore their taunts and lashings. When she saw the men were taking their argument outside, she darted over, opened the door for them, and practically shooed them out.

Once the kitchen was clean, she went out to the barn to begin the preparations for making cottage cheese. She placed a pail under a cow and sank to a stool. It had been forty minutes since the men had walked out of the house. Forty, *wonderful*, and uninterrupted minutes of fantasizing about Daniel. She sighed leaned her head against the cow, closed her eyes, and imagined Daniel's arms folding around her and her lips rising to meet his.

"Emily! Watch what you're *doing*," Steven hollered, standing over her with a bale of hay set on a shoulder.

She straightened, lowering her gaze to a puddle of milk in the lap of her skirt. Shaking it out, she made the proper adjustments and went back to milking. She couldn't imagine what he thought catching her with her lips out like a baby bird begging for a meal. At least it was him and not anyone else. Although she had a growing need to tell Daniel how much she cared about him, she had no desire to spread the news.

That night she propped herself up in bed, opened her journal, and poured out her heart to Daniel in a letter. When she finished, she read it through. She didn't go as far as to tell him she loved him. But what she revealed was enough to make her wonder if she dared give it to him.

Friday rolled around with the anticipation of seeing Daniel—until Francine showed up with empty jars and a sack of lids. They went out to the garden, picked cucumbers and canned them. When they finished, they butchered chickens. They made lunch for the men— which Emily ran out to them. It was late afternoon by the time they finished storing the jars of pickles in the basement and putting the last of the chickens into the freezer. Like usual, after a long day, Francine would stay for dinner.

They were in the kitchen making chicken and dumplings when Emily made up her mind to ask her aunt about her parents. This wasn't the first time she tried. A few months ago, when Emily pressed her, she admitted that her parents were never married. And that Rachael's pregnancy was kept a secret. Her aunt had been out-of-sorts that day, acting peculiar, if not strange. And after the comment, she seemed stunned by her spill and clammed up.

"Aunt Francine. Were my parents in love?"

"Now what brought that on?" Francine snapped as she hacked the wings off a chicken.

"I have a right to know about my parents."

Francine threw the carving knife into the sink and turned to Emily. "What if your grandfather walked in. You should know by now that nothing gets him angrier than being reminded of what he lost. Sometimes we just have to accept what's done, and let it be. Now, I don't want to hear another word about it. Your parents are gone and that's that.

For the first time, Emily realized her grandfather wasn't the only one who hadn't dealt with her mother's death.

*A*fter another fourteen-day stretch of not seeing Daniel, Emily was finally on her way to the schoolhouse, earlier than usual, and thankful she got away. Her stomach was in knots, afraid he had given up on her this time. As she passed his turnoff, she glanced that way seeing only plumes of rising dust and a few tumbleweeds drifting across the road.

When she reached the schoolhouse, she headed for the swings to watch for him. Halfway there, she thought she heard something and stopped to listen. From the back came the steady thump, thump, thump of a basketball. She rushed around the building. And when Daniel saw her, he grinned and stuck the ball under an arm, flicking his hair back.

"Decided to finally make it, huh?"

"I did my best. You're early," she added, aching with the memory of missing him. She wanted to fling her arms around him.

He pulled the ball from under his arm and made a shot through the hoop. They played their usual games as they bantered back and forth. But something had changed for her. She wasn't even sure what it was, although she had felt it coming on for a while. It was just that when he brushed against her, she felt a mixture of elation, frustration, and at the same time, weak from wanting him near. Finally, she became so overwhelmed she caught a rebound and walked off.

"Hey, where you going?"

She bolted across the grass and drop-kicked the ball towards the swings. "Last one over is a dead rat!"

He shot past her, already on a swing when she got there. She hopped on next to him and pumped her swing up.

"I let you win," she teased.

The wind caught her breath, and she squealed, happy that he was willing to share this experience with her. She loved the laughing and joking as they flew back and forth, sometimes touching fingers as they passed, other times gliding together to exhilarating heights.

When the sun hit the mark, her heart dropped, and she stopped her swing and stood.

"It's time for me to go."

He jumped off his swing and retrieved the ball. Tucking it under an arm, he took her hand, and they started up the road. At his turn-off, he leaned over and kissed her cheek.

"See you next week," he said, turning for home.

She smiled and watched him walk away, hoping he wouldn't regret the kiss this time.

"Hey Daniel. I probably won't make it until the week after."

He stopped and looked back. "See you in two weeks then?"

"Yep, week after next."

As he continued up the road, she called to him once more.

"I'll be in the sycamore tree at sunset! And I'll be thinking about you!"

He swung around, walking backward with a smile winding up his cheeks. "I'll be at my bedroom window! And I'll be thinking about you too!"

Any doubts she had about Daniel, disappeared. She was certain that the something stirring inside of her was also stirring inside of him. Nothing was going to get her down these next two weeks.

Everything was just as she promised herself it would be. Every meal she cooked, every floor she washed, and every trip to the barn didn't seem like a chore because it would lead her back to him.

*E*mily took two loafs of bread out of the oven, set them on top of the stove and went to stand by the window. It had only been three days since she had seen Daniel. But she missed him so much it hurt. Until now, she never knew a heart could ache in this way. The remarkable thing was that all she needed to do in order to end the pain was to go see him. What a simple solution.

She looked around at the clock. If she hurried, she could be there and back within an hour. She untied her apron, laid it across a chair, and slipped out of the house, moving at a clip up the driveway.

"Where you goin' Mud," Claude taunted from outside the tool shed.

Her gaze drifted to a patch of flowers. She strolled onto the grassy area and nonchalantly began to pick dandelions, giving him a glance that said, s*ee? Just picking flowers.*

She hated the way he looked at her sometimes. If she could help it, she stayed clear of him, especially when he was drinking.

When he walked into the shed, she threw the dandelions aside and plodded back to the house. She put her apron back on, emptied the loaves of bread onto the stove, and washed the pans and baking utensils.

That she was so close to seeing Daniel and denied the opportunity ate at her. Things would be much easier if Grandfather would allow her to see him.

"Haven't you ever been in love, Grandfather?"

She walked to the window and watched Claude head back to the fields. Friday seemed like an eternity away. It made no sense that she couldn't run over and see Daniel—even if for a few minutes. The men would be gone for a number of hours. And she was caught up on her work. Well, except for cleaning the stalls—since the men were too busy to do it themselves.

Doggonit. The stalls can wait.

Once Emily put her mind to seeing Daniel, there was no stopping her. If someone tried to stop her, she would make something up. Like... Well... She would claim an urgent need to see Aunt Francine. Female stuff...something that would shock the men to silence.

With such determination, Emily believed she could pull it off. She ran upstairs, paged through her journal and carefully ripped out the letter she wrote to Daniel. Rushing down to the kitchen, she tossed her apron onto the table, folded the letter into her skirt pocket, and zipped through the veranda and down the steps. She checked for Claude as she sped across the lawn and ducked through the fence. Once she reached the trees, she ran full speed, passing her aunt's house, not even looking to see if she was outside. If it ever came up, she would think of something.

She was out of breath as she rounded the back corner of the school building. Resting her hands on her knees and panting for air, she smiled up at Daniel. Stuart, one of the young men who came around now and then, was shooting baskets with him.

Daniel threw the ball to him and walked over to Emily, laughing.

"Are you okay?"

Still catching her breath, she took his arm and pulled him around to the side of the schoolhouse. "I needed to see you."

"Come," he said, taking her hand and leading her to the front steps where they sat.

"I can't believe you're here."

"Honestly, I shouldn't be. And I have to get right back. But...."

She reached into a pocket and pulled out the letter, handing it to him. "I wrote it a while back. Got the notion all of a sudden to give it to you. Only wait until tonight to read it."

He turned the folded letter over in his hands and slipped it into a pocket, giving it a pat. "I'll keep it forever.

"Say," he said, nodding over a shoulder. "How 'bout a short game?"

"I would. But I have to get home before my grandfather finds out I left."

He sighed, looking so disappointed that she leaned over and kissed his cheek. "See you Friday."

She stood, and he took her hand, letting it slip from his as she turned and jogged up the sidewalk. At the road she waved and sprinted homeward.

When she plowed around the tree line and towards the house, the dogs ran to greet her, barking and making a fuss. She scanned the area, making sure the men weren't around.

The house was still when she walked in. She cut a slice of bread, smothered it with honey and went to sit on the front porch. If only her grandfather could see her side of things. But he never would. And it was a shame she couldn't tell him that an on-the-spur-of-the-moment decisions like running to meet Daniel didn't hurt anyone. In fact, it made for a wonderful day. She brushed off her hands, jumped up and went to change so that she could have the stalls cleaned before the men returned home.

Once Emily realized that she was in love with Daniel, she understood the yearning and fluttering of her heart whenever he was near. She understood the wanting to know everything about him. And that there was nothing she wouldn't do for him.

Chapter Seven

Age 14-17

They Leave a Mark

Some come to encourage
they bring words of wisdom

Some come
with a gift of love
they bring hope and peace

Others come
like clouds of darkness
they damage and scar, and take...

Kathleen Janz-Anderson

No matter how many hours Emily gave taking care of the men, how much she loved or sacrificed, it didn't stop evil from coming into her life. Only days before she was to see Daniel and tell him that she loved him, everything changed. Her life, her thoughts, her hopes, and even her dreams would never be the same.

She was up in the hayloft just before dusk playing with a new batch of kittens she was hiding from Claude when he found her. The weight of his body took her to the floor before she knew what happened. A sweaty hand over her mouth muffled her screams.

How she made it back to the house without making a scene, she couldn't say. Early the next morning, she awoke to a damp pillowcase against her cheek and an unfamiliar ache in the pit of her stomach. She yanked the covers back and saw that blood had seeped onto the sheets. Scooting off the bed, she ripped her clothes off, pulled on a bathrobe, carried everything downstairs, and dumped the bundle into the washer.

Mist filled the bathroom as she sat in the tub with her arms around her knees, weeping and recalling the horror, the pain, and humiliation. Why she had seen something in Claude that her grandfather and uncles had missed she wasn't sure. She thought of when her grandmother was dying and started to read Proverbs to her. After finishing one day, she told Emily that she had a gift. And that when she heard bells go off in her head, she should listen to them. Well...she was listening but had no idea what to do. Claude would find her again—he said as much—his warning not to tell anyone made sure of that.

*A*s difficult as it was going about her chores, ignoring Claude, and acting as if nothing had happened, it was the thought of Daniel that kept her from falling apart. She imagined that if she confided in him, he would hold her close with his gangly arms and promise her no one would ever hurt her again. Daniel, with his gentle heart would make things better. Only, she could never tell him. He would be hurt and angry and may try to defend her and have to deal with the consequences. She could never do that to him.

On her way to see Daniel, she was determined not to dwell on what happened. When she neared his turn off, she saw him coming up the road twirling his basketball on the tips of his fingers.

She waved at him. "You're getting really good at that!"

He bit his bottom lip and gave her an even better show. As he approached, he put the basketball under an arm and took her hand.

She did her best to stay upbeat that day. They played basketball, took a ride on the swings, then sat on the grass.

He laid back and pulled her down beside him. She rested her head on his shoulder wishing she could tell him everything, and at the same time, relieved she had the courage not to.

"That letter you wrote me. It's the most beautiful thing I've ever read."

"I meant every word."

The weight on her chest, the ache of wanting to forget, and the longing to embrace the excitement of what they were building was bittersweet. But she knew that he knew she was no longer the carefree girl who gave him that letter only days before. She tried her best to stay positive.

"Emily. Tell me what's wrong."

"I'm fine. It's probably just a cold coming on."

Later, as they parted at his road, he hugged her. "Hope you feel better soon."

"I'll be okay. Oh, and… Just to let you know. My aunt informed me that starting Monday we'd be harvesting and canning vegetables for the next couple of weeks."

Daniel looked up the road thoughtfully. "Well… Don't forget. I'm at the basketball court every day. Any time after lunch."

She knew he was concerned about her when they parted that day. In a way, she was glad the harvest and canning would keep her busy for the next few weeks. It would give her time to adjust and to feel normal again.

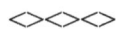

*E*ach time Emily crossed paths with Claude, she did her best to ignore him. He seemed to be ignoring her as well. Still, it would ease her mind if he apologized and promised it would never happen again. That wasn't likely, though. And the least she could hope for was that he felt half as bad about what happened as she did.

She thought about going to talk to Aunt Francine about what happened. Her embarrassment wasn't the only thing that stopped her. Some of it had to do with her fear of the response she would receive. A while back, when her aunt was in one of her odd moods and stumbled through a talk about what happens between a man and a woman on their wedding night, she mentioned something that caused Emily even more confusion on the subject. What struck her the most was when Francine explained that men are different by nature and have ways about them that call for understanding and prudence from a young woman.

For days after her aunt's rambling, Emily had never longed so much for the mother she never had or for the grandmother that was taken from her. They would have helped her through anything without hints of blame.

Thankfully, as the weeks passed, it became easier not to think about Claude's attack on her. Her mind was set on Daniel and forgetting that horrible day. Picking corn, and carrots, peeling, slicing, canning, and hauling jars to the basement and cleaning up afterward kept her busy. But it never stopped her from thinking about Daniel. If nothing else, their time apart made her love him even more.

She knew that school would start soon, and when fall and winter came, a number of things would change. Not only would it get dark earlier, but the men would be around the house more, maybe not in the house, but near enough to where they would notice if she left. She had to prepare herself.

Things were ramping up for the flood of activity that was about to happen around the farm. But for the next two weeks, she was thrilled about the time she would be able to spend with Daniel.

—

That Friday, the men took another trip to Kankakee. And Emily was on her way to see Daniel feeling like her old self again. When she arrived at the school, things had livened up. Some of the students had come back from vacation and were meeting at the school. Sally brought her little sister and young friend along to swing and play on the merry-go-round. And even though Sally had a hard time even dribbling the ball, she joined in the basketball games. Her bumbling attempts to make baskets had everyone roaring with laughter. It was all in good fun, but the best part of the day for Emily was the excitement that everyone saw Daniel as her boyfriend.

There wasn't as much time alone with him as before, but more than ever, he made the world right. Her heart was filled with so much love for him that she didn't think anything could take that joy from her.

When she arrived at the schoolhouse the following week. Stuart, several older students, and two girls, who turned out to be visiting cousins, were playing basketball with Daniel. As Emily approached, someone threw the ball at her, and an exhilarating rival game ensued. Throughout the games, Daniel would touch her hand as he passed by and give her that sweet smile of his that left her quivering with anticipation. As the last game was winding down, Emily took Daniel's hand and led him to the oak trees.

"Say, um... Did you know I planted these?"

"You did?"

"The first day I came to school."

"Weren't you about ten? What made you decide to plant them?"

"I was nine. And it was my mother's influence. She used to plant oaks."

Daniel looked up through the branches. "Of course, as they started growing I noticed them. But I thought the school had decided to spruce up the place.

"What do you do, just bury the acorns?"

"Pretty much. But the planting doesn't always take. And you know, they won't make acorns until they're twenty years old. Can you believe it? But then again, some of them live for over a thousand years."

"Mm. Such interesting facts. I haven't spent much time around oaks but I suddenly have a new respect for them.

"I'm glad you planted these. It's like you left your mark."

"I never thought of it like that. But thanks. Only for me, they're a tribute to my mother and Haity."

Emily knew it was time to go, but being with Daniel under the oak, it was hard to end the day. He brushed strands of hair off her face. And when she gazed into his eyes, she would have surely been late arriving home if not for the others nearby.

Daniel was considerate of the rules her grandfather put on her. And he took her hand as they headed for the road, trailing behind the others. When they all reached the turnoff, Stuart hollered to Emily.

"I'm inviting everyone to my house for ice cream. I'd like you to come too."

"Oh... I wish I could. And thanks. But I'm expected home."

She looked at Daniel, thinking how nice it would be to go along, already missing him so much it hurt.

"We have chicks coming next week," she said, trying to cover her disappointment.

"Oh, really. That sounds like fun."

"I'm looking forward to it.

"Lots of things are happening. So...if I can't make it next Friday. I'll really try the following week.

"I'll miss you," she added quietly.

"I'll miss you too."

The others were heading up the road, and someone called out.

"You coming, Daniel?"

Daniel glanced over a shoulder and back to Emily. "I should go. But I'll see you soon," he said, squeezing her hand.

Emily watched them walk up the road with a lump in her throat, forcing back tears. He had left her there many times before. And she wasn't sure why this day hit harder than the rest, except that she longed to go with them.

A few hours before the baby chicks arrived, Emily turned on the heat lamp and made sure the space was ready for them to stay for the next six or seven weeks. She prepared the area for when they had grown feathers and were taken to the other side of the chicken coop. Once that happened, another load of baby chicks would arrive.

At first, Emily was angry and resentful that she couldn't get away to see Daniel. She missed him terribly. But she couldn't deny her delight when she was told the responsibility of caring for the chickens would be all hers.

The chickens arrived in a frenzy of excitement that was more of a fun and learning experience than work. Sometimes she had to pull herself away to do her other chores. And Grandfather scolded her several times for her rush to see the chicks, but things settled once she grasped the obstacles of her new role.

She had been so busy that she spent very little time thinking about Claude. He came to the house to eat now and then but they barely spoke. She believed that with time she would forget the loft incident ever happened. And she was happy to move on.

*A*t last, the day arrived for Emily to see Daniel again. She got up early, did her chores, peeled potatoes, and cut up chicken for that night's dinner so she wouldn't have to rush back.

The men had lagged with their coffee after breakfast so she was running late. And to make things even worse, clouds were moving in and she heard a distance rumble of thunder as she hurried to meet Daniel. She hoped the rain would hold out so the men wouldn't arrive home before she did.

Since she was late, she didn't expect to see Daniel at his turnoff. And when she saw him coming up the road, she was surprised he wasn't carrying his basketball. He smiled at her, but it wasn't the same.

Instead of taking her hand, he slipped an arm around her shoulders as they walked to the schoolhouse. Their silence wasn't unusual for them. They were comfortable being together whether they talked or not. But this was different.

They neared the school, and Daniel led her to their spot against the building and sat. She slid down beside him, thinking this was a good time for them to discuss their future.

"I missed you, Daniel."

"Me too," he said, attempting a smile.

Oh, Daniel, I love you, she wanted to say.

A blond curl fell over his right eye, and she brushed it back.

"This is where it all began, remember?"

He looked over at the empty court. "I do. I'm not sure if I was more excited or nervous that day."

"Was it your idea that I join you guys?"

"No. But I volunteered to ask."

Daniel tapped her foot with his. "I noticed you long before."

There was a pained expression on his face. He seemed restless. And when he sighed, Emily was sure something was bothering him.

For a moment, it seemed he was about to tell her what was on his mind. Instead, he got up and headed to the swings.

Emily jumped up and followed him. *"Daniel."*

He stopped, waited for her to catch up, and took her hand. The gesture felt that of *love*, although his eyes were downcast. She wasn't sure, but it seemed he may have been brushing away tears. As much as she wanted to ask him what was wrong, she was afraid of what his answer would be.

Once they were on the swings, she hoped their usual lighthearted merriment would turn things around. If there wasn't an art form in swinging, she was sure their collaborating freeform made it so, never going past the limit where they would go over the bar, but higher than any teacher would allow. This day Daniel brought an intensity she had never seen before, and much higher than normal.

"Not so high, Daniel!"

All at once, he bailed out and landed on the grass several feet beyond the dirt. She stopped her swing and ran over dropping to her knees beside him.

"Daniel. Please tell me what's wrong."

He lay back on the grass with his arms cradling his head, staring at the rolling clouds above. She settled beside him and placed her head on his shoulder. He slipped an arm around her.

"We're moving to South Carolina. My father and I are leaving with a truckload on Sunday. That's why I was late. We're loading up."

Emily sat up. "But you can't! I thought we were—"

"I told you we sold the farm."

She moved to her knees and glared down at him. "You can't go. You can't leave me! You, ca…."

—

Her voice broke as tears streamed down her cheeks.

He bit his bottom lip, his eyes narrowing, staring straight up, not at her. This made her so angry she sprang to her feet, went over and heaved herself on a swing, pumping higher than she had ever been.

Daniel jumped up and darted over. "Come on now! Slow down!"

She didn't care if she went over. In fact, she hoped she would.

"I'm sorry, Emily. I don't want to go. I thought you knew I'd be moving."

"Makes no difference now, does it… Daniel!"

No words would stop the pain. Begging wouldn't change a thing. She had already lost him, just like everyone else who cared about her.

He stood with his arms ready for just the right opportunity. And as the swing rushed towards him, he grabbed the ropes and brought it to a stop. She hopped off and started for home. He caught up with her and took her hand.

"We almost moved close by. But someone quit at the company where my uncle works. And they need someone right away. It's a perfect opportunity for him."

There was so much to say. Yet she was too numb to say anything at all—even that she was sorry for yelling at him. It wasn't his fault they were moving. Now that she thought about it, Daniel had told her just as the school year ended that his father sold the farm. So, of course, they were moving.

Daniel didn't stop at his road like usual but kept going. "I'll walk you to the corner."

At the turnoff, he wrapped her in his arms as drops of rain began to fall. "I'm sure going to *miss you*," he said, his voice cracking.

"I'll miss you too, Daniel."

When he released her, she saw tears rolling down his cheeks.

He reached into a pocket, pulled out a folded envelope and handed it to her. "I wrote you something."

She stared at what she knew was a goodbye letter, wanting it to disappear.

"Emily?" Daniel said, jarring her from her stupor. "I snuck off. And I know my father's looking for me. So, I've got to go. I'm sorry. I'm so sorry."

"I know." She reached for the letter. "I'm sorry too."

He took her into his arms again and held her tight.

"Goodbye, Emily," he said, his arms dropping from her shoulders. Tears flowed down his cheeks as he squeezed her hands and turned for home.

She wanted to beg him to stay a while longer, to tell him it was okay that he was crying.

"It's okay to cry, Daniel! Goodbye!

"Goodbye, Daniel."

She watched him walk away, becoming smaller and smaller. At his corner, he looked back, waved and kept going. That was it. One last wave and he was gone out of her life.

That's when her sobs began as drops of rain turned into a downpour. She clutched the letter to her chest weeping and hoping he would come back to her. When she couldn't wait any longer, she slipped the letter into a pocket and turned away from the one thing she wanted most.

A mixture of rain and tears streamed down her cheeks as she raced home dodging puddles of water and hoping she would beat the men to the house. But when she arrived, her uncles were sitting in the veranda having a beer. Knowing what was coming, she stopped at the kitchen door and took a breath before walking in to face her grandfather.

"Where in the...!" he began, as she sailed across the room to wash her face at the sink.

"Every... Everyone's waiting to eat."

He said no more...didn't even yell as she expected.

"It won't be long," she told him quietly, thankful for whatever made him hold his tongue, relieved when he grabbed a beer and went to join Steven and Timothy.

She splashed her face at the sink, dried off, and lit a fire to heat the stovetop and oven. Putting water on to boil, she fanned dried her skirt and blouse near the heat then slipped on an apron. With two pans of chickens frying, she dropped the potatoes she peeled that morning into the boiling water. All the while, tears flowed down her cheeks until the front of her apron was soaked from wiping them away. When her heart was so heavy that it seemed her joy was lost forever, her grandmother's voice came to her.

"You can make it through anything with perseverance, my Bella Bambina. Always remember that prayer and perseverance will get you through."

The first time those words were spoken to her, she was much younger and upset over something childish. She wondered if her grandmother knew of her struggles. And if she realized how much her words still meant to her.

After dinner and clean up, Emily went up to her room and sank to the floor next to her bed. She had managed to keep her emotions close when the men came in to eat, but as she opened Daniel's letter, sobs burst from her lungs.

Dear Emily,

By now you know that my family is moving to South Carolina. If there was a way for me to stay, I would. Trust me, I tried. And I'm very sorry it turned out this way.

Spending time with you these last few months has meant more to me than anything I've ever experienced. I'll never forget you for as long as I live. Please don't forget me. I hope we meet again one day.

Daniel

P.S. I will never think of swings in the same way. Be assured, that every time I see one, I'll think of you.

His comment about the swings made her smile. She folded the letter and slipped it into the envelope. Pulling herself up, she went into her closet. She kissed the letter, stood on her tiptoes and pushed it to the corner of a shelf. It would be safe there, hidden away, until she found a way to deal with her broken heart. She went to her nightstand and opened her journal.

Something struck me, and I know that it's true. At least for me — A heart that is broken by a love so deep and pure it could shake a king from his throne must find its own way, or it may never heal.

Replacing the journal, she went to look out a window wondering if one day she would see Daniel again. The rain had stopped. And she had to force herself not to run up the road to see him. If she did, her senses told her it would make things worse. The best thing for her was to forget.

She gathered blankets from her closet and made a spot on her bed for Kidders and her new litter. Going to the barn, she brought Kidders up first, then went back and brought the kittens up to her room.

As much as she tried to ensure there wasn't an overpopulation of cats, it seemed at least twice a year, there was a new batch of kittens to contend with. Keeping them away from Claude was her number one priority. And she was thankful that Steven, even though irritated at times, was still willing to help.

Someday, she would leave for town too and never come back. But for tonight, she would lay beside Kidders and her precious furry clowder and allow their purring to lull her to sleep.

*F*or weeks after Daniel was out of her life, as much as Emily tried, she couldn't hide her tears. Whatever the men thought of her condition, they kept to themselves. She zipped through her work like someone possessed, and they didn't have much of a chance to complain.

Emily hadn't visited her treehouse as much as she did before Haity died. But after Daniel moved, whenever she could get away, she began to go up more often. She would read and write in her journal. Sometimes she enhanced the picture she had drawn on the cover depicting her in a fairytale escaping the farm. Other times she snuggled with the cats or watched the dogs play below.

Something about Claude's demeanor had given her confidence that he found some decency and decided to leave her alone. But just when she was secure in her freedom from him, he followed her to the treehouse.

"I know you're up there."

She closed her book and peeked through a crack in the floor. When he leaned against the tree, chewing on a piece of straw, she knew he wouldn't budge until she spoke with him. If she ignored him, he would hold her up so she would be late making dinner, or he would invent or exaggerate something to rile her grandfather.

"What'd you want, Claude?"

He looked up at her, spitting out the piece of straw.

"You've been ignoring me. You know I hate that."

"Go away."

She cringed the moment she said it.

He picked up a chunk of wood and wacked it against the tree. Throwing it aside, he started up.

Emily yanked the door open, climbed out, and started down. The treehouse held a special memory of Haity—since she had helped finish it. And she would never allow Claude to mar that.

When she jumped to the ground and headed for the house, Claude grabbed her arm and pulled her back.

"You see... Once we consummated our relationship. It can't be undone. That's just how it is."

She wanted to scream that she didn't belong to him and she never would. It wasn't easy to keep her tongue. And sometimes she couldn't help herself. But she learned the hard way—that it was easier all the way around to appease him.

*I*f Emily was forced to name a silver lining in the messed-up relationship she had with Claude, she would have to say that it overshadowed her loss of Daniel. And gradually, her memories of the boy she once loved drifted away.

Even though it was a hopeless battle, Emily did everything she could think of to keep away from

Claude. She washed and painted the veranda walls, painted the stair railing, and the front porch—things she wouldn't have done otherwise. And if she could help it, she didn't go into the barn unless Steven or Timothy were nearby.

As time passed, sometimes she got careless. Like the day Steven was repairing the horse stall in the barn. She went up to the loft to check on a new batch of kittens that came by way of a stray cat. As she held one of the litter, she heard someone come up the steps. Scooting in front of the other kittens, she covered the one on her lap with her skirt, calling to her uncle.

"Steven? Is that you?"

The footsteps continued up, but there was no answer.

"You're not fooling me." Claude chuckled as he stepped into the loft and strolled over.

"I know there's kittens up here."

He squatted in front of Emily, looking down at the kitten peeking from the folds of her skirt.

"They don't hurt you, Claude. Can't you just leave them be?"

He reached over and rubbed the kitten's head.

"I may not care for these hairy little beasts one bit. But I know how much you love your cats."

Emily's heart sank as she looked down at the kitten so innocent and unaware of the danger it faced.

"Come on, Mud. Show me how much you love your kitties."

This was her life. Working, taking care of the men, protecting the kittens, and waiting for the day when she would be rid of Claude for good.

Chapter Eight

1960
Age17-18

*E*mily lifted her arms and wiggled so that the gray and pink checkered dress slid down over her tall, slender frame. Outside, the wind whipped around the house as though it was mid-winter instead of early spring. Goosebumps shot up her arms, and she shivered as she zipped up her dress and tied her hair into a ponytail. Wanting a good peek outside, she stood on her bed and pulled back the curtains.

The night before, the skies had been clear. Now snowflakes whirled with the moan of intensifying winds. She thought of Aunt Francine and that she had planned to walk over that day and check on her. With snow already piling up and no boots to wear—unless the sun came out and melted the snow—she didn't know how she would make it over.

Claude was coming across the open yard from the barn hunched over in his hooded jacket. She had managed to keep away from him for over a month, never losing hope that he would leave her alone, get a steady girl or get tired of her. When he looked up, she dropped the curtains and went to finish dressing.

She pulled on a pair of knee-high socks and stepped into her sole-worn saddle shoes. Lacing them up, she grabbed a sweater off the back of a chair. She was ready to go down, but something made her stop, go to the dresser and pull out her mother's sapphire ring. Although she had tried it on numerous times, until a month ago, she had only worn it a few times since her sixteenth birthday. She placed it on her finger and headed downstairs to fix breakfast.

*T*wo hours later, the men had filled themselves with bacon, eggs, fried potatoes, fresh biscuits, and honey. They were in good spirits as Emily brought over a fresh pot of coffee.

Since this was supposed to be their last break before planting season, the men decided to celebrate with whisky, beer, and a game or two of cards.

They were about to head down to the basement when a gust of wind came like a train and flung debris against the house.

"Son of a bitch!" Steven said. "What was that?"

Timothy flew out of his chair and went to look out the window.

"Ha. Half the arbor just went down. And it's snowing like the dickens."

Grandfather placed his coffee on the table and reached for a toothpick. "Looks like we'd best check on the beef cows before long, boys…make sure they take to the sheds."

"Aw, come on," Timothy moaned. "It's not like it's the dead of winter. It'll stop snowing in a couple hours."

Emily wasn't sure they'd care, but she had to say it anyway. "If you're going out, someone better check on Aunt Francine."

She was right. The men were more interested in the prospect of playing crazy eight and drinking-it-up in the basement. At first, Grandfather sat stone-faced. Although, after two or three shots of whiskey, he joined in the banter.

Emily turned from the sink where she was washing dishes.

"Steven!" she said, louder than she intended. She caught his eye and softened her voice.

"Please, can you just run over?"

"What're you talking about?"

"Aunt Francine. Go check on her."

"Damn it, girl."

"I'd go, but I've got no boots. Remember?" She bent her leg and wiggled her foot. "Look, the soles on my shoes are worn through."

He glanced at the shoe and groaned, "Aw, maybe later."

The men finally got up from the table, stepped into the veranda and rummaged through the closet for winter gear. They looked out the windows and discussed the weather. That's as far as they got before they headed to the basement for a game of cards, and a drink or two, to ward off the chill.

When Emily finished cleaning the kitchen, she went back to the barn to take scraps to the animals. She was glad that Kidders, her newfound friend, Caesar, and the dogs, were sharing the comfortable hideaway she made for them.

By the time she headed back to the house, the wind had died, and only a few snowflakes were coming down. But there were still at least five inches of snow on the ground, and her feet were already wet and freezing. So, unless it warmed up a good ten degrees, there was no way she would make it to her aunt's. The last time she saw her, she wasn't looking so good. And by the way she had been acting, Emily knew something was up with her. Steven was her only hope. *I'll Tempt him with goodies.* Apple pie was his favorite. Although he would never pass up a chocolate chip cookie.

There weren't too many things more comforting to Emily than a warm kitchen on a cold day and the aroma of chocolate chip cookies and apple pies fresh out of the oven. Enthused about her baking plans, she went inside, placed her shoes by the fireplace, and ran upstairs to put on a pair of dry socks.

Before she finished mixing the first batch of cookies, the orders from down below began. If it wasn't beer, they called up for snacks, cigarettes, or something else they were too preoccupied to get themselves. She went downstairs for the umpteenth time that day, opened a beer for Steven, and shoved it in front of him.

"I'm making an apple pie for Aunt Francine, cookies too."

"Mm."

"A pie for us, the other to take over."

"Sounds good."

He made a play, and there were shouts of excitement, yet no promises.

Back upstairs, she stoked the fires and placed cookies into the oven, noticing the storm was building again. She still wasn't too alarmed and went to the laundry room to wring out clothes.

When she returned to the kitchen, the hourglass sifted the last of the sand indicating the cookies were ready. Wiping her forehead with the back of a hand, she used the other to grab the potholders from a hook behind the stove. As she reached into the oven, a gust of wind hit with such force it sounded like shingles had ripped free and were ricocheting across the roof.

She placed the cookie sheet on the stove, dropped the potholders, and rushed to the window. Snatching the dishtowel from her shoulder, she wiped mist from the pane and peered outside just in time to see the rest of the arbor fall. She sank to a bench and watched snowflakes pile up along the windowsill. Wind whistled along the eaves finding cracks and crevices to chip at. And with each gust, it seemed that things would only get worse.

Leaping to her feet, she dropped the dishtowel over the back of a chair, placed the pies in the oven, and hurried down the narrow basement steps. She moved into the light of the lantern that dangled from the ceiling and glared at the four men. A jug of Jack Daniels, four shot glasses, and half a dozen or so bottles of beer sat on the old kitchen table.

She felt as driven as the storm by now. "Haven't you forgotten something? Remember, the cows? And what about Aunt Francine?"

The men continued with their card game as if she hadn't said a word. She went over to the wood stove they had put in several years back, poked at the fire, and went back to the table.

"I'm telling you. Aunt Francine didn't look so good the last time I saw her."

She waited for a response until she wanted to scream.

"Dang it! The cows are probably all going to die. And for all we know, so will Aunt Francine."

Timothy looked up, rolled his head back, and laughed. "Ooh, look who's worried about dear ole Francine."

He whirled in his chair and stomped a foot. "Boo!" he said, howling with pleasure when she jumped.

She moved to the other side of Steven tempted to smack her youngest uncle, who could go a whole day without uttering a single word, unless of course, he had two or three shots of whiskey under his belt. From the looks of it, he'd had plenty more.

Turning back to the game, Timothy slapped his cards onto the table. "Aces High," he whooped.

He laughed so hard he almost tipped his chair. "Another win for me. That makes you all *three-time losers*."

This didn't go over well with the others. Steven picked up his brother's cards, took a count, and pitched them back onto the table.

"You're a cheat. Either that or you don't know how to add. Now where's the other card?"

Emily noticed a card on the floor. She picked it up and dropped it in front of Steven.

"Are you going or not?" she asked quietly, although he was still brooding over Timothy's questionable win. He picked up the stray card and turned it over several times.

In the meantime, Claude pulled a cigarette from his mouth and blew smoke her way. "Go yourself, Mud. Shoo!"

Brushing smoke from her eyes, she moved behind Steven and placed her hands on the back of his chair.

"I'd go, but I've got no boots. You want me to get frostbite?"

She looked around at a window in the corner that was almost blocked by snow. "Have any of you thought about looking out the window lately?"

Grandfather, who had been silent, slammed a bottle into a garbage can that sat next to the table.

"If I were you, I'd close that son-of-a-bitching mouth of yours, young lady."

A shiver ran up her spine as she headed back up the steps. With all the booze burning inside their bellies, she shouldn't have expected anything different. It was clear now that Aunt Francine was on her own.

Upstairs, Emily made a pot of hot chocolate, poured a cup for herself, and took a plate of cookies to the table. She sat and listened to the wind break against the house. Each time it let up, she looked out the window half expecting to see the sun peeking through the clouds.

Aunt Francine had taken care of herself for years. Logic said she was fine, but something still nagged her to get over there. She looked at her shoes sitting next to the fireplace, knowing they wouldn't get her to the end of the driveway.

Nearly five hours ago, the men declared that if the weather got worse, they would go out and check on the cows. Now, all fired up with whiskey and beer, they rumbled up the steps and into the kitchen.

They grumbled as they finished dressing, slipping on parkas, hats, and gloves. Finally, Grandfather pulled on a thick furry cap and disappeared out into the storm. The others buckled up and scrambled after him.

Emily closed the door behind the last of the men and watched out a window until they wandered out of sight. She took the pies out of the oven. And recalling the mess in the basement, she picked up a pail and a dish rag and headed down the steps.

Chapter Nine

As dusk approached, Emily rekindled the wood stove in the kitchen. After pitching several logs into the fireplace, she sat by the hearth on one of her grandmother's hand-woven rugs and watched flames dance around the crackling wood. This kind of pleasure without interruption from the men was a rarity for her. And she longed for her mind to be still. But something continued to beckon her to go to her Aunt's until she finally gave in.

She leaped to her feet and pattered up the stairs. In a whirl of activity, she gathered winter clothing from her bedroom, headed back down, and dropped everything next to the fireplace. Grabbing the sharpest knife she could find, she went to dig out an old pair of Steven's boots from the veranda closet, pulled them to the fireplace, and jabbed two slits at the top of each boot. Knowing the threat of frostbite, she rummaged through the men's drawers for flannels and two pairs of thick wool socks. After putting on the socks, she grabbed a pair of jeans and overalls, and dumped them next to the other clothes.

She unzipped her dress and let it slip from her shoulders onto the floor. Kicking it aside, she put on the flannel union suit, jeans and shirt. Stepping into the overalls and holding them around her knees, she sat and pulled on the boots and the bottom of the overalls overtop. She secured the boots with four pieces of twine strung through the knife slits and fastened to the jean belt loops. Standing, she buckled up the overalls, pulled on a parka, cap, and gloves, and wrapped a scarf around her neck as she walked to the china cabinet. She gazed at her reflection in the back mirror.

"Sheesh… I look like an overstuffed rag doll."

She hugged herself, twisting her shoulders and flipping up a heel. The security she felt all bundled up gave her a boost and some needed courage.

Feeling as ready as she would ever be, she made her way to the door noticing the pies on the counter, deciding her aunt would have to wait for hers. The wind was picking up again as she stepped from the veranda, carefully making her way down the steps, across the yard, and through the rubble of the arbor.

Snow reached halfway to her knees. And each step was a challenge, although she was determined that nothing could stop her now. As she neared the end of the driveway, she heard a rush of wind coming across the yard where it caught her from the side and thrust her, feet flying, into a snowbank. She sputtered and spat, wiped snow from her face, and pulled herself up.

The house begged her to rush back inside to the warmth of the crackling fire and her soft bed upstairs. Tempting as it was, she lifted the scarf over her nose and turned up the road. This was her first trip over at night, but she was used to the whistling and groaning of wind.

As dusk gave way to darkness, Emily counted on the reflection off the snow to light a path to Aunt Francine's. Seeing a few feet ahead was all she needed. There were trees to her left and a fence to her right. And as long as she didn't hit either, she knew she would be okay.

Her mindset was helpful, but the storm turned for the worse, and squalling wind barreled through the trees in clouds of blackness. She braced herself as gust after gust beat against her back. Every few minutes, she stopped with hands on her knees to catch her breath before trudging on again. By now, her teeth were chattering, and her toes, fingers, and cheeks burned with frostbite as she fought on even when it seemed like a battle she might not win.

At last, there was a lull in the storm. And soon, the outline of her aunt's mailbox appeared within the mist of flakes and crystal snow. When she reached the driveway and turned into the yard, a branch snapped above her head and a mound of snow whumped to the ground beside her. Then all was quiet except for the sound of her feet crunching through the snow on her way to the house. She climbed the front porch steps and knocked, opening the door.

"Aunt Francine! Hellooo!"

Brushing snow from her parka, she stomped her feet, and stepped inside, making sure the door was closed all the way.

"Hello. Aunt Francine. It's Emily."

There was no movement, only shadows melting into the darkness. Beyond the couch, a low-burning wick sat on the coffee table, and in the far right corner, a pile of embers glowed in the wood stove. Even with the cast-iron doors wide open, little heat escaped.

Emily shed her gloves, top layer of clothing, and boots. Rubbing her hands together for warmth, she headed for the bedroom. Halfway there, something made her stop and turn around. There, just beyond the coffee table, in the shadows of the burning wick, Francine lay on the couch beneath a mound of blankets. Her hair was spread across a pillow like a silvery halo, and her face was drawn and thin. Her eyes were closed. A glass of water sat on a small stool next to her. On the floor was a box of Kleenex and a paper sack.

Emily held her breath as she approached and leaned in just as the old woman's eyes popped open.

"What're you doing here?"

Her aunt's voice was husky from a cold.

Emily bolted upright. "I… I um… Well… I haven't seen you in a while. And with the storm and all, I was worried that—"

"You caught me by surprise, that's all. I didn't expect anyone to show up today."

"Are you okay? You don't look well." Emily placed a palm on the woman's forehead. "You've got a fever too."

Aunt Francine looked up, almost timid...so unlike her. "It's not so bad, now," she said.

Emily smoothed back her aunt's wiry strands of hair and fluffed her pillow. "Think I'll get more light in here. Get the fire going."

She looked around the room. "Now where're those matches?"

"There, against the wall," Aunt Francine said, pointing to a mantel above the old fireplace that had been turned into a bookshelf.

Emily fetched the matches and set about lighting lanterns. She noticed the woman's thoughtful gaze following her about the room.

"You know, Emily," she said in a softer tone than Emily was used to hearing from her.

"I've never minded being alone, and to a large extent, preferred it, really. But tonight...well, I guess you could say the last couple of weeks or so...I, um... Well, I'm just glad you're here."

Emily lit several more lanterns about the living and kitchen area and turned to face her aunt. "I had to come. I was worried. Something told me I should."

She almost told her how the men had played cards and drank from breakfast until early afternoon. This was something she wouldn't normally do. Except, there was something so different about her aunt. Deciding not to mention the men, Emily replaced the matchbox and pitched the last log into the stove.

Deciding to fill the wood box, she dressed for the weather and made numerous trips out to the shed for logs and kindling. Once she got a good fire going, she tossed in several more logs.

"Wish you felt better Aunt Francine," she said, poking at the fire.

"Oh, don't worry about me."

The old woman struggled to sit up, bringing on a cough that left her gasping for air.

"Stay right where you are," Emily scolded.

She dropped the fire iron into the wood box, rushed to her aunt's side, and helped her back onto the pillow.

Aunt Francine caught her breath and took a few sips of water, pointing to a jar of Vaseline sitting on a sideboard at the kitchen entrance. "Fetch that for me, will you? My nose is burning like crazy."

Emily took off her gloves, retrieved the ointment, and knelt on the floor beside her aunt, dabbing Vaseline over the raw skin around her nose.

"I don't deserve this, Emily. What've I ever done for you?"

"Showed me how to take care of the house, for one."

"And I couldn't wait for you to take over. What were you, seven?"

"No," Emily laughed, "more like ten."

"Well, I left you on your own for days at a time…long before."

Emily sat back on her heels, wiped her finger on a piece of tissue and twisted the lid back on the jar.

"I did pretty good on my own."

The old woman chuckled. "That you did."

"Besides Aunt Francine. You still come over to help with the canning. You've always helped churn butter and make lard. You taught me to sew. Grandmother taught me to count and started me on the alphabets, reading, and math. But if you recall, you helped with that too."

"You pleaded until I gave in. And you were damn good at it. Besides, I was grumpy as hell the whole time."

"Well, yeah. But the reading and math did wonders when I started school. Remember, I skipped two grades."

"Mm. I never told you this, Emily. But... I was proud of you for that."

"Thank you for telling me."

Emily placed the jar on the coffee table. She stood, gathered supplies to start a fire in the cookstove, and headed into the kitchen.

After the stove was lit and heating, she took off her parka, hung it on the back of a chair, and gathered utensils, bowls, and cooking pots.

"The fire sure feels good," Aunt Francine said. "I'll rest up a bit...get my old limbs warmed and put on some supper for you."

"Oh no, you won't. I'm already working on it. How about some soup?"

"Nothing for me... Well, maybe some hot tea. Oh, and add some of this."

She reached under the couch and pulled out a bottle of whiskey.

"I haven't felt much like eating these last few days. Thought this might help my ailing. I did manage to cook some oatmeal last night, though. Or... was that the night before."

Emily went over and picked up the bottle of whiskey, noticing it was three-fourths empty, shocked, that she had it at all.

"Looks like you need some food."

With two pots over the heat, one with water, she dumped canned vegetables along with some broth she found in the root cellar, in the other. While waiting for everything to heat she made herself a spam sandwich.

When the teapot whistled, she poured water, spooned the tea, and waited for it to brew, all the while glancing at her aunt and wondering how long she had been drinking. It made no sense, not with the way she scolded the men for doing the same.

Emily placed the whiskey-laced tea and a bowl of soup on a tray and carried it to the coffee table. She set the cup of brew on the stool and persuaded her aunt to take in some nourishment.

Later, while her aunt slept, she went to kneel in front of the bookshelf, pulled out *A Study in Scarlet,* and thumbed through the pages. Francine had told her she was too young to read many of her books, especially the mysteries that lined the bottom shelf. But that was when she was barely thirteen. And it wasn't as if she hadn't already read something her aunt wouldn't approve of. In truth, by the age of sixteen, she had read most of her aunt's mysteries by sneaking them home and reading them late into the night.

Emily replaced the book and pulled out *Mr. Polton Explains*, her favorite mystery in a series and her aunt's last purchase. She was so intrigued by the story of a watchmaker turned lab assistant and manservant, who helped solve a case, that she thought if she hadn't already planned to be a teacher, she just may have become a detective. She smiled, recalling her plan to be a dancer before going to college. At the time, the idea was a thrilling possibility, but now she realized it was just a far-fetched fantasy.

Outside, the wind was howling again as Emily stood and placed the book on the coffee table. She felt cozy as she washed, dried and put away the dishes. When she finished, she got a pillow and several blankets from the bedroom closet. Making herself a comfortable spot on the floor at the foot of the couch, she opened *Mr. Polton Explains* and began to read.

*A*unt Francine woke and reached for the cup of brew.

"Did the sleep do some good?" Emily asked, setting the book aside.

The old women's hands trembled as she took a drink and returned the cup to the stool.

"It did, a little."

"You sound better."

Emily got up and went to her aunt. "Now that you're rested. I think you should stand and move around a bit."

Francine chuckled. "You probably know best."

After Emily helped her aunt up, giving her a chance to move about, freshen up, and settle back in again, she returned to the spot on the floor at the end of the couch. She leaned with an elbow next to her aunts tucked-in feet.

"Say, Aunt Francine. Um... When I saw you last, you seemed to be troubled by something. Was it the being alone stuff?"

"Nah, that wasn't it, not at all. I guess the being alone stuff came after the fact."

"After the fact, meaning what?"

"...Well... When you were here last, I meant to tell you what you should've heard long ago." Her voice was weak compared to the crackling fire and rumbling storm, but the words rang clear as a trumpet.

"You're a good girl, Emily. And I've been realizing more and more that I should've done better for you. I mean, who else did you have. Not that crew back at the house, that's for sure. Oh, I went over and helped. And I knew Steven took you to town now and then, and I thought that was enough."

Francine thought for a moment. "It would've been an altogether different story if your mother... Well...everything changed after that."

The old woman took a breath and sighed. "Should've taken you to church like your grandmother asked me to. And those men and that damn drink." She looked down at her mix sitting on the stool and chuckled.

Emily couldn't help but to smile. "What's so funny?"

"Not so funny, I guess. Except for the absurdity of it all. You know… I'm ashamed to admit it. But I think we're a bunch of alcoholics. Steven, not so much, but all of us, off on binges too often. Oh, maybe alcohol has its place. But it can be a deceiver. And it can ruin lives. You'd think a person would learn after a while. Nothing more irritating than a hangover when there's work to do. Course I'm old. Makes no difference now."

Emily was stunned by her aunt's confession and curious to know more. They fell silent as the wind beat against the front door and whistled outside the windows.

Aunt Francine fumbled with a fingernail and looked up. "Why I've come to my senses now, I'm not sure. But I'm glad I have."

"Don't worry, Aunt Francine. I've done fine. It hasn't been that bad."

"Fine? You say you've done fine? You've been treated no better'n a slave much of the time.

"You know, my father, your great-grandfather. He was a drunk, even more so after returning from the war. I remember the rantings followed by glum silences during hangovers that lasted for days. Best thing for you is to never start on the brew in the first place. Should've taken my mother's advice on that subject myself. Not that it ruined my life like it has for many. It's what I should've accomplished that's left its mark. Just don't do as I've done."

Emily had turned to her aunt and was resting both arms on the couch. She felt warm inside like she belonged right where she was.

"I won't. But Aunt Francine. I didn't know that you—"

"Drink like a fish? Huh. Don't recall is more like it. But after a while, I'm sure some things'll stir your memory. I know, I know. You're probably asking yourself, why blurt this out now."

Francine laughed ruefully, followed by a vigorous cough, a sip of water, and some brew before continuing.

"I think part of it's the God your grandmother spoke of knocking on this old heart." She tapped her knuckles against her chest. "But the whole the truth is, I had a dream that gave me the shakes for days. I don't know if that was a message from the man upstairs or not, but that's what got me thinking.

"Whatever the case, I've decided to turn a new leaf and give you some help. I guess it's better late than never."

"You're helping me? With what?"

Francine leaned over with another coughing spell, wiped her nose, and dropped the wad of tissue into the brown grocery sack. She shifted to her side with her head resting on an elbow and set her gaze on Emily.

"My guess is that you'll want to leave soon."

Emily sat up, folded her arms over her chest, quivering with excitement. "I *have* thought about going to New York City."

"New York? Mm… That's a hard town, massive. Best to keep that in mind. But… Wherever you decide to go, you say anything to your grandfather, and he'll put a stop to it."

"Grandfather, let me go? I'm sure he wouldn't."

"Gracious Aunt Matilda," Francine chuckled, "how would he ever pay someone else for the work you do around there.

"You know, Emily. Your grandfather wasn't always such a grouch. Nor stubborn as hell. Ha, I guess none of us were.

"Nevertheless, I haven't seen him look happier then when he met your grandmother at the World's Fair in San Francisco back in 1915. Martha had come to San Francisco planning to check out college. When she stopped by the Festival Hall, we were there listening to an organist. Rupert was never much of a music lover. But something about that organ got to him. And something about your grandmother caught his eye. That was over forty-five years ago. Makes me realize how times have changed."

Francine pointed at Emily. "Don't let anything stop you. Get out of there. The sooner the better."

"I'm surprised you're telling me to just up and—"

"Well, believe it. And believe me when I tell you to plan ahead. Plan carefully. The best way out will be for you to take the train from Watseka to Chicago. From Chicago, you can go anywhere you like.

"You know...come to think of it. Steven goes to Kankakee quite often. If it works out, catch a ride with him. Course you'll have to be sneaky about it. You know how he and Timothy cater to their pa. There's a Greyhound bus in Kankakee just off Highway 52. That's the road he'll take from Watseka. But if that doesn't work, the train from Watseka will do. It'll be more expensive, though.

"Speaking of funds. I don't have much cash, but there's a silver bar that your uncle Carl stashed away that'll get you wherever you want to go. Take it to a pawn shop in Chicago and they'll give you what it's worth. It was supposed to have been for our retirement."

"Aunt Francine. I... I don't know what to say."

"There's no need to say anything. As far as I'm concerned, you earned it. There were four silver bars to begin with, but three of them seemed to have vanished into *thin* air."

"Oh dear. What do you think happened to them?"

"Who knows for sure. But I think it was Carl and your grandfather. Well, to be honest, mostly Carl's doing. But Rupert didn't help any.

"Boy, those two were quite a pair back then. I warned Carl more than once that it was either me or the gambling."

"You were going to leave him?"

"Aw, I doubt I would've gone through with it. Nevertheless, about a week before he died, the two of them went to a poker game in Chicago. Thought they were fooling me. Ninnies. You should've heard 'em carry on when they showed up around six the next morning. I stuck my head out the window and tried to hear what they were saying. All I could tell was that supposedly someone won a jackpot."

Francine squinted and scratched her head. "Whoever it was, it sure wasn't them. Anyway, that silver bar is just been sitting up in the attic collecting dust. You'll find it on top of the last rafter all the way at the end."

"Aunt Francine. Are you sure?"

"I certainly won't need it.

"You're probably tall enough, but if not, there's a chest directly below. You can use it to stand on.

"Oh, and make sure to bring a flashlight with some good batteries. Mine are all dead. I doubt I'll be around long enough to get more."

"Don't say that."

"Well, it's true.

"Listen... I've had a decent life. At times it's been difficult without Carl. But I lived my life the way I wanted. Maybe not the way I should've, but…. I hope this'll make things right.

"You know, Emily. As you find your own way through life, I want you to take heed. There'll be hard times. Life can be a beast. It ain't fair. But, of course, you already know that. Just remember. Don't ever give up."

"I won't."

They sat for a few minutes in silence before Francine spoke again.

"I'm not sure why I haven't told you this. But I've held onto something that's yours. It's a...it's a necklace."

"A necklace? Of mine?"

"It's yours all right, and it's not just any necklace. You see, at one time, it belonged to your great-great-grandmother. She received it back in the eighteen-hundreds from some wealthy Prince. The legend goes that the two carried on an illicit love affair."

Francine rolled her eyes. "Whether that's true or not is beside the point. The important thing is that it's part of your heritage from your mother's side. I put the velvet necklace box inside a brown box. Carl set it next to the silver bar."

Emily was shocked by her aunt's revelations. She attempted to tell her how grateful she was, but the woman was in a hurry to confess everything. It was as if she was afraid her time would run out before she had a chance to finish.

"One of the last things your grandmother said to me was that she wanted you to have the necklace. It was sitting in the back corner of your grandparent's closet. I didn't give it much thought. Then one day, I got to feeling sentimental or something. I went over and picked it up, planning to give it to you when you could comprehend its importance. I didn't tell my brother at the time, didn't think he'd care. But when I mentioned it to him, classic Rupert blew up."

Francine coughed into a Kleenex, dabbed her nose, and reached for the brew.

"Let me get that for you," Emily said, starting to get up.

"Never you mind. I have it. I've been doing it for years all by myself."

She took several sips and set the cup down.

"Now, where was I? Oh yes… A couple weeks after I mentioned the necklace to your grandfather, I came home after rabbit hunting and caught the old boy snooping under my bed."

"Oh no," Emily said, trying not to giggle.

"You laugh now. You should've been there. Boy, what a sight. There he was, in perfect form, with me pointing a gun at his backside. I said, get up, you old goat, or I'll shoot your blasted tail end off. He just about knocked himself out getting up. Didn't make a peep, though, just left embarrassed and rubbing his head. We haven't discussed it since."

"Why would Grandfather want a necklace?"

"Aw, I don't know. Maybe sentimental reasons, in part. But beneath it all, he's likely afraid you'll use it as a tool to leave him without a housekeeper.

"You know, there was a time when many of the children of farming communities stuck around home all their lives. Even though things have changed, I doubt Steven and Timothy will ever leave. But I certainly wouldn't expect that of you. Anyway, I'm sure your Grandfather is waiting for my demise before making another move."

The old woman chuckled. "I think sometimes he's afraid of me. 'Course, he hasn't seen me lately."

Francine settled back on the pillow. "How ironic life is sometimes."

"In what way?"

"Oh, a slew of things that happened. Nothing for you to fret about." Francine thought for a moment and cocked her head. "Show me that ring of yours."

Emily held out her hand. "See? It's sapphire, for my mother and my birthdays. Sure is pretty, isn't it?"

"Yes, it certainly is."

Francine laid her head back and smiled. "Just the other day, I thought how excited your grandmother was when she bought that ring... You know, for your mother. When she realized it was missing, she was, devastated. The day you found it, she was on top of the world. Where'd you find it again?"

"Remember? Outside, next to Grandfather's bedroom. Near the crabapple tree."

"Oh, yes, yes, of course."

Emily spread her fingers, admiring the ring.

"I've been wearing it more of late.

"I hoped Grandfather would've forgotten about it. He might have, I'm not sure. Although when I was pouring him coffee the other day, I caught him staring at it. Before he could say anything, I told him you gave it to me for my birthday."

"Smart move.

"Say... Speaking of birthdays, you'll be eighteen soon, won't you."

"Yep. September the fourteenth."

"Boy, it sure is hard to believe you'll be an adult. Mm. I was just thinking here the last few days about how you've blossomed into a beauty the likes of which I've never seen. I don't expect that a mere click of the camera would even do you justice.

Francine laid her head back and sighed. "I just want you to have a good life, Emily."

She closed her eyes while Emily sat silently, comforted by the words and the change in her aunt.

A few minutes passed before Emily looked up, alarmed by how still the old woman had become. She rolled onto her knees and leaned forward to make sure she was still breathing. Reassured, but no less worried, Emily settled back onto the blankets and gazed at the fire.

"Don't leave me, Aunt Francine. Not now."

Minutes turned into hours as Emily read, stoked the fire, and took another trip to the shed for more wood. Finally, she sank to the floor and pulled a blanket under her chin.

There was more she wanted to say to her aunt. But she didn't know how to sift through all the feelings their talk had brought to light. Before today, Francine had never told her she cared. Yet, Emily realized it didn't matter any longer that for years she had to beg for help or attention or that her aunt had been as sour as stale milk more times than not. Not always, though, like those peaceful times when they read together. Deep down, she knew that Francine had a good heart. And now, without a clue or warning, she had come through with something that would change her life. Emily didn't want to break the spell.

"Thanks, Aunt Francine."

Emily closed her eyes, soothed by the warmth of the blankets, crackling fire, and her newfound friendship with her aunt.

The two slept until morning, waking when Steven and Timothy walked through the front door with the apple pie. Seeming relieved to find Emily and Aunt Francine in good condition, they got to work without a word of reprimand.

They chopped wood and brought in enough to last for several weeks. When they finished, Emily put on coffee and sliced the apple pie. Francine was sitting up, wrapped in a blanket, as Emily brought her a piece with a cup of coffee.

"Looks mighty good. Thank you."

Francine turned to the men. "I appreciate you fellas helping out."

Steven forked a piece of pie and looked over. "Sure thing, Aunt Francine."

Timothy nodded with a grunt.

Emily dished herself a piece and went to sit next to her aunt. They watched the roaring fire and listened to the men talk about the snowstorm and how the beef cows had made it through just fine.

"It's good we made it over before things got worse," Steven said.

He thought for a moment and glanced at Emily. "Sometimes you have a sense about these things."

When the men were preparing to leave, Emily went to Steven.

"Aunt Francine is still running a fever. And with that cough. I think I should stay with her for a few more days."

He glanced at the old woman. "It's probably best. In fact, I was thinking the same thing."

Emily stood on the front porch and watched the men head down the steps and to the pickup.

She called to Steven. "If Grandfather gets too cranky about me staying, tell him I'll catch up on everything soon as I get home."

When she walked back into the house, Francine had gotten up and was wandering off to her bedroom to prepare for the day. It wouldn't be long before she was resting on the couch again, but her will and determination were encouraging.

Emily covered the leftover pie and washed the dishes. She wiped up the floor, cut the flames in the kitchen lamps, and pitched more wood into the stove.

With the fire blazing and her aunt settled in, Emily straightened her makeshift bed and curled up on the floor. She sighed with pleasure as she picked up *Mr. Polton Explains*, thinking that when good things happen, it makes the bad much easier to bear.

Chapter Ten

*T*he day Francine McTune died, Emily tearfully pictured everyone in a front row pew singing *Amazing Grace* with the spirits of her mother, grandmother, and her great-aunt helping to mend the family. When she mentioned having the service at a house of worship, Grandfather's response was a grunt and a look of horror.

Early morning, on the day of her aunt's funeral, Grandfather and Claude left for parts unknown while Emily and her uncles went to the graveyard. Hoping the two would show up for the service, Emily stood between her uncles, clutching a basket of flowers.

She looked over to where her mother and grandmother were buried, recalling how sad her grandfather was after her grandmother died. And yet, it wasn't until his eyes fell upon his daughter's grave that he fell apart.

"They're not coming," she said to Steven.

"How do you know that?"

"I just do. They're not coming."

Steven stood for a moment, looked up the gravel drive, and motioned to the minister to go ahead.

Following the service, Emily walked to where her mother and grandmother lay. It felt comforting to be there for the first time in nearly twelve years. As she stood at their feet with a breeze ruffling her hair, she felt their presence gently pressing against her chest as if they were sharing the sounds of rustling leaves, fluttering of bird wings, and the swaying of the grass in the wind. The whole thing was uplifting, and she hung onto the feeling for as long as she could.

She went over and crouched beside each of their headstones and left a bouquet of marigolds.

"You ready to go?" Steven said, coming up beside her, dropping his gaze to his sister's grave.

Emily rose and they stood together reading her headstone. The breeze picked up as Steven walked the length of the graves and stopped to gaze back at his mother's headstone. Emily knew he missed his sister and mother, but she was surprised when she caught him wiping away tears.

She looked to where her aunt was just laid to rest and noticed Timothy throwing rocks at a tree stump. It seemed like his father and aunt, Timothy also tried to avoid reality.

Steven nudged her and she followed him to the pickup.

"I'll ride in the back," she said already climbing onboard.

As they sped off, she positioned herself in the corner against the grocery bin, lifting her face to the sun. The wind brushed against her cheeks, sweeping through her hair with its fingertips and sighs as it streaked away again. She wondered where the invisible force of wind came from and where it went. And if it would return to touch those who lived in the future as it had done so long ago, tugging at her grandmother's hair, and long before that, her mother's.

> "When there's a stirring in your heart, my Bella Bambina," her grandmother used to say, "that's the God of the universe telling you something. Listen, and be patient, even in trials, for they will pass."

Tears, warmed by the memory of those who had loved her, rolled down Emily's cheeks. A soft wind came and whisked them away, perhaps to live in another day and another time.

Back at the farm, she started lunch for her uncles. There still wasn't a sign of Grandfather and Claude. She noticed on the way back from the gravesite that they weren't at Francine's. Although, it was just a matter of time before Grandfather would go there. Taking this into consideration, she knew it was urgent that she head over herself to retrieve the necklace and the piece of silver her aunt left her.

Eager for the men to eat and leave so she could be on her way, she cut the bread into thinner slices and added less meat and lettuce in their sandwiches. When it was time to sit for lunch, she ate faster than usual in hopes that it would inspire them to do the same. Finally, she stood and started clearing the table. They didn't seem to notice her urgency, just took their sandwiches and left.

After she cleaned the kitchen, she went upstairs and pulled a flashlight and a potato sack from the closet shelf. She draped the sack around her neck and placed the flashlight into a skirt pocket she had sewn on for a purpose such as this. Excited to be on her way, she slipped out of the house to retrieve the legacy her grandmother left her and to claim the gift from Aunt Francine that would buy her freedom.

She called the cats to accompany her. "Kidders! Caesar!"

When they didn't respond, she tried to coax them from their hiding. "Kiiddeers! Caeesar!"

Still nothing. "All right, you rascals, it's your loss."

She wasn't exactly superstitious. But most of the time, whenever she left the yard, they tagged along until something distracted them.

The moment she stepped inside the cottage, she heard voices of warning telling her to get out before the old man showed up. This strange feeling stayed like a cloud as she hurried to the bedroom and pulled a stool to the middle of the room. She climbed on top, pulled the rope attached to the ceiling doorway and lowered the makeshift stairway.

Carefully making her way to the top step, she slipped the flashlight from her skirt pocket, flipped the switch on, and climbed into the attic. It was dark as coal up there and the beam of light was weak as she set off across the old dusty floor. A few steps out, a creaking sound from behind made her stop in her tracks. Chills pricked the back of her neck as she swung around and pointed the flashlight to the attic entrance.

"Grandfather? Is that you? Claude?" She held her breath, waiting for an answer, and went over to take a look. When all was still, she turned back and continued on, brushing away cobwebs and trying not to focus on the pitch-black on either side of her or whatever might come up those steps.

When she reached the far end of the attic, she stubbed her toe on something and dropped the light to the chest Aunt Francine mentioned. Only the chest wasn't what she came for, and she pointed the flashlight at a rafter, moving the light until there they were—the silver bar and the box containing the necklace.

She set the flashlight upright on the floor next to the wall, stepped on the trunk, and reached for the box that held her necklace. Wiping it off with her skirt, she slipped it into a pocket and carefully picked up the silver bar. Stepping from the chest, she lowered the piece of silver to the light. Noticing it had markings, she brushed away dust and revealed a pure shiny surface that gleamed a sixty-ounce marking.

"Ooh. I'll bet its worth at least fifty bucks."

She picked up the flashlight, pulled the potato sack from around her neck, placed the bar inside, and rolled it up nice and tight. Ready to head back down, her curiosity got the better of her. She set the sack on the floor, lifted the trunk lid, and pointed the flashlight inside. At the bottom was a folded military uniform. On top of that was a large brown envelope containing old documents and funny-looking pictures of people she didn't know. There was also a stack of faded letters wrapped in a red ribbon that her uncle Carl McTune sent from Italy and Germany, dating back as far as 1917, addressed to Francine Rezell in San Francisco. Another letter tucked down the side caught her attention. It was addressed to Francine and sent from a man named Samuel Dimsmoore. The return address was a post office box number in San Francisco, dated July 1942. She closed the trunk and placed the letter and a package of stamps she found inside. Lifting the potato sack, she set back across the room.

Emily had only taken a few steps down the ladder when she heard the kitchen door creak open. Trying to get down and out the window in a hurry, her skirt became entangled on a nail or such up in the attic. She grabbed a chunk of fabric and pulled. When nothing happened, she tightened her fingers into a fist and gave a fierce yank. Her skirt made a ripping sound and set her free, although she lost her balance. The sack holding the silver bar slipped from her hand and tumbled down the steps, followed by the flashlight, and she right behind with her fanny bouncing off the steps to the bottom where she lay sprawled on the floor.

Flat on her back and stunned, she looked up to see both cats in the doorway.

"Oh, now you show up."

Clambering to her feet, she returned the room to its original state. Gathering up the newly cracked flashlight and the potato sack, with the silver bar still in one piece, she rushed out the door with the cats beside her.

On her way home, she watched and listened for her grandfather's pickup. While shifting the potato sack to her other arm, she noticed that a piece of cloth had ripped away from her skirt along the poodle imprint.

"Look, Kidders, my favorite skirt is ruined."

The cat rubbed up against her legs for a moment and disappeared into the field with Caesar.

"Oh, like you care."

Back at home, she hurried upstairs to the safety of her bedroom, placed her new treasures on the dresser, and peeled the letter open.

July 21, 1942

Francine,

My hope is that my friendship with Rachael would at least be worth a response from you. I haven't heard from her since arriving in San Francisco. I've been wondering if she's moved, or if she married that guy she was seeing. If nothing else comes of this, I'd just like to know how she's doing. I'll wait to hear from you, or her.

Samuel Dimsmoore

Emily went to sit on the bed and reread the letter. Upon reading it through the first time, it seemed that the man her mother had been dating was her father. Her hope was that Samuel would have known him. Although after reading it through again, she realized that her mother and Samuel had been close friends. But he only knew the guy who was supposedly her father as the person Rachael was dating.

She wondered why her aunt kept the letter or if she even meant to keep it. There was a good chance her uncle Carl thoughtlessly put it in the chest before taking it to the attic. She would never know for sure, although she was grateful, nevertheless.

Goosebumps raised the hair on her arms when she contemplated that a personal friend of her mother's, someone who cared about her enough to write, may still be hoping to hear from her.

The revelation from her aunt Francine regarding how her grandparents met in San Francisco, fascinated Emily. It was hard to envision Grandfather as young and happy. She wondered if being in the town where her grandparents met would make her see him in a different light. The idea was intriguing. *Maybe...just maybe, San Francisco has more to offer than New York City.*

"San Francisco."

Just saying it felt good on her tongue. The City by the Bay and the Pacific Ocean. As her teacher used to say in geography—beaches, warm weather, tall buildings, cable cars, and the Bay Bridge.

Aunt Francine said New York City was a hard place to live, massive, and in the same breath, hinted that there was a better choice. Maybe she should go west instead of east. Besides, New York City without Haity wouldn't be the same.

"That's it," she said, sitting up. "I'm going to San Francisco."

Feeling exhilarated, she picked up the letter again, but all too soon her spirits dropped when she heard the familiar sound of her grandfather's pickup rattle and clank into the yard. When another vehicle tore in right behind him, she stood on her bed and looked out the window, pushing it open a crack. Grandfather had already climbed from his pickup when a long brown car pulled up. The driver jammed on his brakes, bolted from his car, and the two began a fist-flinging brawl. Emily noticed that the other man was the father of

Claude's former red-haired woman friend. Nothing new. This wasn't the first time he came to make trouble. The man called out several expletives, got back into his car, and poked his head out the window.

"You might as well pack your bags," he said over the roar of the engine. "Oh! And leave the tools in the shed!"

He popped his head back in and spun the car out of the yard.

Grandfather shook a fist. "Get the hell out of my sight you son-of-a-bitch!"

Emily watched the car disappear, sinking to the bed, and hoping to recapture some of her excitement. But it was no use. Grandfather burst into the house cussing up such a storm that she folded the letter into the envelope. When he slammed out of the house a few minutes later, she knew he could very well be on his way to Francine's that very moment. The thought of what he would do when he realized the necklace wasn't there terrified her. Her plans to leave the farm had to begin immediately. One way or another, she had to catch a ride into town with Steven as soon as possible.

Filled with renewed vigor, she placed the letter inside a book, went to the dresser and picked up the brown box. Inside, she found the black velvet necklace case her aunt described.

When she opened the box, she gasped.

"It's... *beautiful*."

Carefully lifting the necklace, she examined the sparkling red beads, wondering if Grandfather's claim to it was, by chance, that it was worth something.

"Either way, he'll kill me if he knows I have it."

She laid the necklace within the soft velvet of its original case, broke down the brown box, and dropped it into the garbage, looking around for a safe hiding place. Her gaze fell upon a pail she used as a flowerpot. She removed the dried bouquets of irises, violets, and sundrops. Shortening the stems, she placed the necklace and sliver bar in the pail and returned the flowers.

*T*he first inkling that Grandfather had begun to ransack Aunt Francine's cottage, was a fastmoving trail of dust rising above the trees, followed by the familiar tin-canny sound of his pickup. By the way he tore into the yard and stopped next to the house, Emily could feel trouble brewing even before he slammed into the kitchen.

A chill washed over her as she turned from the window to face him. The old man barreled across the room, holding a piece of cloth with an in-print of a poodle face.

"This was attached to some nails up in Francine's attic!" he bellowed.

She stared at the material, knowing she had to do some quick thinking.

He shook the fabric at her. "It came from one of your outfits. I should know, you wear it enough."

She was surprised he even noticed.

He glanced down at her skirt. "At least you used to. So you waited until she died then went up in her attic."

"No. No. I was there a few days before she died. But I wasn't in the attic."

She took the material from him and turned it over in her hands.

"You're right, I did wear a skirt with this print. But this particular piece of cloth came from one of Aunt Francine's dresses that she ruined. I don't know how that happened. Well... I guess I know now."

She looked up to see if he believed her before continuing.

"After she ruined it, she made a skirt out of it that she gave to me. It so happens that I grew out of it."

She raised her eyebrows. "Looks like you found some patching material. Thanks, Grandfather."

Emily was surprised by her confidence, especially something so ridiculous. Francine would never have owned anything of the kind. And it was Emily who had sewn the skirt. She tossed the fabric onto the table and turned back to the stove.

Grandfather didn't make a move. She could almost feel him breathe down the back of her neck. After what seemed like minutes, instead of seconds, he made a hissing sound and headed back outside.

At that moment, Emily knew she had to leave as soon as possible. She found Steven and told him she wanted to ride along the next time he went into town. He grunted but didn't say she could go. And it was urgent that she got a final yes from him.

*R*ight after Francine died, Emily made a supply bag out of a flour sack. She had shortened it and covered it with blue material to fancy it up. There was even a long sturdy blue strap to place over her shoulder.

The bag was nearly full and sat in her closet at the bottom of the clothes basket. Except for her journal and a snack, she had packed everything she would need— including two socks sewn together for toiletries and another for odds and ends. The silver bar was wrapped in a skirt, and the necklace was wrapped in a blouse. She had also packed several photos, two scarves that belonged to her mother and grandmother, her favorite rag doll that her grandmother made for her, two of her favorite books that had belonged to her mother—one containing the letter from Samuel Dimsmoore, along with a stamped letter she wrote to him. The last time she saw Aunt Francine, Emily claimed her mystery books and tried to stuff *Mr. Polton Explains* into her bag, but the weight and bulkiness would have been too much. So she placed it on the bookshelf next to the others she had to leave behind. Near the top left side of her bag was a neatly folded hat she made that was inspired by a magazine cover. Finally, down the right side was a pouch containing enough money for a train ticket.

The night before her departure, she would make sure to put in a peanut butter and jelly sandwich. She had a rope handy to lower her bag from her bedroom window before the men woke.

*E*mily's birthday came and went. If Aunt Francine was still around she would have come over and helped her bake a cake. But at this stage in Emily's life, another birthday meant nothing to her but for the freedom it would bring. Steven had already announced that he was going to Watseka the following Saturday, which was only two days away. And she was waiting for the right moment to talk to him.

The next morning as she was cleaning up the breakfast dishes, Grandfather freshened his coffee and went outside. Timothy had already left for the barn. And when footsteps came up the hallway, she knew it was Steven. She had to get it out before Grandfather came back in.

"So...you still going into town tomorrow?"

"I plan to. Why?"

"Remember, you said I could ride along."

"I did?"

"Yes, you did."

"Aw... I don't know. Seems fine to me." He hesitated for a moment. "Wait till morning, and let Pa know you're caught up on everything."

Steven knew how things worked with Grandfather. To mention anything too far out—anything over a couple of hours—would give the old man a chance to think of reasons to keep her home.

But Emily wasn't taking any chances. *Nope, I'm keeping silent until we're about leave.* Being this close to freedom, she wasn't letting anything stop her from going.

Chapter Eleven

Moonlight flickered through the leaves of the apple tree casting shadows into the second story bedroom window. Emily shivered, pulled the covers under her chin, and watched the reflection of tree branches dance on rose-covered wallpaper.

Knowing that time was precious, she sat up, lit a lantern and took her journal from the nightstand. She gazed at the picture she had drawn on the cover of a girl riding a dove on a moonlit night. Below, shadows of tree branches drifted in and out of a fog. And cradled within the mist was a beautiful rose.

She adjusted the white goose feather that marked her last entry. Picking up her bag from the end of the bed, she pushed the journal inside, then secured the rope that was tied to the strap she would use to carry her bag over her shoulders.

Slipping from her bed, she dressed and stepped into her saddle shoes that were freshly polished and patched with cutout cardboard. Lacing them up, she took her bag and went to open the right front window, sticking her head out. The light in the kitchen was on, and a shadow moved behind the shade—most likely Timothy up for a glass of milk. She had thought of using the back window. But Timothy and Steven's bedroom was directly beneath hers. And unless it was below ten degrees, their window was open.

Hoisting her bag on the sill, she pushed it over the edge, and let the rope slide through her hands until the bag lay on the ground. Dropping the rope, she closed the window and stepped from her bedroom.

She looked down at the pot of acorns sitting outside her doorway. Picking out the healthiest acorn she could find, she dropped it into her skirt pocket, and headed down.

As she neared the bottom of the staircase, the dogs began to bark. She poked her head around the banister and saw that her grandfather's bedroom door was open. That's not what she wanted nor expected. And her heart raced as she leaped over the last few steps and hurried up the hallway. As she turned into the kitchen, his hand was on the doorknob.

"Where're you going?" she asked, rushing across the room.

The old man swung around. "What do you mean, where am I going? And since when is it any of your business where I go?"

"I was just... I-I'm sorry."

"You take them out, then," he growled, shoving a bowl of scraps against her chest. "Shoulda done it last night."

His slippers sounded like sandpaper as he shuffled off. Emily waited for his shadow to disappear down the hallway, then slipped out the door.

Angel and Tokee were at the side of the house sniffing her bag, trying to get at the peanut butter and jelly sandwich she wrapped in wax paper and put in the night before. She set down the scraps for them and begun to untie the rope attached to her bag. Glancing at Steven's pickup sitting next to the barn, she wondered how far she would get if she loaded up the dogs and cats and headed to San Francisco. If she could even get the truck started, she knew it wouldn't be far.

When she had untangled the rope, she stuffed it in her skirt pocket, watching the dogs run to the front of the house for water and where more scraps were sure to follow.

"Well...here I go," she said, lifting her bag over a shoulder and heading towards the barn.

She set her bag inside the barn doorway, pulled the rope out of her pocket and dropped it next to the wall. After lighting a lantern, she fed the cows and milked enough to fill a small pail. When she finished, she gathered eggs and set them and the milk outside the barn door just as the sun began to rise. She reached back into the barn for her bag and headed to Steven's pickup. Stepping onto the footboard, she reached in back and lifted the lid of the storage bin. As she placed the bag inside, footsteps came up behind her.

"What the hell are you doing?"

The lid crashed back to the bin, and she stumbled off the running board, wheeling around to face Claude. She smelled whiskey on him and already knew what was coming.

"I asked what you're doing!"

"I'm riding into town with Steven. H-he said I could."

"This early? Sounds fishy to me."

He brushed past her and confiscated the bag from the pickup. She wanted to jump him. But all she could do was stand by and watch him rip out her belongings and toss them on the ground. With much of her things lying in the dirt, he reached back in, pulled out the brown skirt, and laid it open in his hand.

"Woo! Where the hell did you get this?"

He took a closer look at the silver bar and chucked it and the skirt onto the hood of the pickup. Reaching in for more treasures, he pulled out the blouse containing the necklace and tossed her bag over a shoulder.

Emily tried to grab the velvet box, but he yanked it away and turned his back to her.

"Wonder what we have here."

"That's mine," she said, trying to move around him. "Give it back!"

Elbowing her, he opened the blouse and lifted the lid of the jewelry box.

"Son of a gun! It's the necklace Rupert's been grumbling about."

He tossed the blouse and jewelry box on the ground and grabbed her arm as he stuffed the necklace into a jean pocket.

"I didn't know you had it in you, Mud. Looks like the ole man didn't either.

"You know... I could forget all about this notion of yours. That's if you'd be *reeeal* nice."

She tried to wrench her arm free, but it only made him tighten his grip again.

"Stop! You're hurting me!"

"Shut up," he hissed, slapping her across the cheek.

"You want everyone to hear? Want ole gramps to know you were running off with the necklace? Is that what you want?" He gave her a shake and let her go.

"The necklace is mine," she snapped, stepping back as she nursed her cheek. "Besides, I'm eighteen now. I'm free to go as I please."

"Oh, and I'm forty. Big deal. Around here, all eighteen gets you is more work and less time to live."

"Please. Just give it back."

Claude nodded at the barn. "Come on then. Let's go up to the loft and talk about it."

"No."

"No? You realize...things would be just fine if you weren't such a *priss*."

He glanced over a shoulder towards the house and back at her.

"Let's go."

It was clear what he wanted, but she had sworn, on her life, this would never happen again. She darted around him. But he grabbed her arm again, digging his claws into her as he pulled her back.

"Ouch. Let me go... Ooouch!"

He clamped a hand over her mouth and walked her into the barn—she kicking, trying to twist free as he manned her up the ladder. When they reached the top step, he shoved her to the loft floor.

Her eyes moved to the opening used to bring baled hay into the barn. She considered the twenty-foot jump. Of course, this time it would be without a truckload of hay as cushion.

He followed her gaze to the opening. "Oh, now that'd be a smart move."

He climbed the last step and yanked her to her feet.

"I'll tell you what. You jump and if you don't kill yourself in the process, I'll put you out of your misery myself."

He grabbed her by the shoulders and slammed her against a pole. The wood dug into her back as he buried his whiskered face in her neck, slobbering his liquored breath on her. She had never seen him so fierce—like a rabid dog. When he worked his way up her chin, she swung her head to the side ready to die before he dared to take the one last dream she still owned.

No… no… this can't happen! Never! Never again! You have to stop him! Stop him!

She wrenched an arm free and slammed an elbow into his chest.

"You bitch!"

She pulled free and bolted. But he grabbed a clump of her hair with such force that her roots crackled.

"Ow. Claude. Stooooop!"

"Sure, Mud." He gave her hair another yank and flung her to the floor again.

She lay in a daze screaming inside and knowing that she had no one to save her, but for herself.

"That'll teach you not to avoid me." His boot caught her on the shin. "You know how angry that makes me."

Her leg ached, and her cheek and arm burned as she pulled herself off the floor, all the while, planning an escape.

"I… I was going to tell you something." She took a breath, forcing back a sob and every name she could think to call him. "If… If you wouldn't get so upset and let me get a word in."

"Go on then. Tell me." He pulled out a cigarette and lit up.

"I haven't meant to avoid you. It's just that I've been… I've been busy."

"So, you gonna forgive me for catching you running off, aye?"

She nodded, yes, but her mind scrambled for a way out. She thought of the last four years and how he used her state of mind and vulnerability after losing Daniel. How he used every threat, trick, and lie imaginable so that she would succumb to his whims.

Tears stung her eyes when her gaze fell on the spot where he had taken her innocence. To think, less than an hour ago, he was out of her life for good. *And now this!*

She had to get away from him. But first, he had to be stopped. Her heart heaved in her chest, knowing exactly how she would conquer the demon inside him. She swallowed, giving herself time to gather courage.

"I know... You didn't realize this, but…."

Look at him! Make it believable! You have to dig deeper. Remember what he did to you? You were so young that first time, so innocent.

She looked him in the eyes. "I… I've been thinking about…you know, way back when…" Her hands shook as she reached for the top button on her blouse. "When we played, *the game*."

Pushing the button through the hole, she slid her fingers up the collar. "Remember…you turned around and, I… I got rid of these." She flicked her collar.

"You sure were shy back then, weren't you."

He took a drag from his cigarette, tossed it on the floor and stomped it out.

The game was her idea. It was a way of control over what would happen anyway. It meant less time with him next to her, less demeaning the way he went about things. As time passed, she was no longer his new conquest. But, of late, he had been asking for a repeat. She understood exactly what he wanted.

"You've been thinking about that too, huh?"

"Mhmm."

"I knew it. Me too."

"Well?" she said, motioning with a finger.

He whipped around, facing the wall—and she continued the ruse as planned moving backwards while keeping an eye on him. She had only taken a few steps when he whirled around. With the most daring smile she could muster, she moved her hand to the next button.

"I knew it. I just knew it," he said, spinning around.

Continuing to inch backwards, she glanced up and quickly down again, seeing a pitchfork at her feet. An instant later, Claude's belt buckle hit the floor. A blast of heat washed over Emily as she plucked the fork into her fist and leaped towards him, only meaning to scare him off.

"I'll kill you!" he roared, lurching at her, his legs entangling at the same time her feet caught a loose board, sending both flying towards each other, his eyes wild as the pitchfork slammed into his chest.

She yanked her hands from the handle, stumbling back as he staggered forward and dropped to the floor. Dust settled around him and everything was quiet.

"Claude? Claude?"

She edged forward closer and closer until she saw the blood and the rest and knew he was dead. Crushing a hand over her mouth, she turned for the exit and rushed down the steps, her shoulders heaving as she forced back sobs.

Once downstairs, she stopped at the water tank next to the door. Flipping pieces of straw and seeds to the side, she splashed her face and dried off with her skirt. Moving to the exit, she peeked outside.

All was quiet as she walked to the truck with daybreak spreading like satin across the yard and over the prairies—almost tauntingly beautiful. Her heart was heavy, wrought by the horror she left up in the loft and the loss for the morning that should have been, knowing it was lost forever.

Her knees trembled as she squatted, reached for her bag and gathered her things off the ground. When she picked up the necklace box, she stood and looked at the barn thinking of the precious jewelry in Claude's pocket. The thought was almost too much for her. Still, she couldn't force herself to go up and take back what was rightfully hers. Brushing off the velvet box, she returned it to the bag, the bag to the bin, sank to the footboard of the truck, and wept.

She wondered if anyone would believe what had been going on, that, if not for the words and actions put on her, it hadn't been by her choice. Who would believe such a thing? She was afraid her family would be first in line to condemn and blame her, just like Claude said they would.

"Please, God, please help me. Help me to know what I should do."

Wiping away tears with her skirt, she looked up at the fleece of clouds that were scattered across the sky desperate to find direction.

She wanted to believe her grandmother had been right, wanted to believe in God's love for her and that he would take this horrible thing from her. And yet, in this predicament, she wondered where he had been for the last hour. For that matter, where had he been for the last four years? She closed her eyes in regret.

"I'm sorry. I'm so sorry. You didn't make me do it. You didn't make Claude do what he did."

She wondered what would have happened if she had told someone the first time Claude forced himself on her. It was easy to look back now, but she wished she had gone to Francine. Maybe that would have saved Claude from himself, and her from the horrible mess she was in.

She was still repenting when the dogs showed up and licked her face. Kidders and Caesar stopped for a look from their play next to the barn. At least she could count on them not to hold anything against her. Whether this was a sign or not, she had to pull herself together because the last place she wanted to be was in jail.

Looking across to the fields and the lonely miles of fenced-in pastures, she wondered if she should start running. Maybe she could take Star and head north until she reached the Canadian border. The urge disappeared quickly. Her only hope was to stick with her original plan. She would be with Steven when he left for Watseka.

Chapter Twelve

Like any normal day, Emily walked into the house with a pail of milk and a basket of eggs. She put on an apron, opened the shades, and switched the radio station to music. The cooking heat was low, so she stoked the fire in the wood stove and began the task of fixing breakfast for three men she didn't want to see.

She jumped at every sound, nicked herself peeling potatoes, and when she dumped the batch into a pan, splatters of hot grease burned her fingers. Her hands trembled as she pulled strips of bacon from the wrap and placed them into a frying pan. Every few minutes, she took a deep breath and forced back tears. She arranged plates, glasses, and silverware on the table, filled glasses with homemade tomato juice, and set out salt and pepper and a jar of honey. On her way back to the stove, without meaning to, she stopped in front of a window, her gaze drifting to the barn....

"Where've you been?"

She jumped, tripping over her feet as she hurried to the stove. Grandfather stood in the kitchen doorway drying his hands with a towel. The straps of his overalls hung at his waist, and his belly jiggled with each movement.

"I-I was out milking cows and gathering eggs," she croaked.

"You took long enough. Did you finish patching my shirt?"

"It's in the hall closet."

He seemed satisfied for the moment and shuffled off.

Timothy came from the bedroom a few minutes later and headed to the fireplace where he dropped to the hearth. For once, she didn't mind his morning ritual when he grunted like an injured animal as he pulled on his work shoes or the way he let his shoelaces drag along the floor on his way to the table. She still didn't understand why he nearly always waited until after breakfast to tie his shoelaces.

When Steven walked in, he went straight for the stove, as usual, and poured a cup of coffee. He took a lengthy slurp that ended in a contented, "Aah."

Each morning, she got satisfaction hearing that display of pleasure from him. Well, except for the morning she forgot to make a fresh pot. That morning there were no pleasantries, just a cuff across the back of the head after he spit the cold coffee onto the floor and ordered her to clean it up. That took her by surprise because Steven wasn't one for physical harm. She knew it was really about the breakup with Bernadette spurred on by a hangover from the night before.

"What time you heading out, Steven?" Grandfather asked as he walked back into the kitchen. He turned the radio off and took a seat.

"Soon as we bring in the bales of hay. Shouldn't take long."

Emily poured coffee and sat in the chair closest to the stove. She kept her eyes on her plate, slicing her toast into strips and the strips into smaller pieces. When she looked up, Steven's gaze was on her. His frown made her wonder if there were telltale marks on her face from the smack Claude gave her. She pulled a clump of hair over her left cheek.

But Steven had other things on his mind. "Think I'd better go into town alone today," he said nonchalantly.

She reached for her coffee, attempting to cover a gasp. He didn't seem to notice her despair and went on to explain.

"There's someone I need to see. That'd leave you on your own for some time."

"I don't mind waiting in the pickup, honest. I... I can... I can bring a book."

"You heard 'em," Grandfather growled. "He's going alone."

He reached for the last of the bacon and shoved the empty serving plate towards Emily. "There's lots to do around here."

Her mind was whirling as she went to the stove for more bacon. When she placed the plate on the table, Steven handed her his coffee cup before she had a chance to sit.

"Here. And grab some jelly while you're at it."

She filled his cup, still agonizing over a way to change his mind. When she went for the jelly, a thought hit her. She brought Steven his coffee and set the jelly on the table.

"I need canning supplies," she said, pulling her chair to the table.

"I'm out of lids, and the jars and rings are low too. This is the time of year for sales. I'll save at least ten bucks, if not more."

She thought her announcement would go over well, but they obviously didn't see the urgency.

"Once I ran out of lids and couldn't can for weeks."

There wasn't as much as a grunt from any of them— —only the sounds of them devouring their food, and the incessant ticking of the clock above the refrigerator.

"S-Steven? I—"

"There's no need for you to go!" Grandfather blared. "Steven can just as well pick up what you need."

"Well, wait a minute, Pops. I was just thinking that since she does the gardening and canning, I'd rather she take care of it. I don't know the first thing about buying lids."

The old man gave it a moment. "Doggone it, just do what you want then."

He glared at Emily. "I'm running over to Francine's. When I get back, if everything's not done, you're not going no matter what Steven says."

Steven let his father's statement sink in before giving a final decision. "Just get everything done," he told Emily.

She was tempted to jump up and give him a hug. He was more concerned about details and turned to his younger brother.

"By the way, how's the gasoline holding up?"

Timothy licked the edge of the honey jar and plopped the container onto the table.

"Don't need any," he said with his early morning bark. "Maybe some oil. Four cases'll do."

Grandfather frowned at Emily.

"Where is Claude anyway? You see 'em when you were out?"

"*No.*"

"Well, I heard him drive in the yard like a crazy fool about four this morning," Timothy said. "Out all night. Tomcatting, I'll bet."

Grandfather nearly cracked a smile. "Uh, you know him. Just likes to have a little fun."

The smell of bacon grease and the mention of Claude's name was too much for Emily, and she jumped from her seat. As she gathered empty plates, she noticed blood spots on the inner part of her sleeve. There were also telltale marks left by Claude's grubby hands. She looked up and caught Steven's gaze on her again.

"Dang barbwire," she said, turning away. She went to deposit the dishes in the sink, dropped her apron on a stool, and rushed up to her bedroom.

Tears welled when she looked in the mirror and saw that Claude's hand had left her cheek deep red and slightly swollen. She touched the spot, grateful her tone was dark enough to where it may not be noticed.

"Don't you dare fall apart."

When she went to the window for a better look at her clothes, she was shocked. Blood had not only seeped through her left sleeve, but there were tiny spots splattered down the front of her skirt and blouse.

She went to the closet door, took off her blouse, and tossed it aside. As she unzipped her skirt and let it drop to the floor, the acorn fell out of a pocket, rolled across the room, and hit the wall. She kicked her bloody clothes into the closet, planning to take them out to the burn barrel.

There was a slight cut and a bruise on her left arm. Although with the bleeding virtually stopped, all she needed was a piece of fabric cut into strips to use as wrap. Once that was taken care of, she put on two long-sleeved blouses to hide the bulge, tying the top one at her waist. She pulled on a black calf-length skirt, zipped it up, and went to retrieve the acorn. Such a small thing it was, but she had so little to hang onto. She tucked it into her pocket and headed downstairs.

Steven was the only one in the kitchen. And she felt awkward facing him again. He set his coffee cup on the counter and was about to leave when his gaze dropped to her sleeve.

She pulled her arm back. "Do you think we'll be leaving within an hour?" she asked before he had a chance to say anything.

He ambled across the room and put a hand on the doorknob.

"That's my plan. Forty minutes, maybe." He looked out through one of the long narrow windows and settled on the barn. "Guess I should rouse Claude so he can help you feed the animals."

"Don't bother. I-I'd rather do it myself."

He paused, thoughtfully, his gaze still on the barn. "Oh, I don't know… There's no reason he can't help. You've got plenty to do before we head into town."

"Not that much." She glanced at the mess around her.

"I'll get it done before we leave, easily."

"Weeell, you'd better make sure you do."

When he left, Emily crammed dishes into the oven, and the rest under the sink. She set the garbage next to the door just as Grandfather came down the hallway and into the kitchen.

"I've half a mind to keep you home, young lady," he said on his way across the room.

Slapping on the same cap he wore whether rain or shine, he turned at the door. "You still didn't get the last of the carrots picked."

He glanced around the kitchen. And she leaned back against the cupboard, wiping an imaginary spill along the edge of the sink.

"I started on the carrots last night. It'll only take fifteen minutes to finish. And I'll can them tomorrow. Even if it takes me all night," she added, boldly.

He dug a toothpick out of a shirt pocket, stuck it in his mouth, and slammed out the door.

Chapter Thirteen

A sense of doom filled the air as she headed for the barn that suddenly looked dingier than she remembered. Gusts of wind picked up dust, whirling it in every direction. Tiny mounds of dried earth that formed with the last rain crackled unusually loud beneath her feet. Even the muffled sounds of the animals seemed strange. She wondered when she had stopped noticing the aroma of leather straps and saddles and of soiled hay and manure—the smell was there now as she approached the building and forced her hand around the latch. The hinges creaked and her stomach churned as she pulled the door open and stepped inside.

She stopped at the entrance, her gaze drifting to the left where steps led up to the loft. Her instinct was to rush back out. She was thinking of doing just that when a gust of wind slammed the door behind her.

Claude's presence permeated the air like a black cloud. She wanted to turn and run, but she had no choice. Her legs felt like rubber as she crunched across the straw-covered floor. The pigs grunted with anticipation, and the rush began as she sprinted back and forth between the feed bin and troughs. Each time the old building settled, she held her breath and turned her eyes up to the loft.

Finally, it was her last round. She hurried to the bin and scooped up a bucket of oats for the horse, took it to the stall and dumped the contents into a tub. Star had always been part of her life—nearly twenty years old now. Emily recalled how the opportunity to ride her mother's horse had been limited to evenings. If she drifted out of sight, Grandfather would throw a fit—as if he feared she would leave with his prized possession and never return.

Before this morning she thought of coming back one day to visit the animals. But her fate was sealed, and she had to move quickly.

She rubbed the spot between the horse's ears. And with the food and water supply restored, all she had time for was a quick goodbye before rushing from the barn. When she collided with Steven, it was like running into a brick wall.

"Hey! Watch where you're going," he said, pushing her aside. "You done in there?"

She stepped back to the door and rested against the frame with a leg out—as if that would stop him from going inside if that's what he wanted.

"They're all fed, watered, and content as could be. Listen. Not a peep."

Mumbling something about a *blasted truck,* Steven headed to the toolshed. He stopped at the door and looked back to where she was still watching him.

"Hey! Have you seen Claude?"

"He's sick. Got some milk and left."

Steven nodded and continued into the shed.

Emily closed the barn door, grasping how easily she had lied. *Now what do I do? Confess? Should I confess? Maybe... Just maybe they'll understand.*

"Oh sure...."

Even if they did, or at least Steven, he wouldn't be the judge and jury. Besides, Claude had stooped as low as to threaten her with jail—how he would arrange that he didn't go into detail. Although when she was eleven she had stolen a red pullover sweater when she rode to town with Steven to buy new shoes. Longing for store-bought clothes like many of the girls at school, on the spur of the moment, she had dropped the sweater into her bag on the way out of the store. For months, she had been wracked with so much guilt that she never wore it. Instead, she left it in the barn loft, where she took it after returning home from town that day. She wondered if Claude had seen her try it on and guessed that she had stolen it. Eventually she threw the sweater into the burn barrel and forgot about it—until now. Nevertheless, whatever Claude knew or didn't know, he had warned her about what happened to the young and beautiful behind bars. That...she would do everything possible to avoid.

On her way to the house, she looked out to the field to where Timothy's head was under the hood of the truck. Confident that's where Steven would go, she hurried inside, up to her bedroom, where she gathered her stained clothing. Picking up the trash as she left the house, she went to the burn barrel that sat next to the barn. She lit a match and watched evidence of the dreadful morning go up in flames.

With smoke still rising, she walked around the corner just in time to see Steven go into the barn. She dashed to the entrance. And when she stepped inside, he was climbing the ladder.

"Nooo!"

He turned to the commotion as she rushed towards him and up the steps.

"What in the...?"

"Th... the cat!" she screeched, pointing to Kidders who was peering down at them from a step near the top. "I was about to check on her. I... I think she's having kittens."

She slipped past her uncle. "What'd you need? I'll get it for you."

He sighed and headed back down. "Bring me a pitchfork. And make it quick."

She scooped Kidders up as she stepped into the loft. When she checked around for a pitchfork, she noticed, besides the one planted in Claude's chest, there were two up against the wall just beyond where he lay.

"Emily!" Steven called from below. "What're you up to? There's a pitchfork by the railing."

I'll be right there," she said, letting the cat jump to the floor. When Kidders streaked down the steps, Emily rushed over to Claude and dug her necklace out of his pocket.

"I'm coming up!" Steven hollered.

"Don't bother. I've got it!"

She stuffed the necklace into her skirt pocket and darted to the wall.

Hearing Steven's footsteps, she grabbed one of the pitchforks, bolted past Claude, and down the steps, meeting him halfway.

Steven snatched the pitchfork out of her hand. "You're acting mighty peculiar, Emily."

He tromped back down, and she sank to a step just in case he thought of something else he wanted from the loft. Kidders scampered back up and rubbed against her legs. She stroked the cat's fur watching Steven fork straw into the pens as if he had all day. Claude's presence was at her back, and she wanted to scream at her uncle to hurry.

At last, he leaned the pitchfork against a pole and headed for the door. "Let's go," he called on his way out.

She leaped to her feet. Bounding down the steps to the door, she stopped and looked back. Star was contently eating straw. A mouse had already distracted Kidders, and Caesar lay on a stack of baled hay looking like a king. Thankful for their indifference, and for the safety of their future off-spring, she rushed outside and hopped in next to Steven.

The pickup rattled to a start, and they moved across the yard. When she was ready to breathe a sigh of relief, Steven pulled up to the house and let the engine die. He didn't explain, just got out and went inside.

Emily tried to concentrate on the dogs romping around the front lawn and stepped out for a few minutes. They wanted to play, and she threw them a couple of bones. But, knowing Grandfather was due back at any minute and seeing her would remind him of the unpicked carrots, she gave the dogs a final hug and went to wait in the pickup.

She felt the bulge of the necklace in her pocket as she gazed up the road, watching for the old man. It wasn't long before he pulled into the driveway and parked no more than two feet away.

Like a deer caught in a headlight, she watched him walk around Steven's pickup, up the walk, and take the steps to the top. He took the last drag from a cigarette and tossed it into a pail of sand next to the wooden sidewalk. Watching it burn for a moment, he turned his gaze on her. Their eyes met in a flash before she was able to pull her eyes away.

Steven came out onto the porch and exchanged words with his father—something about a new engine. He headed to the truck and was about to get in when his father called to him. Hearing him out, he peeked in at Emily.

"Pa wants to know if you picked the carrots."

Emily recalled the dozen or so jars of carrots already stored for winter. "They're in the basement."

"She said they're in the basement," Steven hollered as he climbed in.

Grandfather waved absently and disappeared into the house. The old Ford pickup made its usual sputters and coughs as they left the yard and headed up the drive. They passed Aunt Francine's old property. And when they turned onto the main road leading to Watseka, Emily sighed.

"Finally."

Steven glanced over. "Mm? What'd you say?"

"Oh, nothing."

If only she could leave it at that, but she knew there was a lot of things she would have to deal with in her own mind. And as much as she knew the horrible secret she carried would burrow a hole in her soul if she kept it to herself, she couldn't tell him.

Chapter Fourteen

Since Emily's first trip to Watseka, which only occurred two or three times a year, the novelty had never worn off. Now, instead of the usual excitement, she was terrified the police would grab her before she had a chance to catch the train. Getting the address and a departure schedule was vital if she wanted to leave that night. And in order to get that information, she needed to use a telephone as soon as possible.

Steven didn't seem to notice her distress and appeared to have forgotten her odd behavior back at the farm.

"After I pick up supplies, I'm going to stop at Joe's Tavern," he said. "The movie hall is just down the street. Thought I'd leave you there for a few hours."

"Oh, that'll be nice. Thanks."

She tried to sound excited, wondering if he had finally found a new girlfriend. For his sake, she hoped so.

The only movies she had seen were *The Three Stooges* and *Singing in the Rain*. And that was several years back. She couldn't even recall where exactly the movie hall was located. At first, she was disappointed Steven chose this day of all days to let her see another movie. Although, after some thought, she realized that by him thinking that's where she was, she would have more time to catch the train.

When they turned into the store parking lot, Emily scanned the area for a place to hide her bag. A paved area alongside the store with a stretch of trees and shrubs looked like a good spot.

Steven parked, stepped from the pickup, and studied the sky. "Looks like we're in for some showers," he said as rolling thunder rumbled in the distance.

Emily closed the door on her side and followed his gaze. She hoped the showers would wait until she was on her way out of town.

They were heading into the market when she noticed the telephone booth that sat next to the street was empty. As soon as she could slip away, she would retrieve her bag from the grocery bin and hide it in the bushes before making the call to the train station.

Shopping had always been a treat for her. But now, she was a pack of nerves as she grabbed canning supplies and walked up and down the aisles picking up things she would never use. They were in the back of the store when she made her move.

"Um… I need to pick up some personal things," she told Steven.

With a nod from him, she made her way to the front of the store, checking to make sure he didn't notice her heading to the exit.

Outside, a gust of wind blasted her face with hot air. As she walked to the pickup, she noticed a man was in the phonebooth. She lifted her bag from the grocery bin and walked around to the side of the building to a row of bushes. Looking around to see if anyone was watching, she lowered her bag until it almost touched the ground and gave it a slight pitch into the underbrush.

She went around to the front of the store just as the man in the booth dropped more coins into the phone. Disappointed, she headed back inside before Steven got suspicious. On her way through the doorway, two teenage boys rushed out, and one of them nearly knocked her over.

"Sorry, ma'am," he said.

Catching her balance, Emily waved him off, and walked inside just as Steven stepped to the checkout counter. She went over to help him, relieved that he didn't ask questions.

As they left the store ten minutes later there was a distant lightning strike and a low rumble that seemed closer than before. Emily noticed the phone booth was empty and hoped it stayed that way until she returned for her bag. There was no more room for setbacks.

She wiped her clammy palms on her skirt, climbed into the pickup cab, and rolled down the window. Sitting back, she searched the bushes where her bag was hidden, thinking it felt wrong to leave it behind. She glanced back to where Steven was loading groceries into the bin, cringing to think what he would have done if he had found it there.

The boys she met in the entryway retrieved a ball from two cars down. They ran around to the side of the store and began to throw it against the building. Watching them brought memories of happier days at the schoolhouse playing basketball with Daniel.

When Daniel left, the pain had been so overwhelming she did everything possible to forget him. After months of weeping and torturing herself over the loss, she thought she was over him. But she was fooling herself. And she knew just how much by the emotions that washed over her when she realized the letter he wrote to her was still up in the closet.

The night she had kissed the letter and pushed it to the corner of the shelf, it had been of the utmost importance for her to keep it safe and at the same time forget it was there. *I hope you know that I've never really forgotten you, Daniel.*

She heard the slam of the grocery bin and quickly pulled herself together. Steven swung the door open, slid onto the seat beside her, and they were on their way. Normally, they would buy groceries then stop for farm supplies. Sometimes they delivered vegetables and eggs. Today, things were different.

They headed down Walnut street and took a right onto North Fourth Street. The truck barely geared up before he made a right turn onto Oak. He drove a couple of hundred feet up the street, made a sharp left, and pulled over.

"There it is. The Watseka Theater."

He reached into a shirt pocket, dug out a dollar and a quarter and handed it to her.

"Should be enough for soda and popcorn."

This surprised her as much as the first time he gave her money. Of course, she had nearly embarrassed him half to death right in the middle of the store before he got the hint that sometimes a young woman needs to pick up some things on her own.

A breeze rippled through her hair as she stepped from the pickup, turning as she closed the door and looked at him through the window.

"Thanks, Steven."

He smiled, something he didn't often do. "I'll meet you back here in about two and a half hours."

She watched him shift the gears and pull away.

Although they had never been close as in, *let me tell you my secrets,* she felt a pang of sadness as he drove away.

On her own for the first time in her life, her feet were heavy on the pavement as she headed up the road. She thought of looking for a telephone at the theater, but her first priority had to be the silver bar.

As she walked, she thought of how the day had begun with such promise. Now, for all she knew, the police had been notified and were already searching for her. Her shoulders tensed when a car approached. She wished she had pulled out her hat for camouflage.

Thunder rumbled closer and she picked up her pace as it began to sprinkle. Within minutes, clouds were sending down buckets of rain. When a crack of thunder hit, she took off running.

She found cover under a tree every so often. Then off she went again. Just as she turned onto Walnut street, she nearly tripped over a black cat when it streaked in front of her. She stopped and watched it run up a sidewalk and onto a porch where it snuggled in the corner.

"You don't know how lucky you are, cat," she said as she took off again. She wondered how it would feel with nothing to worry about but a little wet fur and where to wait out a rain shower.

By the time she reached the store parking lot, the rain had stopped, and the clouds had parted enough to let the hot sun evaporate most of the puddles.

The leaves and branches were still wet as she reached into the underbrush for her bag. She had trouble finding it and moved deeper. Still nothing. Her throat tightened, and a sob began to build as she patted the branches and ground in every direction. Finally, she stood and looked up one way and down the other before turning back to where she knew she had placed the bag.

"It's… Right there. That's where I put it."

Diving back in, she frantically flailed her arms. But her search was futile. Everything she owned was gone. Choking back tears, she pulled herself from the bushes, looking each way again and searching for something she may have missed. She felt the bulge of her skirt pocket again, relieved she still had the necklace. It wouldn't get her out of town, though.

A breeze whipped across the parking lot. And she looked around at the building where the boys had been playing ball earlier. Recalling the apology from the one who ran into her, gave her hope.

She swooshed her hands across the wet leaves, snapped off a branch, and brushed dirt off her skirt. Pulling her damp hair up and twisting it into a knot, she went into the store and approached a clerk.

"Sir," she said, pushing back strands of hair from her face. "I lost my bag. Well…it's a purse but it looks like—"

"Why don't you try the office?" he said pointing her in the right direction.

"Excuse me, ma'am," she said to a woman sitting at a counter desk. "I lost my bag. It's blue, about half the size of a flour sack. I'm sure someone left it here."

Her heart raced with excitement certain she would soon have it back.

The woman looked at her curiously. "Uh… No one brought in a bag."

"But—"

"I would've seen it."

"I'm certain it's here."

The woman didn't share her optimism, although she attempted a search and looked over each of her shoulders. She turned back to her paperwork, glancing up.

"Sorry. But like I said, it's not here."

"Please ma'am. I saw two teenage boys outside the store earlier. I'm sure they found my bag. Maybe you know them. One has reddish hair a...and the other has brown—"

"May I help you?" a voice broke through the tension.

A middle-aged man brushed past Emily and stepped into the office. Emily noticed a *Manager, Jack Smith* badge pinned to his shirt.

"Oh, thank you sir, I hope so. I'm looking for a blue bag."

She took a breath trying to contain her excitement. "You can't miss—"

The man raised a hand one step ahead of her. "Two boys were in earlier, Alex and Ethan. Nice boys. They come in with their mother quite often."

He reached down into a cupboard and pulled out her bag. "They said their ball rolled into some bushes and they found this."

"That's it! That's my bag. Oh, thank you. Thank you so much."

"This is quite a purse you have here," he said, handing it over.

"You make it?"

"Yes, I did."

She placed the strap over her shoulder and dug in her pocket for the dollar bill Steven gave her, handing it to him. "For the boys. And tell them I said thanks."

Outside, she placed the necklace into its original case and pushed it deep into her bag. Taking out her hat, she pulled it on, tucking in strands of hair as she headed for the phone booth. Thankful for the change Steven gave her, she placed the coin into the slot and dialed.

"Good morning. Watseka Union. May I help you?"

"Yes. I'm looking to catch the next train to Chicago. I... I'm headed to...to New York. And if you'd be so kind, sir, and give me directions. I'm at Fourth and Oak."

"Let's see. There's a train leaving in twelve minutes. But you'd better plan on taking the one this eve—"

"Sir, I... My cousin is waiting. And I... I... Just give me the directions, please."

"Well, okay. You'll go up to Fourth Street until you reach Second. Take a left and head up that way. We're just past Walnut on your right."

"I'm on my way," she said, already out of the booth. Reaching back in, she dropped the receiver on the hook and scampered up the sidewalk, securing her hat every so often. She made it to the corner lickety-split and raced down Second. A street sign caught her eye, and she knew if she was on the right track, it had to be Walnut.

As she neared the crossing, a train whistle blew. *Just a warning, that's all,* she told herself. Her legs were already spent, but she strained her limits as she barreled past Walnut.

A few more steps, and there it was, the building, and amongst a rise of trees in the back sat the train. Hope urged her across the lot with a willful sprint. But the groan of the engines and the grinding wheels stopped her cold. She stood open-mouthed watching the train move away. Eyes stinging with tears, she hobbled to a tree and leaned to catch her breath.

"Gosh darn! Now what?"

She looked around the tree and across the parking lot, visualizing directions from a scanty map she was able to dig up at home. From the looks of it, if she continued up Walnut where the train was heading, it would eventually take her to Highway 52 and straight to Kankakee, just like her aunt said. Once in Kankakee, she would take the Greyhound bus to Chicago. She still had to find a ride, so she wasn't out of the woods yet. Although she was filled with renewed energy.

With a plan in place, she took off again, slower now, reminding herself to keep an eye out for police, and at the same time, a place to hide if one approached. She patted the top of her head. At least no one would be looking for a female in a floppy black hat.

She hadn't been walking more than ten minutes when she came upon a gas station. There at the pump sat a truck loaded with baled hay—a familiar sight for her. Wherever that truck was headed, it looked to be going north. An attendant prepared to fill the truck with gas while the driver checked the wheels and went into the building. Emily hurried over and walked in behind him.

Directly inside, next to the door, was a stand that held maps. She picked one up and found that Walnut street turned into Highway 1, then Highway 52 into Kankakee. Replacing the map, she looked around just as the driver walked to the counter with pop and an arm full of snacks.

"Headed up north, ay?" The cashier asked.

"Yep, Kankakee. Taking a load over."

The gas attendant came inside, and Emily knew she had to think quickly. She looked out the window at the stacks of hay in the truck and noticed they cut short of the tailgate. And there was an opening in the middle section with just enough room for her to hide. She glanced over at the young man again, wondering if she should ask him for a ride.

He'll ask questions. What if I fall to pieces?

Thirty seconds later, she had spun out the door and was crouched between three layers of baled hay. She tucked her hat into her bag, holding her breath as the man approached the truck. He walked around and stopped next to the door.

What're you waiting for, mister?

Finally, she smelled cigarette smoke and heard the clink of the door handle. The engine started and they were on their way out of town. She leaned back with a sigh and closed her eyes. The wind against her cheeks, and the hum of the engine, was the distraction she needed. That's where she kept her thoughts until they approached Kankakee forty-five minutes later.

The moment he stopped, she had to go for it. She clutched her bag and worked her way around to the side of the truck bed and waited. The driver slowed, made a right turn and another shortly after. She peeked over the side and saw they were heading out to a remote area. There was a stop sign ahead. That's where she would get off.

Crouching with a hand on the rail, the moment the truck stopped, she hauled it over the side and was down in the ditch within seconds. She sank into the grass and looked around to make sure no one had seen her.

The driver was rolling through the intersection, and the only cars visible were far enough back to where they wouldn't have noticed her risky move. Waiting until they passed, she headed back to Highway 52.

She recalled her aunt saying the bus station was right off the highway. There were a few businesses alongside the road, no sidewalk, only a dirt pathway. About a fourth of a mile up, she noticed a woman coming from a driveway across the road. She gave Emily a curious look as she pulled over and stopped. Emily was too startled to do anything but watch the woman reach over and roll down a window.

"Hi young lady. I'd be happy to give you a lift. Where you headed?"

"The Greyhou…."

"The Greyhound Bus?"

Emily nodded. "Yes."

"Well. I'm going right past there. Hop in."

Emily wasn't confident in her decision to ride along, but she opened the door and got in.

"Thanks for the lift, ma'am."

"Glad to help out. It's just up the road here."

Emily tried to relax, but she feared the woman would start asking questions. *Say something. Hurry! Anything.* She looked for some kind of distraction and noticed a book on the seat between them.

"So—"

"The Boxcar Children!" Emily blurted, interrupting the woman.

"What's this about?"

"Oh, that. One of my friends is loaning it to my daughter. Haven't read it, but I've heard it's pretty good. Something about four orphaned children who find a home in a boxcar. I think their estranged grandfather becomes aware of them. Oh…but I don't want to give anything away in case you read it."

"I could, possibly very well read it." *Think of something else to say, quick!* "Although…i-isn't it for children?"

"Not necessarily. My friend read it twice, and she's thirty.

"Where you headed, young lady?"

"Florida. To visit my cousin… Lucy."

Emily picked up the book, thumbed through the pages, and back to the first line. "This really does look good. I'll keep it in mind. Living in a boxcar. Hmm. Very interesting."

She pretended to read some more, too nervous to actually read, but hoping the woman wouldn't interrupt. *You better say something.* Emily held her finger on a page as if she were marking where she left off.

"Has your daughter read any of the books in the Nancy Drew series?"

"In fact, she has. I think she's finished them all."

"Boy, that's something. I'm going to do that one of these days too. There's nothing like—"

"Oops. There we are. Next exit. I'll drop you off at the door."

"Thank you, ma'am. You see, my… My cousin. Well…my other cousin had to work, so she…she couldn't drive me." *You're not making sense.* "Anyway, I appreciate the lift."

The woman didn't seem to mind Emily's fumbling terror and soon had her parked in front of the Greyhound bus station. Emily set the book down and slipped out of the car, thanking the woman once again as she closed the door.

Chapter Fifteen

*O*nce on the bus, Emily was greeted by an odorous punch of orange peels, half-eaten apples, Cracker Jacks, and hints of musty luggage. The place was buzzing with excitement as passengers moved up the aisle looking for a spot to sit. Some were stuffing luggage beneath seats, or overhead, while others pulled out books to read and what looked like games to play.

Emily was relieved to be on board, feeling as if she had left a hundred-pound weight outside the bus door. She poked her head over and around shoulders and arms in search of somewhere to sit.

Several rows down, she spotted a seat next to a pleasant-looking woman talking to someone across the aisle. When Emily stepped over her legs to reach the window seat, she did a double take on the woman's brown ankle lace-ups. She sat and looked at her own scuffed-up shoes, feeling funny, thinking how the woman's sturdy pair would've been perfect for the farm—it seemed so pointless now.

The driver secured the door handle and started the engine. As the bus slowly joggled from the building, Emily pulled her bag close. She sat back, reminding herself how urgent it was that she find a pawnshop immediately upon arriving in Chicago so she could catch a train out that night.

Her seatmate swiveled around, moving in so that her piercing eyes gazed into Emily's. "I'm on my way to Alabama," she said over the rumble of the engine.

"Wow, Alabama. That's sounds exciting."

"What?"

"Alabama! That sounds exiting!" Emily exclaimed as the bus reached its final gear, her mind still on finding a pawnshop.

"Well, that depends on what you call exciting." The woman cackled. "You see...my sister Leona just got herself a divorce and I'm going out there to mop up the pieces. Where you headed?"

"Pawnshop... Ch-Chicago," Emily added quickly. She saw by Leona's expression, *Grandma's in Texas,* would've sounded better. The woman nodded and turned back to the group across the aisle.

Just as well, Emily thought, knowing she had carelessly left a trail from the bus station to a pawnshop. The realization that she was utterly alone set a fire inside her for no other reason but to rebel against the voices that beckoned her to fail.

She reached into her bag and pulled out her journal and pen, sweltering with passion as her pain and fear dropped to the pages like smoldering lava. An hour later, she looked up and saw Chicago in the distance. With the feather in place and the pen tucked away, she returned the notebook to her bag and watched in hopeful awe as they approached the city. She couldn't imagine that San Francisco would be any more spectacular.

Once off the bus, she went inside the depot, paged through a phonebook, and jotted down the names and addresses of three pawnshops. Now all she had to do was find her way to at least one that would buy her silver.

Outside, she attempted to ask directions as she headed to a corner to read the street sign. Everyone seemed caught up in their own destination. And she was relieved when a cute little woman, whom she guessed was from Japan, looked at one of the addresses.

"Um, et see," she said, going on to explain with a heavy accent.

The little woman grabbed the pen and paper, drawing a map while explaining and pointing out directions.

"Four blocks, then left, you say?" Emily asked.

Yea, yea," the woman finished, satisfied as she handed back the pen and paper.

Emily thanked her and hurried off. When her stomach began to rumble, she pulled out her sandwich, took several bites, dropped it into a garbage can, and kept moving up the street.

She strained her neck to take in the entirety of structures that were at least thirty floors high. Imagining herself up there looking down, she tried to put her mind on the excitement of the city, the buzz of traffic and bustle of people. But memories of Claude worked their way into her every thought.

Catching sight of her reflection in a store window, she stood agape, realizing she was looking into the eyes of someone who had taken the life of another. Her chest tightened as she turned up the street, pining for what should have been a joyous occasion—if only Claude hadn't shown up.

If only, if only, if only.

If only she could go back she would have left that morning with nothing but the clothes on her back. The way it was, she had to find a way to force the bitter memories out of her thoughts. She took a deep breath, determined to forget his name, forget the terrible things he did, and forget the way it ended.

Twenty minutes later, she pushed through a heavy steel door and emerged into an amazing clutter. The space was dark, dismal, and charged with the musty stench of dusty books and old furniture. Dozens of shelves held pots and pans, radios, cameras, and hundreds of other items. Some of the objects were so strange she couldn't imagine what their purpose would be.

She worked her way out of the clutter to where jewelry and finer accessories were ensconced inside glass cases. A stocky man with black collar-length hair greased into Presley-style was leaning over the counter, thumbing through a magazine. She reached into her bag, unraveled the silver bar from the skirt, and gingerly set it on the counter.

"Mm," he said, lifting it for a better look.

"Where'd you get this?"

"My... My aunt."

"You don't say."

He turned the silver over in his hand as he walked to the end of the counter, where a man with a wild head of white hair was busy rearranging a display. The pair mulled over the silver bar, glanced at her, and mulled some more. She pictured herself running over to snatch it away and flee out the door. The older man slipped behind a black curtain—she suspected to call the police—while the heavyset man headed her way.

"We'll give you two hundred dollars," he said, placing the bar on the counter. She couldn't believe her ears until he repeated the offer. "We go by market price. Today it's value is two hundred. Tomorrow it could be less, or it could be more."

She gaped at the man until she realized he was waiting for an answer. "Yes, yes, two hundred is good."

"What's your name?" he asked, pulling out a pen.

"My name?"

"Yes. For the check."

"I don't have time for that. I'm just passing through, heading east."

He placed the pen over his ear, twisted his mouth into a pucker, rubbing his chin. "Hmm. I just went to the bank about an hour ago. Well... Let me see. Hold on."

He ducked behind the curtain, and she kept an eye on the spot until he returned.

"Exactly two hundred dollars," he said, counting out five twenty-dollar bills and two fifties into her outstretched hand. "I hope that'll help you out."

She stuffed the money into her pouch, already scooting towards the exit. "You'll never know how much, sir," she said. "And thank you, thank you so much."

The door closed behind her, and she faced the excitement of the busy street. It felt good to have that out of the way and have a substantial amount of money in her bag.

Chapter Sixteen

*S*omeone whistled up ahead. Emily turned just in time to see a man bolt into the street and wave down a cab. It pulled up to him, and he hopped inside, slamming the door before it came to a complete stop.

Her luck wasn't as quick in coming. After several attempts, she was ready to try another spot when a bright yellow cab tore around a corner and stopped a few feet from her. She stood transfixed as the door flew open. A couple, laughing and hanging onto each other for dear life, tumbled out and walked up the street entwined like one of her grandmother's hand-woven rugs. The driver stepped on the gas and ripped up to where she stood.

She wrenched the door open and hurled herself into the back seat securing her safety with a solid yank of the handle as they sped off.

"Where're you headed, young lady?" the driver asked as he adjusted the meter, nearly hitting a car as he switched lanes.

She wished he would keep his eyes on the road.

"The train station, please."

"Which one?"

A horn blared as he swerved between two cars. He looked into the rearview mirror and narrowed his eyes for a better look at her.

"There's at least five."

Emily clutched her bag with both arms and looked out the window, sure it must be against the law to drive like a maniac in the middle of town. She held her breath when another cab nearly sideswiped them.

"The closest one, please," she said, moving away from the door.

The radio blared country western tunes. She expected to hear a news-breaking report about a murder and a suspect named Emily Alexis Rezell. But, to her relief, there were no news breaks. And in less than fifteen minutes, the cab pulled up in front of Union Station.

She paid the taxi driver, stepped out onto the sidewalk, and stared up at the grand building. When she walked through the door, she was astonished at how massive it was on the inside. The domed ceiling had to be at least fifty feet high. She took the marble steps down to where long wooden benches held travelers from the very young to the very old. Attendants in red caps pushed carts loaded with luggage in a variety of colors, textures and different sizes. She approached one of the red caps.

"Excuse me, sir. Can you tell me where I can buy a ticket?"

"Just around the corner, young lady." He pointed at an archway.

The ticket area buzzed with travelers, some standing in line or sitting on benches patiently waiting, while others wandered about taking in their surroundings. At the far end were partitioned windows made into black-barred cages with a uniformed man behind each. Up on the wall, boards showed destination and departure times. She noticed the last train to San Francisco, *City of San Francisco,* was scheduled to leave at six-thirty. She located a clock and saw it was five fifty-seven. That meant she had thirty-three minutes to make sure she was on that train.

Visions of police dragging her from the building in the middle of the night set her rushing across the room to the ticket counters. She found a spot at the end of a line furthest from the entrance where she could keep an eye on the door. No one seemed concerned at the slow-moving lines. But she checked ahead and glanced at the clock and entrance every other minute.

She wondered if Steven and the others knew what happened to Claude by now. Trying to appear steady while her insides were in turmoil wasn't easy. She could just hear the yapping blather back home, the guilty verdict in, and the drinking binge already begun.

Every step forward preceded another wait, more visions, a quick check of the clock, and another to the entrance. Finally, at six-eighteen she was at the front of the line. With just minutes before the train was to depart, she marched to the counter and peered through the bars.

"I'd like to buy a ticket to San Francisco."

"For which day would that be?"

"For tonight, the train that leaves at six-thirty, of course."

He looked up over his glasses. "You realize you should've made reservations weeks in advance."

"How was I to know?"

He waved the passenger list. "Everyone knows to buy tickets in advance."

"Obviously, not everyone," Emily blared.

She noticed the sudden quiet around the cage.

"Please, sir," she said, leaning closer. "I have to leave tonight. There's an emergency. My grandmother died. I... I can sit on the floor."

She pulled out her pouch, dug for money, and slipped a fifty-dollar bill under the bars. The man had turned away to exchange words with another clerk.

"Looks like we have a cancellation," he said when he faced her again. "Departure time is set for seven."

She pulled her hand back. "Seven? But, that's the morning train. I... I can't wait." She checked the clock and moaned when she saw it was six thirty-five.

"Ma'am? I'm talking about the train that leaves tonight. It was scheduled for six-thirty. But it's running late. If you hurry, you can still make it. Will that be round trip or one way?"

"Oh, yes, yes, one way, sir. Thank you."

"That'll be forty-four dollars and twenty cents. You'll be on train one, track twenty-one. It's preparing to leave so you'd better hurry."

*T*he ticket felt like a precious stone in her hand as she hurried to the main lobby. A sign led her through another door to endless rows of trains. People were scrambling here and there. Locomotives sat humming, waiting to leave, and bells rang as trains pulled in. When she noticed wheels turning as a train backed out, she took off running, keeping an eye on the signs above that indicated track numbers.

She passed waiting trains on tracks twelve, thirteen, fourteen, fifteen, and sixteen. Track seventeen's train had already left. Warning bells began to ring as a train on track eighteen pulled in. One platform over, men were loading up the last of the steps on train nineteen. Emily noticed that the crowd was thinning. It looked as if everyone with a ticket was already on board. Her heart sank until a man with a suitcase in each hand scrambled by as the train on track twenty began to back away.

As the way cleared, lo and behold, there on track twenty-one—in all of its yellow and black-trimmed beauty—was her train to freedom. Her excitement took her through the gate to where a man in uniform greeted passengers.

"Where to, young lady?" he asked, holding up a hand to indicate he didn't need her ticket.

She shoved the piece of paper into a pocket. "San Francisco."

It sounded just as good as the first time she said it.

He pointed to the back of the train.

"That'll be six cars down."

"Thank you, sir," she said, rushing off again.

"The conductor will collect your ticket onboard," he called after her.

Chapter Seventeen

*T*he inside of the train was much like Emily had seen in pictures with light blue and a gray interior, high-backed seats, curtained windows, and silver framing. She spotted a window seat and moved around a little girl who was talking to her mother across the aisle.

"But, Mommy," the girl said, "what if they don't find it?"

"I let them know honey. That's all I can do for now. I'm sorry."

Emily concentrated out the window, trying not to eavesdrop on their conversation. She was relieved when the train began to roll, backing towards the exit. Everyone became silent as the rumble of the engine built into a steady drone. A minute later, as they emerged from the dark cavern into the sunlight, the quiet anticipation of the passengers exploded into chattering delight.

"Miss?" came a voice from the aisle.

Emily turned to see a man in uniform.

"Your ticket, please?"

"Oh, sure."

Emily pulled the crumpled wad from her pocket. "Sorry," she said, trying to smooth out the creases before handing it over.

He stuffed the ticket into an envelope along with others and continued up the aisle.

As they left the city, the train gained momentum and headed into the countryside. The little girl maneuvered her way around Emily and stood next to the window for a better view. The sad look on her face was troubling. Emily leaned forward, trying to break the spell.

"You ever ride on a train before?"

The girl nodded, keeping her eyes on the scenery.

"My name's Em…"

She stopped for a moment but decided she was far enough from home to use her real name. Besides, if she forgot and used two different names, that would look more suspicious. Just in case someone asked, Tennessee would be her home.

"My name's Emily. What's your name?"

The little girl turned to her. "Sophie."

She pointed across the aisle. "And that's my brother Mister over there and my mother. Everyone calls her Eve."

Sophie's long chestnut hair bounced with every word, and Emily couldn't resist. "Your hair is beautiful," she said, brushing back a wayward curl.

"That's what my daddy says. I bet you can't guess how old I am."

"Mm, I'll bet you're uh… Twelve."

The girl laughed, shook her head and stuck out a hand, fingers spread. "Nope, I'm five. And guess what? We're going to live with Grandma in Reno, Nevada. But my dad can't come with us…."

She turned her gaze out the window before confiding once more. "I forgot my doll at the train station."

"Ooh, that's too bad. I'm sorry."

Emily remembered the doll she brought with her and dug it out of her bag. "See this?" she said, holding it up. "I've had it since my third birthday. My grandmother made it for me."

Sophie reached over and squeezed the doll in several places.

"She's made of cloth."

"Yes. And she's stuffed with cotton. Here, I want you to have it."

Sophie took the doll and rearranged the hair that was made from strings of yarn.

"Is it for keeps?"

"Yes, it's for keeps."

"Thanks.

"Look, Mommy," she said holding up the doll. "The lady gave it me."

"Are you sure?" Eve asked Emily.

"Yes, I'm positive."

Sophie took a seat and placed the doll on her lap. "Where have you been, Sissy?" she said sternly, playing pretend—something about Sissy running away. It wasn't long before she tired and curled up with her new companion wrapped in her arms.

"Mind if I tuck her in?" Emily whispered across the aisle.

"Oh, you don't have to, I'll—"

"Really, it's no trouble," Emily said, already up, pulling down a blanket and pillow.

With the little girl comfortable, Emily pushed her bag under the seat, leaned back, and gazed out the window. She wondered if this would be the last time she saw the flat lands, dairy farms, and wheat fields being prepared for winter. Even the horror she left behind wasn't enough to keep her from feeling the loss of home.

She closed her eyes and listened to the low rumble and the clickety-clack of the wheels. The commanding urgency of the iron beast reminded her of when she would lie in bed and listen to the distant thrum and wail of train whistles fading into the night. Her dream had been to one day live the adventure of riding a train across the country. Instead, the weight of what happened back at the farm continued to haunt her.

*W*hen Emily awoke the next morning, the children she barely knew were standing over her. She sat up, brushing hair out of her eyes and rubbing the crick out of her neck.

"Oh, Um...uh... Good morning."

Sophie pushed two cookies at her. "Chocolate chip and ginger snap."

Emily looked at the well-done cookies.

"Go on, try one," Sophie urged, holding them closer. "I helped make them night before last."

Emily took one, then the other.

The children were waiting for her to take a bite. There wasn't an easy way out. So she bit down hard enough to get a chunk out the ginger snap. "Mm, not bad."

"And there's more if you want," Mister offered. He placed a box on the seat next to her.

Emily wiped crumbs off her chin. "More...cookies?" She gulped.

"Nope. It's a game. We want you to play with us."

"Please. You say please," Eve chided, looking up from her crocheting.

"And Emily. We have an overabundance of those cookies, so don't feel obligated to finish them."

"Oh, no... it's not a burden. They're actually pretty good."

Emily was grateful for the children's company that day. Their enthusiasm kept her sane. Later that evening, she found herself alone and restless, unable to keep her mind from wandering back to the farm.

Finally, she went to the lounge car and bought chips and a soda, taking a seat just as the sun was setting. It wasn't long before stars began to appear. Ever since she could remember, she thought of them as twinkling eyes winking at her. The moon rose from out of the horizon spreading a soft glow across the still prairies. With the lights flickering from an occasional house, the scene spun a picturesque frame. Everything seemed still and peaceful. Even the quiet murmurs and laughter from other passengers was comforting.

But no matter how soothing or serene the atmosphere was, something as trifling as a smoker's cough or a fleeting laugh a bit harsh reminded her of Claude. A sob built in her throat, and she pressed a hand over her mouth, struggling to hold it in. *Don't think about him. Not ever! Don't allow him to win.*

For sanity's sake, she had to try and forget. And yet, it seemed by the tears streaming down her cheeks, and the pain in her chest, she never would. *Please, God, please help me to find a way through this.* All she asked was to be able to put the horror out of her mind until she could deal with it in a rational way. She imagined that if she found a trusting friend she could share this horrible thing with, that would be the best she could hope for.

Midnight approached, and the lounge car was nearly empty. Emily found a pillow to place on the armrest, curled up, and gazed at the full moon as it moved across the sky. She took a deep breath feeling her mind and body begin to relax as the train raced like a yellow comet into the night. Soon, the low hum, and the wheels against the track, lulled her to sleep.

*E*mily opened her eyes as the sun crested the eastern skies and spread a blanket of light across the frost-covered plains and distant hills. Warmth streamed through the windows of the lounge car, where two early risers chatted in a corner, drinking coffee and feasting on muffins.

All too soon, those few glorious moments upon waking became flashbacks of her last hours at the farm. Her long-awaited freedom turned into another day as a fugitive. She jumped from her seat and dashed from the lounge, moving through the cars, letting the noise and breeze in the vestibules, and the throaty yawns and morning whispers from each car, take her from the awful memory.

By the time she reached the luggage area down below, she was fully awake. She freshened up, combed her hair, and brushed her teeth. Back upstairs, all the passengers were up and preparing for the day.

"First call for breakfast," a man in a gray uniform announced as he made his way up the aisle. Emily had never eaten in a restaurant before and thought breakfast cooked by someone else would be good for her.

When she reached the dining car, the maître d' sat her with an elderly couple celebrating their fortieth wedding anniversary. She was glad for the distraction and didn't mind that they shared their entire trip with her in explicit detail as she enjoyed pancakes and a cup of hot chocolate.

After breakfast, she went back to her seat and was writing in her journal when Sophie ran up the aisle.

"Don't run!" her mother called after her.

"Look, Emily, I got a lollipop. And I've got another for Sissy.

But I don't think she likes chocolate. You want it?" She held out the candy.

Emily laughed. "You're so thoughtful. But I bet by tomorrow you'll wish you had another. Maybe you should save it."

"Okay, but if you change your mind, let me know." She popped her candy back into her mouth and stuffed the other into a pocket.

They deposited toys and games and were starting off to lunch when Eve stopped and turned back.

"You're welcome to join us."

"I just ate. But thanks anyway."

When Emily finished writing in her journal, she picked up the leftover chips from the night before and headed to the lounge. By the time she saw the man, it was too late to turn around. He didn't say anything, just gaped from beneath a brown hat with stone-gray eyes. It took her a moment to collect herself before flying around him and up the aisle, but not before she caught the intent expression in those familiar eyes.

Her first instinct was to go back to her seat and hide under a blanket. But she knew that would never work. She continued to the lounge and took a seat at the furthest corner.

Now where've I seen him? A trip to Watseka? Did he come to the house? He doesn't look like a farmer.

Wherever they had crossed paths, she knew by the expression on his face, that he too was considering where he had seen her. How ironic that she traveled hundreds of miles from home just to run into someone who could turn her over to the police.

She opened the bag of chips and absently consumed them as she contemplated her predicament. It wasn't as if she knew a lot of people. Although that wouldn't keep someone from knowing who she was. She tossed the bag into a garbage can, resting her fist beneath her chin as she gazed out into the countryside and considered who this man was. Finally, his identity came to her as she watched three men rounding up a herd of cows.

The man had stopped by the farm when she was nine. She had just walked outside as he drove into the yard. Grandfather was in a hurry to get back to the fields and spit out a nasty, "We don't need whatever you're selling."

In the meantime, she had walked to the grove of trees out back and climbed up to her treehouse for a break. When she heard a noise, she looked down and there he was staring up at her with those gray eyes. She

180

had been too shocked to react. And he seemed set on asking questions, such as, how she liked living on the farm and what she liked to do the most. She told him that living on the farm was fun, and that she liked to read, study the skies, ride the horse, and play with her cats and dogs.

After Emily contemplated their unusual meeting, she decided the best thing for her was to get off the train and take another to San Francisco. If he didn't already recall who she was, another meeting would be sure to trigger his memory. He would likely have relatives around Watseka who would keep him up to date on the local news.

When a crew member announced that the next stop was Rawlings, Wyoming, in ten minutes, she rushed down to the baggage area to wait.

Once she got off in Rawlings, there was a slight setback. The next train to San Francisco wouldn't leave until the following evening. Disappointed, she took a seat and pulled out her Nancy Drew book, ready for a long wait. She had only been there a few minutes when she saw him again, talking to a man no more than ten feet away.

She bolted from her seat and sent her book sailing to the floor. When she stooped to retrieve it, she glanced up and saw that he was watching her. She grabbed the book, flung her bag over her shoulder, and dashed for an exit hoping to get back on the train.

"Emily?"

She hesitated for a split second then darted out the door. When she was sure he wasn't following her, she looped around the building and back to the train. The horn blasted a warning, and a crew member lifted the last stepping stool. He looked around surprised to see her rushing over.

"Cutting it kinda close, aren't you?" he said, placing the stool back onto the ground.

She gave him a breathless, "Thanks," and climbed on board.

Chapter Eighteen

It came unexpectedly
like lightening through her veins
as a soft wind tempting.
It came like the hot sun against her cheeks
like a flower waiting for rain.
It came like a book ready to open
by a curious heart yearning.

On the way down the aisle, Emily bumped into a woman and sent her flying back into her seat. The group of women she was with roared with laughter.

"Young lady, are you all right?" someone asked.

"I'm fine. Sorry, ma'am."

Emily realized how odd she must look, flustered, shaking, and out of breath, maybe even a little wild-eyed in the midst of all these light-hearted travelers.

The women were still chuckling as she charged up the aisle into the vestibule and right into the arms of a young man.

"Are you okay?" he asked, holding her by the shoulders.

"Sorry," she said, too embarrassed to look up.

She pulled away and meant to rush off until one of his hands slipped to her elbow.

"Miss?"

His voice came again so soft and pleasing that she couldn't help but to turn back and look at him. He was probably mid-twenties, several inches taller than she was. His stylish hair was a deep golden brown with just enough curl to be noticed. His dark eyes sparkled.

"I... I'm fine." She pointed a thumb over her shoulder. "Just...late, that's all."

He dropped his hand, and she wrenched her eyes away and slipped through the doorway, trying to salvage her composure. That little episode back there was ridiculous. She knew it the moment it happened. *How silly of me. How silly,* she thought again as she made her way through the cars and collapsed into her seat.

Maybe from the very first, she made a big mistake by running. It probably made her look guiltier than ever. She wondered again, desperately, if things would have gone differently if only she had told someone about Claude.

As she thought about the mistakes she made, about the regrets, and all the possibilities, it struck her that the man with the stone-gray eyes had come to the house around the time she was starting school. Considering the timing, that visit had obviously been on behalf of the school board. She wondered how he would have reacted upon seeing her on the train if she had asked for help instead of running from him.

Exhausted from wrangling with herself about what she should have or not have done, she rested her head on a pillow and looked out the window. Although the sun was shining, it was easy to imagine herself on the tail end of a comet zipping through space. She closed her eyes and played it like a movie in her head until she drifted off.

*W*hen Emily woke, Sophie was sleeping across the aisle huddled up with her mother and brother. To see them so peaceful and secure in each other's love was comforting. It gave her hope for the future.

That's if you get through this.

She groaned, wishing to silence the jeering voice that came to torment her. *Stop listening then,* she told herself. *Occupy your mind with good things.*

Grabbing her bag, she started to get up and go to the lounge when the train jolted and squealed with sounds of metal on metal as it braked. She didn't have time to hold on and flew head first into the seat in front of her.

Dropping back to her seat, she pulled a tissue from her bag and placed it on her forehead. When the train stopped, Mister lay on the floor, and Sophie dangled off the seat, still hanging onto her mother. Everything was quiet for a few seconds before the train came back to life.

"What happened, Mommy?" Sophie asked as her mother helped her and Mister back on the seat.

"I don't know, sweetheart."

She noticed Emily dabbing her forehead with a tissue.

"Oh, Emily, you're bleeding. Are you okay?"

"Yeah. Just smarts a little."

"That was cool," came Mister, gazing out the window.

A few moments later, a crewmember moved up the aisle. "Is everyone okay, anyone hurt? You okay, ma'am? Sir, any injuries your way?"

"Over here," Eve called, motioning towards Emily. "She's bleeding."

The man accessed other passengers as he continued up the isle and stopped at her seat. Emily lifted the tissue long enough for him to see the damage.

"Oh, yes, you do have a gash there, don't you. Just sit tight, young lady. It won't be long. We're in the process of gathering medical volunteers."

"Sir," Eve called again. "Can you tell us what happened?"

He had already started up the aisle but stopped and turned back.

"We hit some cows, Ma'am. That happens once in a while. No need to worry. Everything's under control."

Not more than ten minutes later, the same young man, who Emily ran into in the vestibule, walked up the aisle and stopped at her seat.

"Oh... Hi," he said as their eyes met in a fleeting moment of recognition. "I see you've got a little cut there. How're you doing?"

"Okay. Just startled more than anything, I think."

"I'll have that patched for you in no time," he said, taking a seat and placing his supplies between them.

He opened a leather bag with well-organized compartments of medical supplies and pulled out cotton and disinfectant.

Sophie leaned over the armrest. "Hey, mister. You a doctor?"

He turned for a moment, smiling. "I'm working on it."

"Is it bad?"

The young man chuckled. "No, not at all. I think it looks worse than it is."

Emily tried to concentrate elsewhere, but her gaze kept drifting back to his dark eyes. She winced when he swabbed her injury with disinfectant.

"Sorry."

"That's okay."

She would make sure not to flinch again.

"Is it just your head?" he asked, reaching for a Band-Aid.

"Yes. I hit it on the back of the seat."

He ripped the Band-Aid open and placed it over her wound. His hand lingered for a moment then gently moved to the spot still bruised from the wallop Claude gave her.

"Is that sore?"

"No, not at all. I... I bumped into something a couple days ago."

"Sir," a crewmember called from the doorway.

"When you're done here, there're several people two cars down that need looking at."

"Certainly," the young man said, glancing at the train official, "I'm just finishing up."

Turning back to Emily, he gently pressed the edges of the Band-Aid again. "So, there you are."

She thanked him, watching as he gathered up his belongings and stood, imagining herself tugging on his sleeve and asking him to stay.

Sophie jumped to the floor and yanked his pant leg. "Is my friend okay?"

"As good as new."

She held up her doll. "See what she gave me?"

"That was very kind of her," he said, turning to Emily. "I hope you enjoy the rest of your trip."

He ruffled Sophie's hair and turned up the aisle.

Sophie sat next to Emily, hugging her doll, and smiling up at her.

"I'm glad you're okay."

"Oh, Sophie, I'm glad you are too."

As the train sat for the next several hours, Emily caught herself looking for the young man whenever someone walked by. Finally, she saw him as she went to the diner with Sophie and her family. Their eyes met just long enough for them to exchange smiles and for Emily to experience an excitement that sent shock waves through her. Daniel had made her heart flutter, made her want to do crazy things like fling herself onto a swing and take it higher than she should have. She had thought of his beautiful green eyes and sweet smile as she watched sunsets. And chores no longer seemed like work whenever she thought of him. Yes, Daniel had made her jump for joy and laugh and made her cry with longing when he was gone. She would never forget him and would probably always love him. But this... This was like a flame rushing through her veins and into every cell of her body as it took her breath away. It made her forget what she was running from. And it made her happy again.

You don't deserve one speck of that happiness, came the tormenter. *It's a distraction. That's all it is.*

But those feelings weren't something Emily could stop any more than she could stop her heart from beating or her lungs from needing air.

Chapter Nineteen

*M*ost of the passengers were asleep as the train rumbled into the night. Emily lay awake thinking about the handsome young man who saved her life with disinfectant and a Band-Aid. Well...not exactly saved her life, but her wound was clean and healing, which was what he had set out to do.

She was barely awake when someone stopped by her seat and changed the Band-Aid. That it wasn't the handsome young intern was disappointing.

All during breakfast, she chided herself for thinking that just because the soon-to-be doctor took care of her measly wound—by code of honor, no doubt—and looked into her eyes and smiled a few times, that she meant anything to him.

She began to wonder if the romantic feelings she had so soon after living through the nightmare with Claude was normal. *Normal enough to recall the times he forced me into the barn loft to have his way with me.* Her hand slid to her cheek. *After all the pain he caused, how can it not be normal to try and forget, and to find some happiness.*

*E*mily spent most of the afternoon playing games with the children while their mother went to the lounge with some other travelers. When Eve returned, Emily picked up her bag and went to rinse her face with cold water, taking special care not to wet the Band-Aid. She changed into a white blouse with a standup collar and wooden buttons that matched her skirt. With a quick check in the mirror, she set off for the lounge and found a seat facing the window. She pulled out her Nancy Drew book and began to read, glancing up now and then to watch the passing scenery.

A crowd begun to gather and fill the car with cheer and conversation. Some of the passengers played cards, and discussed football, while others talked about their family and their travel plans. Finally, Emily gave in to the temptation and closed her book, allowing herself to enjoy the atmosphere.

When she had all but forgotten about the young intern, he walked through the doorway. Her gaze shot out the window, so excited she felt like a whistling teapot ready to bubble over. As he sat a few seats down, her heart beat so fast she was sure he could hear. She was relieved by the distraction of grinding wheels and the pull of gravity as the train slowed and began its climb into the Rocky Mountains.

"How's your forehead?"

She nearly lost her breath when she realized he was talking to her.

"Oh, it's fine." She touched the Band-Aid. "Someone changed it for me this morning."

"That's good."

"Thanks for putting on the first one."

She wished she hadn't said that. It probably sounded as if that's all she had been thinking about.

"That's my job. You'll be able to take it off by tomorrow," he added, turning his attention out the window.

She looked out, too, pretending to notice the scenery more than she was, feeling disappointed he would have no reason to speak to her again—now that he knew she was okay. Not that she was ever in danger.

"Where're you headed?"

"San Francisco."

"Oh, really. Me too. Actually, I'm across the Bay at the university. So, are you from San Francisco?"

"No. This is my first trip out west."

"I'm sure you're going to love it there."

He got up and moved to the seat next to her.

"By the way, my name's Michael."

"I'm Emily.

"Sorry about running into you in the vestibule the other day." She cringed, wondering why she said that after everything else that had happened since. He would know she had been thinking about the moment they met and how she had practically flung herself into his arms.

"Aw, that's fine. I didn't mind."

He didn't mind. He said he didn't mind that I fell into his arms.

There was no turning back now. She looked down at what appeared to be a medical book on his lap.

"So…you're going to be a doctor."

"Yes, I am. I'm about to start my internship at Berkeley. That's where my father graduated from. He worked in the Bay area until my mother became ill and they moved to Maine to be closer to her family. That's where I've been, visiting my mother. My sister and I take turns going out since her heart surgery."

"I bet she appreciates that. Is she okay?"

"We hope so. She's at home now, still recovering. Thanks for asking."

They talked for some time before Michael looked at his watch.

"Oh dear. I have to run. I need to return a book to a gentleman who decided to get off the train early. But… They have this dish in the diner. Prosciutto Gouda. Each time I head across country, I make sure to have at least one. All it is, really, is a crescent with cheese and dried ham. But let me tell you, there's nothing simple about the taste. I think it's mostly in the bread. And their soup de jour is always the best. At least as good as Grandmother's.

"So…" he said, smiling at her. "How about it? Would you like to join me for dinner?"

"Oh. Well… Sure."

"Say about…twenty-minutes? In the diner?"

"I'll be there."

Emily went back to her seat, wondering if she had the right to feel so happy.

When she reached her car, the children were excited to see her.

"Hey, Emily," Mister called, "you're just in time to play a game of checkers with us."

"I'm sorry. I can't. But I will, later."

Sophie tossed a pair of checkers across the board. "Why can't you play now?"

"I ran into someone in the lounge and um...we're meeting in the diner."

Eve grinned. "By any chance is this a young man you're sharing dinner with?"

"Someone's got a *booy* friend," Mister teased.

"Someone's got a *booy* friend," Sophie chimed in.

"All right, kids. You're being rude."

Emily chuckled. "Oh, they're fine."

"Still, you kids know better," Eve admonished sternly.

"Say, you guys listen to your mother, and when I get back, we'll play a game or two before your bedtime."

The children agreed and apologized for teasing her.

She fixed her hair, slipped money into a pocket, and stuffed her bag under the seat. Straightening her clothes, she gave Eve a how-do-I-look motion.

"You look beautiful, just beautiful."

"Well. Here goes."

On her way to the diner, Emily had a moment of hesitation. But when she saw Michael waiting for her, any doubt she had, vanished. There was a candle on the table, two salads, and a bottle of red wine.

"I hope you don't mind that I took the liberty of ordering salad and wine."

"No, this is nice. Thanks."

The wine reminded her of Aunt Francine's warning about the downside of alcohol. But as far as Emily was concerned, a little certainly wouldn't hurt. Besides, why ruin the mood.

When Michael finished pouring their wine, he set the bottle to the side and lifted his glass for a toast.

"Here's to your trip out west."

The wine was tangy and bitter at the same time with a curious taste that became less bitter with each sip. The effects came all at once, and Emily rather liked the mellow feeling it gave her as they talked and ate salad.

The waiter brought their main dish, and they started on the Prosciutto Gouda and soup.

"What do you think?" Michael asked after a bite of the Prosciutto.

"You're right. It is *delicious*."

Emily tried the soup. "Mm. This really is *almost* as good as Grandmother's."

"See why I can't resist?"

When he finished his wine, he picked up the bottle, and offered some to her.

"Yes, please," she said, pushing her glass over.

He poured her wine, picked up his glass and sat back. "So. Where're you from?"

"Illinois," she said, immediately realizing her mistake, hoping he wouldn't ask more questions.

"W-we live up north. Where it's nearly flat... Well, except for some ravines and a few hills."

You're double-talking, she scolded herself.

She looked at his handsome face and smiling eyes that seemed to say he was interested to know all about her. But right now wasn't the time.

The train had gone through several tunnels and over the Wasatch Mountains, and it slowed all at once, bumping onto a trestle.

"There it is. The Great Salt Lake," Michael said, explaining its name came from its high content of salt. "Did you know it's the largest lake of its kind in the Western Hemisphere?"

"Aah... It does go on forever. It's astonishing."

She concentrated out the window until the wheels were on solid ground. Leaning back in her seat, she caught a glimmer in his eyes that said he had been intently observing her.

"If I'm not mistaken. I'd say that was the first real lake you've seen."

"Nothing even close to that."

"Well, I'd love to see the look on your face when you get your first glimpse of the Pacific Ocean."

The waiter came to clear the last of the dishes off the table. And Emily recalled her promise to the children. She pulled a five-dollar bill from her pocket and held it out to him.

"Oh no, you don't. It's on me, remember? I asked you."

"Are you sure?"

"I'm positive. Put your money away."

She replaced the money and stood. "I'd better go. I promised Sophie and Mister I'd play some games with them. So, Um... Thanks for dinner."

He stood and took her hand. "Thank *you* for joining me. It was lovely."

"It was. And thanks again."

She smiled, slipped her hand from his, and wandered off, wishing he would call her back. She wondered if he liked checkers.

After returning to her seat and playing several games with the children, they went down together to brush their teeth. When they returned to their seats and the children had settled in for the night, Emily picked up her bag and went to her favorite spot in the lounge.

Pulling out her journal, she began — *Maggie had dinner with a boy she met today.* She scratched out *boy* and replaced it with, *young man.* She thought for a moment, scratched out Maggie, and replaced it with, *I. He's going to be a doctor. He listened when I talked, like every word was important to him. He's kind and thoughtful. To have him come into my life at this time means everything to me.*

Shadows from a row of trees passed by the window as she looked out at one of the most beautiful sunsets she had ever seen—at least as beautiful as those she witnessed up in the Sycamore.

That's when she saw his reflection. She couldn't hold back her joy as he walked over and sat next to her.

"I hoped you'd be here," he said.

She closed her notebook, trying not to show her excitement.

"Hi, Michael."

"Wow, that's some picture," he said, referring to the picture she drew on the cover of her notebook. "You never told me you were an artist."

"Oh, I'm not. Just something I started long ago. I call it *The Dove.* See?" She pointed to writing on the bottom right corner. "At the time, I imagined a big bird would...."

She stopped, seeing how foolish her childhood fantasy would seem to him.

"Don't sell yourself short, Emily. I've attended several art exhibits in college. And from what I see, you have a unique and interesting perspective. One of my cousins draws beautifully, and when I was younger I thought it would be wonderful to be gifted in the arts."

"Well... It took me several years to draw that, so... I don't know if I'm exactly gifted in that way."

She looked at him and smiled. "Although... Caring for others is probably the most important gift of all. So... Why'd you choose medicine?"

"I was always intrigued by the science of the human body. Not only that, but my father, grandfather, and several uncles chose medicine."

Emily couldn't help but to admire him and his selfless profession, although it was a reminder that he was about to graduate from college. From what he said, he came from a family of college graduates. In that sense, they weren't in the same league. Although she thought her voracious reading and plans for studies should count for something.

As they continued to talk, a group of young people sitting near them were becoming livelier by the minute. When they noticed the two gazing at them, someone asked if they wanted to join them in a game of scrabble.

To Emily's delight, she and her new friend became a couple in the midst of fun-loving prattle with a flask of whiskey passed around—until Michael said they'd had enough. Emily had been ready to say yes to more. And she couldn't help but to wonder if she would have had enough sense to stop at all. Michael's attentiveness made her like him even more.

Later, after the group split up, they were sitting back across the car. Most everyone had left, and it was still, except for a few murmurs and soft music playing on a radio. Emily looked out the window just in time to see the full moon rise from behind a mountain. It was stunning. She wondered if Michael noticed it too.

He put an arm over the back of the seat, and she held her breath as he slipped it around her shoulders. When he pulled her closer her heart raced—not sure if she was ready. But she was ready, she was…and she closed her eyes as he leaned towards her. Just when the tension was too much to bear, he kissed the temple at her hairline. Her disappointment was quick, and her lids flashed open. Their eyes met and he moved towards her again. This time, his lips settled over hers, soft and warm, urgent and yet as tender as she had believed it would be. He held her for a moment, kissed her forehead again, and gave her a gentle squeeze.

Michael pulled his arm from around her and leaned with his elbows on his knees.

"I wasn't planning to do that," he said looking at her with a sheepish grin. "Hope I wasn't being presumptuous."

"No. You weren't. Not at all."

"I'm glad.

"You know, Emily. I really do care about you." He sat back and gazed out the window. "I'd like to get to know you better."

"I'd like that too."

Sure, you would. Tell him about Claude and see how much he likes you after that.

"There's something I'm curious about," he said after a few moments of silence. "You never mentioned why you're going to San Francisco."

"I didn't?"

"No... You didn't. What's taking you all the way out west?"

A flash of cold spread across her shoulders and down her arms. She longed to look at him and smile as if there was nothing wrong. On the other hand, she wanted to tell him everything.

"Well... At first, I planned to go to New York. But my aunt told me how my grandparents met in San Francisco. I thought it would be a great place to live."

"So, you have family there."

"Well, I did. But I don't, not any longer."

She noticed the moon had disappeared. Even he felt tense beside her all of a sudden.

"I mean…it seems as if you've been avoiding talking about your family. Why's that? What about your family back home? Up north."

She was taken aback by his questioning and couldn't think of one good thing to say to keep their fun-loving friendship from fading away. There was too much bad that came to her all at once. She was desperate to confide in him. But this wasn't the time to tell him about her life. They'd had such a wonderful time together. And now there seemed to be no way forward. Tears rolled down her cheeks, and she brushed them away.

Michael placed an arm around her shoulder. "Emily. What's the matter?"

"It… It's nothing."

More tears clouded her vision, and she blinked them away. Everything she had managed to forget these last hours rushed back with Claude's face right where she left it. She shook her head to lose the vision.

"Please tell me why you're crying," Michael said, placing a hand over hers.

"…. It's my grandmother."

She hated to lie to him. And although it wasn't a complete fabrication, she couldn't tell him the whole truth.

"It's been difficult without her. And I miss her every day."

"I'm sorry. I didn't mean to—"

"It's all right. I think part of it's that I haven't slept much." She patted the seat. "And this isn't the most ideal thing to curl up on."

"You slept here? Must've been very uncomfortable."

She nodded. "It wasn't too bad."

He glanced at the seats around them. "They don't look like they were built for comfort, that's for sure."

"For about five, ten minutes."

"Say... I have an idea. My room's small, but it's clean, and the bed's comfortable. The guy next to me is the one who decided to get off at the last stop. You can stay in my room, and I'll stay in his. That's the least I can do."

"No, I can't do that. I'll go back to my seat."

"Okay. But...the room is yours if you change your mind."

He got up and pulled Emily to her feet. They walked back to her seat where they found Sophie sprawled out like a cat. Her mother and brother were sleeping as well.

"Aw. So sweet," Michael said, nudging her. "You don't want to wake her, do you?"

"No. Of course not."

"Come with me."

He smiled, took her hand, and led her to his room.

"Go on, have a seat," he said, closing the door. She sat on the bed, and he pulled a suitcase from a shelf and began to pack his clothes and toiletries.

"You sure it's okay if I stay?"

"Absolutely. Don't worry. You won't be bothered. There's a lock, see?" He reached over to demonstrate how it worked.

"We should meet for breakfast," he said, zipping the suitcase.

"What do you say? Is seven all right?"

"Yeah, I'd like that."

He picked up the suitcase, his medical bag, and stepped to the door, glancing back.

"I had a wonderful time tonight."

"I did too."

"Goodnight, Emily. I'll see you in the morning."

After he left, she got up, turned the lock, and flipped the light off. She slipped out of her shoes and crawled under the covers. Hearing him move about next door was comforting. To know she would see him first thing in the morning made her shiver with delight.

She looked out the window and searched for the moon. It hadn't shown its face again. But she didn't need the moon to tell her how she felt about Michael. She sighed peacefully and settled her head on the pillow.

◇◇◇

"Next stop, Sacramento, forty-five minutes," came a voice over the intercom.

Emily opened her eyes, knowing at once that she had overslept. She scrambled out of bed, expecting Michael would be there at any moment. Her clothes were a mess. And she wet her hands from a pitcher of water and while pressing her clothes out, she noticed that a button on her blouse was missing. Checking the bedcovers, she found the acorn, dropped it into her pocket, and continued searching the floor, the garbage, and shelves for the button. Finally, admitting she could have lost it anywhere, she went next door.

"Michael?" she said, knocking.

When it was obvious that he had already left, she headed up the passageway. He would expect to meet her in the diner.

She stopped to freshen up, grateful when a woman gave her a safety pin to replace the missing button on her blouse. It was too big, although better than nothing.

On the way to the diner, she adjusted the safety pin so it wouldn't look so conspicuous. Once she reached the diner and realized he wasn't there, she took a seat anyway, sure he would arrive at any moment. She placed an order and kept an eye on the entryway.

By the time breakfast arrived, she decided the oats and fruit didn't look so good after all. When it was apparent that Michael wasn't going to show, she convinced herself it was just as well. She would never have to tell him about Claude. *It's for the best*, she reminded herself. That didn't stop her from looking around the diner once more before she left to check the lounge—he wasn't there, either.

When she returned to her seat, she was disappointed to find that Sophie and her family were gone. She sat, hoping Michael would come to find her. He knew where her seat was.

She pulled the acorn from her pocket and gazed at the familiar memento. It was such a small thing, yet a comforting essence of her mother rising from the very dirt they both walked on. She held it to her lips, rolling it back and forth, wondering if her parents had loved their daughter even in the womb. *Love...that elusive word so many have taken to their graves.*

Reaching into her bag for her grandmother's scarf, she draped it around her neck and pulled out the photo of her mother and Grandmother standing beneath the arbor.

> *"Perseverance, little Bella Bambina. That's all you need. Prayer and perseverance."*

Emily visualized the reunion that would take place in heaven one day, seeing her grandmother and her aunt again, and finally meeting her mother. That assurance always brought her peace—for a time.

Tucking the photo away, she wrapped the acorn in her mother's scarf and shoved it to the bottom of her bag. The acorn wouldn't last much longer—she knew that. But for now, it was a comfort.

Wondering what happened to Michael and still hoping he would come to her, she gazed out the window as the train rumbled across what someone said was the Carquinez Strait Bridge.

When they pulled into the Sacramento station, she leaned forward to watch the departing passengers. All at once, she gasped and swung back from the window. *Why's Michael getting off here?* He lived in Oakland, and from what he said, that's where he was planning to get off. She looked again. He stood just a few feet beyond where she peered down at him. His luggage sat next to him. She willed him to look at her. But he could have been a million miles away because he didn't notice her. His attention was on the beautiful raven-haired woman who rushed into his arms. Tears rolled down Emily's cheeks as she watched them wander off through the crowd, arm-in-arm.

She sank back in her seat as the train began to move, wondering what could have happened. He had been so kind and attentive. The worst part was that he hadn't bothered to say goodbye. She wondered if it was the whiskey that made him kiss her, made him think he cared about her. Maybe he woke up with a different mind-set and panicked.

Serves you right. Claude probably isn't even buried yet, and here you are, pretending to fall in love.

*A*fter the stop at Berkeley, the train never picked up much speed. When they arrived in Oakland, a man announced the train would turn around and head back east. He added that those intending to go to San Francisco would take the ferryboat across the Bay.

Emily slipped on her jacket, slung her bag over her shoulder, and made her way to the exit stooping with curiosity to look out the windows on her way down the aisle.

Salty sea air filled her lungs as she stepped from the train and followed the other passengers to the cavernous shed where the ferry waited. The engines hummed and the floor vibrated beneath her feet as she stepped onboard. Men brought on carts of luggage. Soon, the vessel inched from its binding—screeching and hawing like an old building. And as the foghorn blared a warning, they set off across the Bay.

There was talk of a spectacular view of the Bay Bridge. Not wanting to miss a thing, she buttoned her jacket and walked out onto the open deck, moving with the crowd. When she gazed at the Bay Bridge nestled within a blanket of fog, she was captivated by what seemed to be a phenomenon. She pulled up her collar to ward off the chill, watching in awe as the fog silently shifted and rolled creating an illusion that the bridge was suspended within a cloud. The scene was mysterious and beautiful.

Mournful wails of the foghorn sounded as she made her way to the front of the ferry. She squeezed in between two passengers to claim a premier spot at the railing. As the fog lifted, beams of sunlight glistened through the haze and across the churning swells of water. In the distance, with tall buildings partially covered in a silvery fog, there in that moment of stunning beauty, she got her first glimpse of San Francisco.

Chapter Twenty

The good and bad entwined
by a winding sundry of choices, as pathways,
like brooks, lakes, and rivers spilling into the sea.

By Kathleen Janz-Anderson

*T*he ferryboat moved across the water as fog lifted and made way for sunlight and blue skies. Seagulls raced alongside the vessel as it came to shore and was moored at the dock.

Emily moved to the exit, energized by the panorama of activity and the scents as foreign as the sea. On the way down the gangway, she leaned over the railing and watched pigeons scampering about the pier, snatching up crackers, dry breadcrumbs, and other bits of food.

Once off the boat, she wandered into town, exploring streets and looking through shop windows. On a whim, she walked into a store, bought a pair of brown lace-up shoes, and tossed her old pair into the trash on the way out.

She looked over her shoulder to where slivers of water glistened, and the melancholy sound of ships blasted their horns. Before she knew it, she was at the waterfront sitting on a rock and looking out over the harbor. She scanned the horizon for a glimpse of the ocean she knew wasn't far away by the cool of the salty mist.

The Bay Bridge, now parading full and clear, was a sight to see. It was astonishing to her how it held up under the weight of all the trucks and cars. She studied its length to where it ended at Oakland, wondering if Michael was with the woman from the train station or if he was already there preparing to start his internship in Berkeley.

She took a healthy breath of San Francisco air, determined to focus on something that would help her instead of bringing her down. With the wonder of something never experienced, she gazed up and down the bay watching seagulls and various kinds of boats move across the water. In the distance, two fishermen stood in-between rocks waiting for a nibble. Just down from her, heading to the boardwalk, two women strolled along the waterfront discussing things that made them howl with laughter, arms flinging, heads back or down at their knees. Emily couldn't help but chuckle herself.

Her eyes moved to where several people stood on a raised platform gazing out over the bay. Something caught her attention, and she looked below the platform at a man in a gray baggy suit. He glanced in either direction, pulled something from a pocket and stuffed it in a groove beneath a step. Moving into the sunlight, he stared across the bay for a few moments, slowly turned, and settled his eyes on her.

Whatever fascination this town held, she knew when nightfall came, that everything would look much different in the dark. Still feeling the chill of that stranger, she slid from the rock, hurrying back to the city that sat like a fortress against the ever-changing bay.

"See what stalling gets you?" she said with a self-mocking laugh.

Once she reached the city streets again, she leaned against a building, wondering where to begin. Planning this move back at the farm had been a breeze. Now to actually be in a metropolis of this size was much more complicated.

She had written Samuel Dimsmoore a letter. After thinking it through, she wondered what the point was so many years later. But now, being here alone in a strange city, even a few words with someone who had a connection to her mother would be of comfort. She considered the possibilities with excitement.

Bells began to ring, and she caught the tail end of a cable car as it chugged up a hill. When it disappeared around a bend, her gaze dropped to a sign a few feet ahead—*Mack's House of Food*.

That she had only eaten a few bites of breakfast would be why her stomach was rumbling. She stepped inside the restaurant into a long narrow room with several dirty tables, a handful of customers, but not a waitress in sight.

Except for a few murmurs, the restaurant was silent—until a racket came from the kitchen. It sounded like pots and pans were being tossed around, along with profanities she might've heard from the men back home.

She considered leaving until a man drinking coffee at the counter caught her attention. He looked like the picture of contentment. Across the room, a young couple shared a plate of french fries, staring at each other as if this was the best moment of their lives.

Everything considered, she decided the place may not be so bad.

Picking a window booth, she dropped her bag onto the tabletop as she sat, plucked a menu from its holder, and glanced over the list of items.

The kitchen door swung open, and a lank woman with a tousled blonde updo and a bright pink uniform sashayed into the room. She set a piece of pie in front of the man at the counter.

"Here's your pie, sir," she said with a southern drawl as harsh as the clang of those pots and pans. "Chocolate's a little frozen in the middle, but I just now whipped up the cream."

She leaned towards the metal part of the dessert compartment, applied a red coat of lipstick, and turned back to the man.

"Can you believe ole Mack's got me workin' alone the last hour of my shift?"

She pushed his glass of water aside, leaned on the counter, and poked a long-nailed thumb at the kitchen. "Just between you'n me, I've seen pigsties that look better'n that kitchen looks."

"Maxine, you complain too much," the man said. He emptied his cup and shoved it across the counter. "But you make a killer pot of coffee."

Unfazed by his bluntness, Maxine reached for the coffeepot and filled his cup. "I could threaten to find another job. Hmm... Maybe not such a smart move at my age, you think?"

She set the pot on the warmer, and when she turned back, she noticed Emily.

"Gosh darn. I got a customer."

Gathering supplies, she sailed across the room, slapped a coaster on the table, and placed a glass of ice water on top.

"What's the matter? Lose your best friend or something?"

"No. Not exactly."

"What do you mean...*not exactly*?"

Emily pulled the glass over. "Well," she said, taking a sip. "It's only that, um... I just got into town, and...."

She thought of Michael and forced back tears, lifting her chin.

"I'm going to find a job. I may try to find an old friend of my mother's too. In fact...I have his post office box number. And I just need to send off a letter."

Maxine gaped at Emily's bag.

"You traveling alone?"

"Yes."

"If your mother and this guy are friends, how come she didn't give you his home address?"

"My mother died when I was a baby. I...I grew up with my...my aunt. When she died, I found a letter from him up in her attic." She gave her bag a rub. "I've already written him the letter."

"You notice the date on that letter you found?"

"1942."

Maxine chuckled. "Let's see. That's eighteen years ago. You actually think he's gonna have the same P.O. box?"

"I don't see why not."

"You know how many times I've moved in the last eighteen years?"

"Well, no I don't, but I—"

"Ten, maybe eleven times, I'll have you know. Across country and back, and a number of towns in between. Say...what's your name, anyway?"

"Emily. But I don't think it'll hurt to send out a letter."

"Listen here, young lady. You ever consider that maybe the man got himself a P.O. box so's not to be bothered?"

"People do that?"

"Well, would you give out your home address to just anyone when you didn't want certain people to find you? For instance, the police?"

Emily snatched her drink off the table and took a gulp.

Maxine gazed at her, thoughtfully. "Do you know anyone in San Francisco?"

"No."

"Where you from?"

Emily set her glass down using her thumb to rub moister off the rim. "Tennessee."

"Have you ever had a job?"

This was beginning to feel like one of Grandfather's interrogations. She glanced at her bag thinking it may be time to leave.

"Well, have you? Have you ever had a job?"

"No."

"You're not planning to mooch off your dead mother's friend, are you?"

"No. Of course not. And as soon as I get done here, I'm headed out to look for a job."

"You know how naive that sounds? Coming to a city of this size like a, a...*lost soul*, expecting to find some fly-by-night stranger with a P.O. box from, 1942?"

"Huh. And you expect a job to just drop from the sky without a day's experience. From the looks of it, you haven't seen much more than a mop and a bucket. You need to prove yourself first."

"But I have. I've cooked and baked a-and I've sewn my own clothes for years. In fact, back at the farm I canned shelves full of fruits and vegetables. A number of times they helped us through a bad winter."

Emily thought that would show her.

"Y'all can brag about your homemaking skills," Maxine said, making a point of looking down at Emily's blouse, "but you still need experience."

Emily felt for the safety pin that had worked its way through the buttonhole, pushing it back in.

"Well, I've done enough cooking that it should prove something."

"A job's not just throwing meat and potatoes into a pan."

Maxine lowered her voice.

"You know... My grandma used to cook up a storm back on the farm too, but that's not the same as workin' a real job. Even here in the restaurant, you have to count out change for customers. Have you ever done that? Ever counted out change to a customer?"

"No."

"Well, there you are. I mean, you could send the profits home with someone. You need experience."

Emily toyed with her glass of water, took a drink, and set in down. "I may not have counted out change to customers, but I know my math. And as for getting a job, how do I get experience if I can't get a job?"

Maxine thought for a moment and leaned with her knuckles on the table. "I'll tell you what. I just might have something for you. Why don't you give me your order, get your tummy filled, and I'll get back to you."

She whisked a pencil from behind her ear and pulled a pad from a pocket. "Now... What can I get you?"

Maxine reminded Emily of one of the crabs at the bottom of a creek waiting to latch onto a toe. The moment just before the strike was the worst. The best thing to do was not get too close.

"I'll have a grilled cheese and French fries. Oh, and a Coca Cola."

Emily watched her wander off then whipped out the letter to Samuel and scribbled that she would like to meet him at *Mack's House of Food.* She stopped for a moment, wondering if she should use another meeting place. But since she didn't know of another, she decided the letter needed to get out as soon as possible before she changed her mind. Just in case Samuel didn't check his mail too often, she set three dates when they could meet: November ninth, December first, and December nineteenth—between one and two. At the bottom, she added that a waitress told her she might help her, although she wasn't sure if it was for a job or a place to stay. She sealed the letter, thankful for the stamps she found in the old chest back at the farm.

With Maxine in the kitchen, Emily slipped out of the restaurant and took the letter to a mailbox she had noticed just up the street. On her way back, she saw a telephone booth directly across from the restaurant. She stopped and gave it some thought before heading over.

Digging out change, she searched the phonebook for the name Dimsmoore and anything close to Samuel. After calling each of the Samuel's, Sam's, Sami's and Samson's, she tried a number with the initial 'S'.

"First of all," the lady said curtly, "the initial 'S' stands for Scott. And secondly, I doubt that he's the friend of your mother's, not unless she was about two years old when this friendship took place."

"Well, then. By chance, do you know of a Samuel Dimsmoore?"

"I sure don't. Who is this anyway?"

"An old friend," Emily said, disheartened as she hung up.

She looked down at the last Dimsmoore with the initial '*S*' and dialed.

"Hello ma'am. I'm looking for a gentleman. A friend of my mother's. His name is Samuel Dimsmoore."

There was a long silence followed by a sigh. "I hate to say this, but Samuel...." The woman was obviously choked up. "He was my son. He died...three years ago."

Emily heard tears in the woman's voice and was taken aback.

"Oh, no... Um... Sorry. So sorry for bothering you ma'am. I... I'll let you be."

Emily hung up, immediately feeling terrible that she cut the woman off so abruptly. Knowing how difficult loss was for her grandfather, and Haity's father, she should have known better. She almost called back to apologize but changed her mind and headed across the street.

Her food was on the table when she returned to the restaurant. The place had livened up. And Maxine was taking an order three booths down. Several customers came in as she ate, along with two waitresses arriving for the next shift.

"Well… I've got some news," Maxine said as she stepped to Emily's table twenty minutes later. She folded a piece of gum into her mouth. "It wasn't easy, but I managed to pull some strings."

"With a job?"

"If you wait here while I grab my things, I'll take you to a place that's looking to hire. If the woman decides to take you in, it won't cost you a dime. You'll have a place to stay and money to boot."

"You're saying, just like that, there's a job? And a place to stay?"

"That's right. And it's not something that comes along every day."

Maxine stood with her hands on her hips, working her gum. "You know, if I were you, I'd forget about that friend of your mother's. If he's not in jail, the guy's probably a kook at best." She held out a hand. "Let me toss the letter for you."

Emily had no desire to argue with her. "It's done. I already dropped it in the garbage."

"Good decision. No use clouding your mind with false hope."

◇◇◇

"*I* take the bus," Maxine said as they headed out the door.

She glanced at Emily's clothes. "Once you get rid of those, you'll feel much better."

Emily's cheeks flushed with anger thinking of the effort she put into sewing her skirt and blouse.

"Come along now, here's the bus," Maxine urged when Emily fell behind. "I want to tell you something."

She reached around and nudged her forward onto the bus digging her long fingernails into her back.

"If you keep in mind what I've told you and don't make any waves, you'll do just fine."

What's that supposed to mean? Emily wondered. Whatever it was, she decided it couldn't be half as bad as the mess she was already in.

The bus wound through the streets stopping at every other corner, speeding through intersections, and whining as it climbed hills with the breaks squeaking on the way down. The bus was near empty, the houses secluded, fewer, and further between as it slowed and pulled over alongside a row of trees.

When it moved on and left them standing, Emily followed Maxine about a fourth of a block up a side street.

"There it is," she said, pointing at a white, three-story mansion with black shutters and a chimney up the side. They made their way through a solid iron gate into a spacious yard filled with an array of stately trees, colorful plants, and flowers. The property was hedged on both sides by trees and other greenery. Off to the right, from a separate entrance, was a row of red maple trees circling a long looping driveway with a shot-off paved area that continued to the back.

Moving up the walkway, they stepped onto a large porch enclosed with hanging plants and potted ferns. Emily cupped a sweet-smelling flower in her hand while Maxine stepped up to the stained-glass door and pressed the buzzer.

A woman who looked to be around fifty opened the door. She wore a scarlet red dress with cleavage that swelled like two mountains. Her bright red hair was stacked up into neat layers and sprayed to a freeze. At first glance, at her fiery blue eyes and pointed nose, one might've considered her brazen, although her voice was sweet as pie.

"Oh my. I guess you *were* serious."

"Hello, Miss Bea," Maxine said, her voice trilling with pleasure.

The woman gave Emily a thorough once over. "So, this is the gal. Emily, you say?"

"This is her," Maxine crowed. She put a hand on Emily's back and pushed her forward.

There're those fingernails again. Emily moved out of reach and tried not to make too much of the way the women talked as if she wasn't there.

"Soon as I heard she was new in town with no place to stay, I thought of you right way."

Miss Bea stepped out onto the porch, took Emily by a wrist, and pulled her from side to side.

"Well, young lady, we'll just have to see if we can do something about this dilemma of yours. How about it?"

"I—"

"It's terrible to be all alone in a strange town, isn't it, dearie," Maxine cooed as she stepped closer, craning her neck in order to gaze into Emily face.

Emily wondered why the sweet change in her voice and why she was suddenly calling her dearie.

A bus rumbled in the distance. Maxine took notice and positioned herself for a better view. She turned back, bobbing her head around, peering into the house.

"Ah. Don't you have something for me?"

Miss Bea reached inside the doorway and took an envelope off a stand. Maxine snatched it away before she had a chance to hand it over and made a quick exit down the steps.

"See ya'all."

"Later," Miss Bea said with a chuckle and a shake of her head. She took Emily by the shoulder.

"Come in, come in. Let's have a chat in the parlor."

Chapter Twenty-One

*E*mily stepped onto shiny hardwood flooring and followed Miss Bea across the hallway into an enchanting room with a silk floral rug, and walls of moss green. There were paintings of men in suits, and women in elegant gowns and bonnets, having tea in parlors or sitting in gardens.

Sunlight reflected off mirrors, polished oak, and glass tabletops. Elegant marble sculptures sat about the room. And facing a white stone fireplace, was a sofa and two high-backed armchairs covered with material of peach-colored flowers.

"This is just the beginning of the amenities we enjoy here," Miss Bea said, offering Emily the couch and taking an armchair for herself.

"Where did you say you were from?"

"I'm from down south. N-near Memphis."

"Maxine mentioned that your mother passed on. What does your father think of you moving all the way up to San Francisco?"

"My parents both died when I was still a baby. I… I'd been living with my aunt ever since. She died recently."

"Oh. You really are alone, aren't you?"

She glanced at Emily's bag. "Tell me something, just out of curiosity. How much money are you carrying?"

Emily rubbed her bag. "A hundred and forty dollars. Enough to get a place of my own if I have to."

"Oh my, young lady. I hate to burst your bubble, but you'll never make it on that bit of money."

"But…my rent wouldn't be more than *that*, would it?"

Miss Bea raised her brow. "You really don't have a clue, do you. Well, dear, it's not only the rent and trying to find a safe place to live. But there's food and dozens of other items you'll need. There's bedding, cooking utensils, soap, light bulbs, bus money, and the list goes on."

Her gaze dropped to Emily's clothes. "And there's that getup you're wearing. Gracious."

Emily tried to smooth out the wrinkles. "I've been traveling, and, I—"

"Oh sure, you could go out and buy yourself an outfit or two, but then... Well, it's back to the living expenses."

Miss Bea smiled sadly, shaking her head. "And it looks like you have no friends or relatives nearby that you can count on for help. Right?"

"Well, I... I. No, I don't."

By now, Emily was close to tears.

"You know, dear. Your lack of finances isn't your only worry."

"But I... I don't understand." She had hoped this woman would help her.

"Just a warning."

"... About what?"

"For one, the bums that roam the streets. Stay clear of them, especially at night."

Emily recalled the man down by the waterfront. The look he gave her had frightened her silly.

"You understand, I'm just being realistic."

"I think so."

"You do have a choice."

"I do?"

"Work for *The Palace* and you won't have to worry about any of it. No rent to pay or food to buy. I'll even set you up with a new wardrobe. You'll have nice everyday clothes all the way to some pretty fancy dresses. If you stick around long enough, play your cards right, you'll leave here in about four or five years with enough money to start up a new life anywhere you like. Even buy a home for yourself."

"Me... Buy a house?" Emily chuckled. "How's that possible?"

Miss Bea smiled, flashing long white teeth Emily hadn't noticed before. "This is San Francisco. People are willing to pay good money for the best." She stopped to size Emily up again. "After a little do-over, you certainly have what it takes."

"It's not that I don't believe you, it's just that... I, um... I still can't understand how this is possible. I mean, what'll I do? You know...without experience. Maxine said that—"

"Exactly why she brought you here."

Miss Bea moved to the edge of her seat. Her voice was almost tender. "You'll never get a chance like this again." She tapped Emily's knee. "Trust me?"

"Well. Yes, I do. But... What's my job? What kind of a place is this, anyway?" She looked around. "Is this where I'll work?"

"This'll be your home *and* your workplace."

Miss Bea relaxed back in the chair. "What we are is a... Well... We're an exclusive private club. There's none other like it in the world. As a matter of fact, we have two locations, although my goal is to bring the two together within the next year."

She gazed at Emily and smiled. "I think this is the perfect spot for you. It's smaller than our other location and runs a little smoother."

"It's very pretty"

"Well, thank you. And I'm proud to say that this was my vision, and it's done well for me. And my staff too, of course. At the time, we have over two thousand paying members. As you can imagine, there's too much detail to go into at the moment. But basically, we have a spectacular lounge where guests come to eat the best food around. Afterward, they may want a drink, dance a little, enjoy entertainment, play some poker, and delight in each other's company."

"So, it's a restaurant and nightclub?"

"Yes...that, only much more. Let me just say, that there's a fountain of wealth that flows through here. Many of our customers spend *crazy* amounts of money for our services. We even have clients from across the world who are regular guests. And...well... There'll be plenty of time to discuss the details. The important thing is. Would you like to make big money and invest in your future? If so. Would you like to stay?"

Emily looked into a face that seemed sincere. "It's hard for me to understand how this'll all work, but it sounds like a chance of a lifetime. So yes...I'll stay."

"Wonderful!"

Miss Bea clapped her hands and stood. "Come along then and I'll show you around."

Emily followed her into the hallway.

"My quarters." Miss Bea gestured to a doorway that was tucked around a corner across the hall.

"We usually have between forty and fifty girls working here," she added as they continued up the hallway. They turned right and passed an alcove-like entryway on the left with double oak doors.

"That's our lounge area. You'll see that tomorrow.

"Now, as I was saying, besides you, there're five girls living here. At the moment, I have another forty who come in between three to five nights a week. Several of them are college students, some work full-time, others part-time. Your room will be on the second floor. We have a third floor we call the *loft*."

Footsteps pattered down the steps. A young woman with light auburn pigtails, and yellow ribbons, rounded the corner and nearly ran into them.

"Oh... Miss Bea."

"How many times do I have to tell you, Ginger. No running."

"Sorry."

They were making introductions when another young woman with luminous dark hair flowing to her hips rounded the corner. She glowered at Emily as she passed and entered the lounge without a word.

"What's with Layla?" Miss Bea asked Ginger.

"Oh, who knows."

"I assume you two are preparing for the Perdue party?"

"Yes Ma'am. Early setup in the loft for happy hour." Ginger folded her arms and nodded at Emily. "Will she be joining us?"

"Listen," Miss Bea said firmly, "as you can see, I'm in the process of preparing her. And, no, she won't. Now, run along."

Ginger disappeared into the lounge, and Miss Bea led Emily up the hallway. She stopped at the staircase to straighten one of the flowerpots that lined the hardwood steps.

"You twenty-one?" she said as she straightened.

"No."

"Well, that's fine. Just remember. The drinks are free, just don't overdo it. If you're out dining, no drinks, unless you're with one of us. You hear?"

"Yes."

Beyond the staircase was a large room with the same hardwood flooring, two brown leather couches and matching chairs, a television, and a pool table that sat in the corner beyond a fireplace.

"This is our gathering room."

Miss Bea nodded towards a back entrance. "Out there we have a spectacular backyard with a patio and a fountain that lights up at night. Further down is a place to take in the sun. There's a parking lot beyond the trees, and an additional exit."

They moved down another hallway and through a swinging door that led into a large kitchen so stunning it took Emily by surprise.

The room was a mixture of greens and yellows, with hints of red in the trim and accessories set off by shiny black countertops.

A woman standing in front of the stove turned with a curious smile.

"Emily, this is Toni. Toni, this is Emily."

"Such a pretty one," Toni said, nodding an approval.

Emily shuffled the strap on her bag, greeting the woman who looked to be nearing mid-life, not exactly plump, but healthy with thick shoulder-length hair the color of porridge, large, black-rimmed glasses and determined eyes.

Still caught off guard by the grandiose surroundings, Emily gazed about, noticing an alcove next to a large window overlooking a flower garden. Sitting with a perfect view was a long green table, matching end chairs, and a bench on each side. The flooring was a yellow vinyl with streaks of red and green.

Miss Bea pulled a mug off a rack and poured herself coffee, turning to Emily. "Want some?"

"Uh… No thanks."

"Well, there's always a pot of coffee on and plenty of snacks whenever you like."

Toni placed a lid back onto a pot and turned for a better look at Emily. "I hope you're not one of those finicky eaters trying to live on carrots and chicken wings. You know, some men like a little meat on their gals."

Emily chuckled. "I like carrots, but not enough to live on. And I'll take a chicken breast over a wing any day."

She looked at the green electric stove with silver trim, hoping she would be helping Toni with the cooking.

"I sure like this kitchen."

"See there, Miss Bea?" Toni grinned, scanning the room. "This is exactly what I was trying to inspire when I recreated my aunt Diana's kitchen."

"And why I let you decorate the kitchen instead of the lounge."

Toni chuckled as she uncovered two loaves of bread that had been rising. "Everyone loves it, 'cept you."

"I like it just fine, Toni. It just wouldn't be my choice, that's all."

Miss Bea turned to Emily. "As you can see, besides Toni having an interesting eye for decorating, she makes sure there's enough food for everyone. The late meal is ready around five. We have a girl that comes in for the night shift at six. And another comes in on Saturdays and Sundays. When they're not cleaning or making preparations, they hang in the maid's quarters down the hall."

"You're open all night?"

"In the main kitchen off the lounge, we're open until eleven. This area is for all our girls who come and go as they please." She placed her cup into the sink.

"I guess that's enough for now. So...you ready to go see your room?"

Miss Bea glanced at the cook. "Oh, and Toni, don't forget to bring Emily refreshments later on."

They headed up the stairs, turned left at the landing, and went up another flight of steps to where it opened into a sprawling second story. Emily glanced up the staircase that lead to the third floor. She was amazed how the place was even larger than what it looked from the outside. They walked to the end of the hallway where Miss Bea opened a door to the left. She motioned Emily into a lovely room.

A bed with a colorful spread sat a few feet to the right. Further down, across the room, was a black leather couch with two solid-wood stands, a coffee table, and lamps with shades of red and yellow. To the left of the couch sat a hardwood table with a vase of flowers and two matching chairs. Above the table was a window with open shutters made of moss green wood. Emily crossed the room and looked out into the front yard. The house was a distance from the street, secluded, but Emily noticed the front view from where she stood was partially open.

Miss Bea stood in the doorway resting an elbow against the doorframe. "Tomorrow morning I'll take you shopping for some suitable clothes. Tonight, I want you to stay in your room and relax, get to bed early. The restrooms and shower room are up the hallway, left of the staircase. Just beyond, is the laundry room where you leave your bedding and personal items. Make sure to mark your room number on the basket. Everything you'll need is there in the cupboards."

She straightened, looking around the room. "Now, what else is there. Oh yes. Someone cleans *The Palace* early mornings. But it's your responsibility to keep your own room clean.

"Also, if you need help in a hurry, here's a bell that rings in the kitchen, maid's quarters, and in the council." Miss Bea pointed at a chain dangling next to the doorway. "Give this a pull and someone will come up."

She stepped into the hallway, turning back with her hand on the knob. "I've got to run, but I'll meet you in the kitchen first thing in the morning."

Alone, Emily went to the bed and smoothed a hand over the silk bedspread. She moved about the room, noticing the interesting pictures on the walls that were similar to those in other parts of the house, although more revealing. Everything in the room matched with colors of green, yellow, and scarlet red. There was an oak chest of drawers to the left of the doorway. To the right of the chest was a large walk-in closet with a full-length mirror and a dressing table at the far end. There were shelves and a chest on one side, and on the other, a clothes rack that ran the length of the closet.

She wandered back into the bedroom and sat on the bed. Pulling the bag strap off her shoulder, she untied her shoes, kicked them off, and laid back. After everything she had been through, it was hard to believe she was living in this beautiful mansion. Most importantly, she had a job. It all seemed too good to be true.

Chapter Twenty-Two

Sunlight streamed through the narrow, corner-window shades, along the floor, up over the bedcovers, and across Emily's face. She stretched, yawned, and snuggled back into the silk spread. That's when it hit her exactly where she was. She peeked at the clock that said six forty-five. Back home, it would already be mid-morning. She sat up, looking around the room strangely excited but guarded.

After spending time with Maxine and Miss Bea, she had a feeling that living in a house with a group of women meant she would have to be strong. Whatever she revealed to them, she could never tell them about Claude. She had to try and push back any thought of him. Until she was surrounded by those she could entrust herself to, it was best not to deal with that awful morning.

There was a tray on the table which meant Toni had brought her dinner while she was sleeping. She put on her shoes and took her clothes from her bag, placing the bag in the bottom chest drawer. Hanging some of her clothes in the closet, she used a wet cloth to smooth out the wrinkles. She changed into another outfit, took her soiled clothing to the washroom, and took the tray down to the kitchen.

A woman with shoulder-length chestnut hair sat at the table drinking coffee and reading a newspaper. A basket of bread, and a bowl of jelly, sat to the side. She looked up when Emily walked through the doorway. In some ways, she appeared to be in her early twenties, and in other ways, she seemed much older.

"You must be Emily," she said, setting the paper aside. "I'm Delilah. Big shopping trip today, aye?"

Emily placed the tray on the counter. "Yeah. It's not something I'd normally do."

"Say, how long've you been doing this kind of work, anyway?"

Emily reached for a bag of puffed wheat, glancing back. "I've been wondering exactly what I'll do." She took a jug of milk from the refrigerator, poured some on her cereal, and set it back. "Miss Bea didn't go into detail, except that I'd be... Let's see, serving guests? I presume, waitressing?"

"How typical."

"What?"

"Oh, just thinking out loud. Let me guess. You have no friends, no relatives nearby, and you were in desperate need of a job and a place to stay. Um... A runaway, maybe?"

Emily took a seat and smothered jelly on a piece of bread. Delilah was right. But to admit everything would only mean more questions.

"You're right about a job and a place to stay."

Emily took a bite of bread and wiped crumbs from the corners of her mouth. "You know...I've done a lot of cooking."

Delilah smiled. "We've all learned to leave the cooking to the cook. And you can't get any better than Toni." She picked up her coffee. "Of course, there's the kitchen in the lounge, but that's another ballgame in there. Except for three cocktail waitresses, there're only waiters. Anyway, no need to go into that."

She sipped her coffee, set it aside, and began folding the newspaper. "I think the bottom line is that Miss Bea is expecting you'll fit in like we all do.

"Hey, I'm just curious. How'd you find out about this place anyway?"

"Through a lady named Maxine. I met her at *Mack's House of Food.*"

"Oh, yeah, the waitress. Boy she's one you don't want to cross."

"I figured that.

"So... What brought you here?"

"Me? Oh, you know. I was let go. And here I am."

Delilah tossed the newspaper into a basket that sat on the floor and took her cup to the sink.

"Don't worry about washing the dishes. Toni insists it's her job. She loves to be needed."

"Where is Toni, by the way?"

Delilah broke off a piece of roll, taking a bite as she leaned back against the counter.

"A doctor's appointment."

"Anything serious?"

"Just a couple bunions and an ingrown toenail," Miss Bea trilled as she walked in. She filled her coffee cup and turned to Delilah.

"So, Toni informed me that you're tagging along on our shopping trip."

"If you don't mind. Thought I'd look around while Emily gets fitted. I've got that opera I'm going to in a few months. When're you planning to head out?"

"Soon as you guys get yourselves fed and dressed."

*A*n hour later, the women walked into Poffs Boutique. The only time Emily had been in a clothing store was once a year when she went wide-eyed and yearned into Sears and Roebuck to buy underwear and a pair of shoes. Now she felt like a princess trying on fancy dresses at the boutique and, later, at a department store, clothing she would have been proud to wear to school. She had never worn skirts less than two or three inches below the knees. And it took the two women to convince her that some of the dresses for work were meant to show leg.

When they finished with her wardrobe, they stopped at a jeweler, and on to another store where Emily picked out various colors of frilly undergarments. Making their way across the street, they stopped at several shoe stores before going to purchase makeup. Emily had convinced Miss Bea she could do her own hair. And looking down at a dressing table with jars, odd-shaped containers, and tubes, she was reluctant about having her face painted. But they sat her down anyway, and a woman tweezed her eyebrows and showed her how to apply foundation, rouge, eye shadow, lipstick, and finishing powder. She curled Emily's eyelashes but decided they were so dark and thick there was no need for mascara, and that just a bit of liner would do.

The woman finished with the last touch of makeup and handed over a bag with everything she would need to duplicate the process. Emily thanked her. And when she stood and looked in the mirror, she was stunned— not sure what to think.

"I look like...."

"Like a beautiful woman," Delilah assured her.

"You'll get used to it," Miss Bea said as she turned to leave.

"Come along, girls. Let's go have lunch."

Once they deposited the bags in the chauffeured town car, they headed to a nearby restaurant. As they walked, Emily considered her new attire and makeup and couldn't imagine her job would be serving food or cooking.

Needing answers, she brought this up to Miss Bea.

"You're on the right track, Emily. But just you wait, young lady.

Once you get all decked out and walk into the lounge, your eyes will pop right out of your head."

They approached the restaurant, and a distinguished-looking man walked out and held the door for them.

"Hello, ladies."

"Hi, John," Miss Bea said, all smiles. "How're you doing?"

"Just grand," he said, tipping his hat. He placed a newspaper under an arm and headed up the sidewalk.

Inside, a waitress escorted the women to a table in back. After ordering beverages and turkey sandwiches, Delilah turned to Emily.

"You got yourself some gorgeous dresses today. Just make sure to practice walking in those heels."

"Oh, I plan to.

"It's too bad you didn't find what you were looking for."

"I know. But I have plenty of time."

"So…um…you're going to an opera, you say?"

"My first. So yeah, I'm excited. Raymond, the guy who's taking me, says he's going to culture me."

Miss Bea chuckled. "Do you even know what the opera's about? I'll bet you can't tell us the name."

"Oh gee. It's uh… A romance, I'm told. Oh, what was the name now… Hmm."

"*La Traviata*, which means, *woman gone astray.*" It's a classic tragedy."

"Still, a romance," Delilah said sourly.

"Yes, but no less a tragedy. Did you know it's based on the novel *Camille (Lady of the Camellias)?* Greta Garbo played Marguerite in 1936."

"Aw… Miss Bea. Don't ruin it for me."

Miss Bea raised her glass. "Take my advice, Delilah, and read the book."

She took a sip of her wine and set it aside.

"You'll get more out of it if you do. It's in Italian."

"I knew that."

"Oh, sure you did," Miss Bea chuckled, "sure, you did."

"You're just jealous Raymond didn't ask you."

"I'll have you know, young lady, I've already seen the opera. In fact, I encouraged Raymond to take you. So, there."

Since *The Palace* was closed for business on Mondays, the place was silent when they returned. Emily was relieved to have another night to herself.

A few minutes after five, she looked up from her reading when she heard a squeak-squeak, squeaking sound come up the hallway and stop at her door. There was a warning knock and Toni walked in with a tray.

"Here's tuna on rye and a slice of cake I baked this afternoon." She crossed the room, set the tray on the table, and headed back to the door. "I didn't know if you like milk or coffee, so I brought both."

Emily sat up and put her book aside. "Oh, thanks. It's perfect.

"How're your feet?"

Toni looked at her new thick-soled shoes. "Nothing that a good soaking and, finally, a decent pair of shoes won't fix."

She walked out the door and poked her head back in. "Just to let you know, Miss Bea insists I do a couple days of catering. The leg work ends tomorrow." She chuckled. "To be honest. It's all just a ploy of enticement for the new girls." She gazed about the room. "Looks like you're doing just fine."

She closed the door and left with her shoes squeaking back down the hallway.

The day had been long—and although Emily had to admit somewhat exiting—she slept hard that night.

A man slipped outside through a door at the top of the third-floor stair landing as Emily stepped from her bedroom. A few moments later, a young woman with bleached blonde hair, dressed in a long white robe, came down the steps counting out a stack of bills. She was heading to her room when she was taken aback upon seeing Emily.

"Oh... I didn't realize anyone was here. You're new."

"Yes, I am. I'm Emily."

"I'm Angellee," the girl said, folding the money into a pocket. She reached for a doorknob and looked back across the hallway. "If that's concern on your face, don't worry. This is far better than any place I've ever worked."

Emily hadn't been as concerned as she was curious, but now she was more concerned.

"Thank you. I'll keep that in mind."

She watched Angellee step into her room and went to take a shower. Turning the faucet on high, she stood beneath the spout delighting in the rushing water winding its way down and around her toes. This being the first shower she had ever taken, it was exhilarating. But the thrill was soon coupled with a shocking realization that came with a memory of an article she found at her aunt Francine's. It was about a lady named Sadie during the gold rush area. Emily was certain the memory had to do with what she just witnessed. The man leaving out a back entrance, Angellee's comments, and the image of her counting out money. At the age of fourteen, Emily had been shocked and somewhat intrigued by what she read. Whether or not the recount of this woman was all fact, Emily believed she was living in the midst of one of those establishments that very moment.

She could grab her bag and sneak out the back door. But even if she found a place, Miss Bea said she wouldn't last more than a week or two. And with the police most likely aware she came out west, the way things looked, she might as well put on her fancy clothes and go down.

Turning her thoughts from her predicament, Emily went to her room and concentrated on the luxury of her stay. She went into the closet, sat at the dressing table and used bobby pins to clip her hair up. After putting on a touch of face and eye shadow, rouge, and finishing powder, she thought that maybe Miss Bea was right and that she would get used to making up her face. Although the corset and nylons would need some extra getting used.

When she lifted her arms through a silk underslip, she held her breath as the soft cool fabric slid into place. She pulled on a black dress and zipped it up the back. Clipping on her heirloom necklace, she stepped into a pair of red heels and went to the full-length mirror. She ran a hand across the red beads, comforted that she would have the necklace close to her heart as she entered into this puzzling new world.

Removing the bobby pins, she ran her fingers through her curls as they cascaded down past her shoulders. The heels made her look even taller than she already was. Nevertheless, when she looked into the mirror, for the first time, she felt quite pretty.

At eight-thirty, Emily stepped from her bedroom, headed down the hallway, and descended the stairway in the sleeveless black dress. It was cut a little low for comfort but a perfect spot for her necklace. The bodice fit snuggly around her waist, hugging her curves to mid-calf, and though elegant, it was essential she take the steps with care.

At the landing, she stood for a moment and gathered her bearings before heading down the main staircase. Miss Bea was talking with a man in the gathering room. Emily was startled by how much he looked like Moe from *The Three Stooges*. He was taller than Moe, with slightly longer hair, and attractively styled. And though he looked more professional, he shared the same expressive eyes and thick eyebrows that gave a devilish crown to his narrow jawline. She had a feeling there was more to him than his looks, trailered suit, and fancy shoes.

Miss Bea noticed Emily standing at the bottom of the stairway and called her over.

"Come. I have someone who wants to meet you."

As Emily approached, Miss Bea pulled her over. "This is Donald Schillings," she said in a tone suggesting this was the man to meet.

Apart from Daniel and Michael's gentle gestures, no one had greeted her in such a way. And when this stranger came at her, throwing out his hand, she flinched—although it wasn't Claude coming at her. And she glanced up apologetically, placing her hand into Mr. Schillings' chubby fist. She expected it would be cold as the handle of a water pump iced over. But it was warm and spongy, giving her the oddest sensation like he had just come in from the barn with a fresh pail of milk.

"So, you're the girl that showed up in such a pickle. From what Miss Bea said, you're lucky to have found us."

Emily wondered what Miss Bea told him. And she couldn't understand why anyone would think a dwelling such as this would be a lucky place to end up, pickle or not.

"Here's your champagne," an enthusiastic voice interrupted. A young man in a black tuxedo set a tray of drinks on a table, handing Emily and Miss Bea each a tall glass before strolling off again.

Donald reached into a shirt pocket for a cigarette case and flipped the lid open. "How disheartening," he said, tapping a cigarette out of the box, "to come to a strange town with nothing but a bag of belongings and a few dollars."

He dropped the case into his vest pocked, studying Emily as he pulled a lighter from his suit pocket.

"Well, ladies. I have calls to make.

"I'll be in your office," he said to Miss Bea, placing the cigarette between his lips. He gave Emily a sweeping glance, lighting up, as he headed off.

Emily hoped he wasn't coming for her later. Her eyes dropped to her glass. At least, she would have something to cloud the reality. She took a long drink, welcoming the warmth that spread from her throat into her belly and through her limbs — getting dressed for the night had postponed the inevitable. But now, the moment of truth was stirring her insides.

She looked at Miss Bea. "Why didn't you tell me what kind of place this was?"

"You mean our little family here? I think I did. And don't tell me Maxine didn't mention it?"

"Nope, not a word."

It was obvious that Miss Bea would never take credit for something as obvious as the way she set her up. She could've at least warned her.

Emily listened half-heartedly as the woman tried to convince her that *The Palace* was the best place for her.

"You'll ease right into things. They all do."

Her words drifted into promises of glamour, high society, trips, and money.

"Emily? Did you hear me? I said I was going to explain it all, but I'm still not certain what your assignment will be. Since talking to you yesterday, there's a man that's very interested in you. For a personal position."

She took a sip of champagne and glanced at her office door across the room.

"Oh, why not. I guess there's no reason to keep you in suspense. It's Donald Schillings. He's been adamant for months now about what sort of girl he needs—desperate, really. And he's at his rope's end trying to find the right person for the job. For some reason, he thinks you may fit the bill."

"What do you mean by *assignment*?"

"Just what I said. Although what he has in mind, exactly, I'm not sure. I could use you at *The Palace*. And I hope he finds someone else. Because there's an enormous amount of money to be made for both of us right here."

Her eyes darted back to her office door and back to Emily. "I wasn't thrilled when he informed me of his interest in you. And yet, I can't say no to him. He's got too much clout for that. Not to mention the important clients he brings in."

"I don't know. It just doesn't make sense."

"Of course, it doesn't. And that's exactly why I didn't explain every last detail. You have to grow into something like this. The important thing is. You have the opportunity of a lifetime right here. Remember? You said as much yourself."

Emily looked up the staircase, knowing she didn't want to stay. But being out in the streets alone at night, with police looking for her, wasn't an option.

Miss Bea tapped her on the shoulder.

"Come now, after I bought you all those beautiful clothes. You can at least check things out for yourself. I bet you'll end up having a marvelous time just like all the girls do. You'll have to trust me on that. I mean…what do you know about life? What do you have to lose?"

"Well, I—"

"Listen, Emily… Two young women were found dead last week, raped and stabbed. It's a dangerous world out there for anyone, but even more so for someone as young and naïve as you."

Emily had a feeling she wasn't quite as naïve as Miss Bea or Donald Schillings thought she was. She took a hardy drink of champagne, realizing that, for now, she was at their mercy.

Chapter Twenty-Three

Miss Bea opened the double oak doors and they walked through a stunning round entryway with walls of decorative mirrors and a hanging crystal chandelier. The flooring was polished white marble infused with intricate black designs. It continued into the lounge area and wound around to the left as a walkway that spun to the far side of the lounge to a bar positioned slightly to the right with mirrored walls and soft red lights above a black counter and matching high-backed leather stools.

On each side of the marble walkway, customers were visiting in luxurious sitting areas. The burgundy carpeting was a striking backdrop to black leather chairs, loveseats, and glass table tops set with sculptured bases. Overhead, shimmers of mottled lights hung from the ceiling.

A man noticed Miss Bea and came over.

"Miss Bea, just the person I'm looking for."

"What is it, Randy?"

"Well... I've heard rumors of a new home for *The Palace.*"

"Where'd you hear that?"

"It's not true, then?"

"I didn't say that."

Emily moved away from the two and looked around the magnificent room that was far larger than she had imagined. Approximately fifteen feet straight across from the entry was a step-up with an exquisite black railing that circled a dining area. There were at least thirty people eating at tables draped in white linen and topped with soft candlelight. Down from the dining area was an extension of the lounge where a crystal-lit archway opened into a back room.

Her gaze drifted to her left, just beyond the entryway, where a waterfall, set within greenery, flowed into a pond. When a lovely melody began, she stepped around the waterfall to observe a man playing *Rhapsody in Blue* on a grand piano. She knew that music well and had listened to her grandmother play it on the Victrola many times before the player broke. She stood transfixed to the spot until the song ended.

Miss Bea came up beside her and they stood looking about the room. "Well, what do you think?" she said. "Quite spectacular, isn't it."

Emily's disappointment in her hadn't changed, but the room was more than spectacular.

"It's unbelievable. It's…breathtaking."

Miss Bea took Emily by an elbow. "The area with marble flooring that runs across to the bar is called the *strip*." To the left of the bar, we have a dance floor. A band usually comes in once or twice a week."

She pulled Emily around, pointing to the right of the entryway where a woman sat in a small room behind an open window. There was a man standing next to her who was a giant in comparison. Behind them, steps winding upward, led to another room. Emily looked up to a window directly above that looked out over the lounge.

"That's our council," Miss Bea said. "They're here to ensure everything runs smoothly."

The click of heels approached, and they turned as a young woman walked towards them. Her blonde curls bounced around her shoulders, and her short silver dress sparkled as she came up the strip.

"Howdy. You called for me?"

"I did," Miss Bea said, taking her by an arm.

"Felice, this is Emily, our newest addition. I'd like you to introduce her to a few people."

"Certainly. I'd be happy to."

She turned to Emily and examined her attire. "Nice dress.

"Wow," she said, rolling a thumb across her necklace. "Where'd you guys pick this up?"

"Well, I bought her sev—" Miss Bea took a closer look.

"It's mine," Emily said. "An heirloom."

She raised an arm, twisting her wrist. "I thought it went well with the bracelet you bought me."

Miss Bea looked at her oddly then motioned for the girls to be off.

Felice took Emily's hand and they walked up the strip.

"Hey... Meredith, James," she said as they approached a couple who were about to leave.

Emily guessed upstairs, most likely to the attic, since she didn't think the woman lived at *The Palace*.

"I have a surprise for you. This is Emily."

Meredith was older than most of the other women, probably in her late twenties. She was pretty, in a tomboy sort of way, with shiny brunette trundles cut just above her shoulders. James looked to be in his late fifties. His hair was dark except for graying around his temples. His beard and mustache were speckled with white that popped out like springs from a worn-out pickup seat.

"Mm... a delicious surprise, indeed," he said, gazing at Emily.

James removed the cigar from his mouth and in a suave fashion, took her hand and planted a kiss.

She pulled back when the bristly hair around his mouth pricked her skin.

"Take is easy, ole boy," Felice joked, "she's new."

James released her hand and bowed with a grin. "I apologize, young lady. I hope I didn't scare you off."

"Not yet."

Emily laughed along with the others, thankful for the champagne that bubbled in her veins like a cushion softening her uneasiness.

"He's harmless," Felice whispered, giving James's beard a playful tug.

She tucked an arm around one of Emily's and they crossed the room with more introductions before stopping to visit with a couple who were standing next to the piano.

"Marshall and Pollyanna. This is Emily, our newest girl."

Pollyanna was elegant in every sense of the word. She was tall with short jet-black hair, delicate features, and a beautiful smile. Her strapless floor-length gown was pink crepe, simple, yet as elegant as she was.

Marshall was the man who had been playing the piano earlier. His light-brown hair was shaved neatly around his ears. He was immaculately dressed in a black tailored suit, silk tie, and black leather shoes.

Emily hadn't expected to meet a pair like Pollyanna and Marshall at *The Palace*. It made her wonder about the intertwining paths of those who meet by chance.

"I love your music," she said to Marshall. "It took me back to memories of my grandmother."

"I appreciate your kind words. Thank you."

Felice put a hand on Pollyanna's shoulder. "You realize, tonight is Pollyanna's début. She'll be singing in front of a group for the first time."

Pollyanna leaned against the piano as Marshall took a seat on the bench. "Well, officially my first time."

"Oh, Felice, my girl." A youthful-looking man, no more than thirty-five, whisked over and draped an arm around her.

"The game starts in five," he said. He gave her a peck on the cheek and sailed off again.

"Oh, shoot," Felice said, turning to Emily. I'm scheduled in the poker room tonight. Hope you don't mind if I take off."

"That's okay. I see that Delilah is waving me over."

Emily said goodbye and walked to where Delilah sat at the bar with a man. He wore a white shirt, dark tie, and dress pants. His long tied-back hair seemed almost a contradiction to his apparel. There was something appealing about him, although when she thought Delilah might have plans to bring them together, she found herself comparing him to Michael. Those few hours with Michael riding the train across the country had been one of the most meaningful in her life. Just thinking of him again made her feel like someone had tied her heart into a knot and given it a fierce yank.

"There you are," Delilah said as Emily approached.

"Peter, I'd like you to meet Emily."

The man swiveled in his chair and held out a hand. "Well, hello. It's a pleasure."

Delilah stood and placed an arm around Emily. "I said you'd join him for a drink. Hope you don't mind."

Emily nodded. "It's fine."

"Good. I'll leave you two be, then."

Delilah picked up her drink and strolled across the room singing *Put Your Head on My Shoulder* along with the piano.

Peter motioned Emily to sit, took her empty glass, and pushed it aside.

"Abe," he called to the bartender, "bring this young lady a fresh drink, will you?"

He turned back to Emily. "I couldn't help but notice when you walked in. I haven't seen starry eyes like that in a long time."

"It was that obvious?"

He winked. "Just a little."

Emily smiled. "I may've been starry-eyed. But to be honest, I was just as stunned."

She looked out across the room, thinking the bar stool was the perfect spot to take it all in. "It's like a fairytale."

"This place has a unique ambiance, all right," he said. "Miss Bea has good taste. Or just a fabulous decorator."

A round of drinks came from a patron, followed by another. Emily loved how the champagne fizzed in her mouth, rolled down her throat, and seeped into her veins. Although she was feeling the effects.

When Pollyanna began to sing *Unforgettable*, Emily turned her attention to the beautiful woman with a voice so sweet it brought tears to her eyes.

"Are you okay?" Peter asked when the song ended.

Emily pushed her glass aside blinking several times to ensure no tears would fall. It seemed that wine set better with her.

"I'm okay," she said, rubbing her forehead. "Just a little too much champagne. I feel a headache coming on."

"Champagne will do that."

He motioned to Abe. "Some water, please?"

Leaning back, Peter observed Emily.

"So… Do you mind telling me how you came to work for *The Palace*?"

"Um, well, it's a long story involving more than you'd probably care to hear. I mean… I… I don't know how long I'll be staying." *Now, why'd I say that?* she scolded herself. "You're not going over to tell Miss Bea, are you?"

He looked at her curiously. "I have no intention of doing anything of the kind."

She was still deciding if she should trust him or not when Donald Schillings strolled in with three men. They sat along the strip, just tables down from the bar.

Donald glanced over several times, but to Emily's relief, he seemed to lose interest. Lucky for Miss Bea, others felt differently. It wasn't long before the three men left, each with a woman in arm. Donald sat alone. And Emily held her breath when he glanced at her again. His gaze drifted to Peter for a hard look. A minute later, he got up and wandered off around the corner towards the poker room.

Emily sighed, wondering how she would ever do what Miss Bea expected from her. Of course, it couldn't be half as bad as what Claude put her through. If she looked at it that way, she was better off by far, and maybe she should be grateful.

Peter touched her arm. "Is it the headache?"

She nodded. "Yeah...it is."

"Why don't you let me walk you to your room."

Emily wasn't prepared to go up with him, but what choice did she have. At least it was with someone she liked. They stopped at the council before heading up the stairs. As they walked, she was leaning on him more than she intended and pulled back.

"You're shaking," he said.

She nodded but didn't look up.

When they reached her room, she closed her eyes and turned the doorknob.

He placed his hands on her shoulders and pulled her around.

"I'm not going in with you, if that's what you're thinking."

"Oh." she said, nearly hugging him. "Thank you. I mean.... It's just that, my head—"

"Don't worry. I've taken care of everything. You're free to stay in your room for the night."

He dropped his arms, stood back, and looked into her eyes. "Are you sure you're going to be all right?"

"Oh, yes, I'll be fine." She laughed nervously. "Just *normal* business."

"How's your head?"

"It still hurts. But hopefully a shower and some sleep will help."

"Here… I want you to have this," he said, reaching into a shirt pocket. He pulled out a card, handing it to her.

"I live in Los Angeles and don't make it up often. But that's my address and phone number, just in case. Just keep it to yourself, if you don't mind."

"I will. And thanks, Peter."

When he disappeared down the steps and around the landing, she went to the restroom to prepare for the night, thankful for the supplies and pajamas that were available to the girls.

Back in her room, after putting everything away, she placed Peter's card inside the top chest drawer where she kept her jewelry and crawled into bed.

*B*y morning, Emily's headache had turned into a dull pain, something of a nuisance that kept her from getting the rest she wanted. Finally, she put on a pair of plaid peddle-pushers, a yellow top, slip-ons, and went downstairs.

She was about to go into the kitchen. And when she pushed the swinging door open, Layla was coming out, and the door hit her and knocked a plate of cookies out of her hand.

"Now look what you've done! You…."

"Oh, I'm sorry. Let me help—"

"Just never mind! I've got it!"

Toni grabbed a plate, filled it with cookies and took it to Layla.

"Here. Take these. Go on. I'll clean it up."

Layla dropped the cookie she had picked off the floor, took the plate, and left.

"You're welcome," Toni said with a smirk as she sank to a knee and started on the mess.

Emily went over with a wash cloth and picked up the broken plate and swept up the crumbs.

After they put everything away, Toni turned to Emily.

"I noticed her claws."

"Yeah. She's not an easy one to understand."

Toni Laughed. "That's an understatement. But listen here... I trust you. So I'm going to fill you in on a few things."

Toni looked around the kitchen making sure they were alone.

"You see... Layla's mom was once Miss Bea's assistant. Donald Schillings and her had a fling. And before she died, she claimed Donald was Layla's father. Honestly, I think her mother saw that Layla has no ambition and hoped to set her up for life. Donald probably saw through her scheme and has never accepted her as his daughter. But to keep her quiet, he's made it so she can do more or less whatever she pleases around here. Boy does she take advantage of that. And I've seen how she's caused problems for those she doesn't like. Yes, her mother and Miss Bea were friends, but... I don't know. From what I've seen, Layla has no real bite. She'll try. But what can she really do. Just... don't let her get to you."

"Ha. I'll do my best."

"So... How was your first night?"

"Oh, okay. I met a nice man."

"Can't ask for more than that."

Toni pulled a pan out of the oven. "I've got piping hot muffins here and some rolls I'm about to ice. If you want eggs, it'll just take a few minutes."

Emily put a fork into a muffin and dropped it onto a plate. She picked up a cup of coffee that had been poured for her and headed to the door. "Thanks, Toni."

"That's all you're having?"

Emily checked out the spread on the counter not wanting to hurt Toni's feelings. "I'm sure it's delicious, but...lunchtime, I'll have something more, I promise."

Back in her room, she sat at the table gazing at the scenery outside the window. She ate her muffin, mulling over the fact that her first job would always be *that place* she wouldn't want to name out loud. It was disheartening to think that on her next trip to the lounge she wouldn't have Peter to rely on.

Miss Bea said she would get used to her duties like the other girls had. Maybe so. Maybe she would have to. She wished there was another option. But for now, it seemed there wasn't a safer place for her. At least no one cared where she came from. And there was food and almost everything else she would need.

She finished her breakfast and looked out the door, listening for signs of life. For all the people supposedly in the house, it sure was quiet. She gazed up the stairs to the third floor, curious, but not enough to check it out just yet.

Closing the door, she straightened her room and took her breakfast tray down to the kitchen. A number of girls were gathered around the table. She took an apple from the counter and a chocolate chip cookie from a tray Toni had just taken from the oven.

"My favorite."

Toni smiled. "Everyone's favorite."

Emily noticed Layla sitting on the window seat beyond the table, with her feet up, looking outside. She glanced at Emily and turned her gaze back out. Felice exchanged a few words with the girl and a minute later Layla got up and left.

"Hey, you all. I want you to meet Emily," Felice said, pointing out the girls and rattling off their names – – Poppy, Estelle, and Lorena. Lorena mentioned she was heading to class and just stopped by for breakfast.

The other two said they hadn't left from the night before.

Felice and Poppy decided to go up town and invited Emily along.

"I'd love to go, but I have some things to take care of."

Emily didn't feel safe going outside the gates of *The Palace* just yet, at least not without Miss Bea, who seemed to be accompanied by her driver wherever she went.

Why she felt that way was a secret she would have to keep to herself. If she were relying on mere emotions, she would entrust Delilah with that knowledge, although something told her to hold back.

She wondered what Haity would think if she saw her in a place like this. Knowing her, she would have made sure she was okay, then laugh—a rolling on the floor, barrel laugh. Of course, if she knew everything, she would be blazing angry. Haity would have done anything for her—something Emily knew was rare for even a friend. She thought of the day in church with Haity and her parents and longed for that chance again. But, right now, it wasn't time for daydreams that made her ache and would never come true.

On her way upstairs, Layla barreled down the steps. Emily had a hello on the tip of her tongue, but Layla glowered sour-faced straight ahead and continued down.

*T*hat evening, after a shower and a touch of makeup, Emily pulled her hair back over her left ear and clipped in a red flower. She put on a silver vine necklace and matching bracelet, went to the closet, and took out a white dress.

"You look too stunning in that to worry about the few inches above the knees," was Delilah's comment. When Miss Bea agreed, Emily had given in. Now as she was about to put on that dress, she had a feeling it would be the best part of the evening.

She pulled on silk nylons and fastened them to her corset. Slipping on the white bubble dress, she zipped it up the back, and stepped into a pair of black heels. As she walked over and looked in the mirror, she imagined herself as pure and elegant as a water lily on her way to meet Michael. But when her gaze dropped to her bare legs, she saw herself as she was. It was as if she had backed herself into a corner and there was nowhere for her to turn but out the door and down the stairs to her job.

Chapter Twenty-Four

*B*roken *Hearted Melody* played on the jukebox as Emily entered the lounge, her black heels clicking against marble, turning heads as she glided up the strip, seeming more confident than she was. A waiter in a black tux came with a tray filled with glasses of champagne. She nearly turned him down but needed a quick fix and decided to limit herself to one.

When she approached the bar, she noticed a thin pasty-looking man down at the end with short sandy hair and sideburns like sliver moons. He had been watching her. Yet, when she caught his gaze, he turned away. He reminded her of a broken-winged bird with pondering round eyes and drooping shoulders. She thought he looked as out of place as she felt.

"What do you have besides champagne?" she asked Gabe as she slid onto a stool. She took a sip of her champagne and set it aside.

"Too much gives me an awful headache."

"There's whiskey, rum, vodka—"

"Vodka? Mm. I'll have that."

"What would you like with it?"

"Something with it? Well… Whatever you think."

She watched him make her drink, garnish it with a cherry and a slice of orange.

"Here you go," he said as he set it in front of her. "I put in sour mix. If you don't like that, I'll be glad to make you something else."

She took a sip. "Mm. It's good. Thank you."

Gabe's calm demeanor was appreciated. And Emily could see that he was an asset to *The Palace*. He was a nice-looking man, somewhere in his forties, Emily's height, with honey-blond hair a bit messy—in a boyish sort of way.

Emily took a sip of her cocktail—followed by another, and another. Before she knew it, she was filled with a delightful warmth, as if a ray of sunshine had draped a blanket of joy around her. Wine and champagne relaxed her, but this was something far beyond even that—like a simmering flame of excitement promising to make something wonderful happen.

A new tune played on the jukebox as the thin man walked over, put his drink on the counter, and stood at the chair next to her. She caught his gaze in the mirror and watched his reflection as he turned to her.

"I'm Erich," he said in a voice that sounded as if it came from a distance.

She looked at him directly, although he had already turned away for a drink. He wrapped his long fingers around the glass, lifted it with care, and took down a good fourth with surprising gusto.

"Hi Erich," she said, in the happiest voice she could assemble, hoping to make him comfortable. She wondered what he would think if he knew she had compared him to a bird.

He placed his drink on the counter, slipped onto the seat, and settled back.

"You're new here," he said, peeping at her.

"Yep, my second day. Well, actually my bird... mmy third."

He turned and met her gaze straight on. She noticed he seemed less broken all of a sudden and less nervous. She smiled at him—and why not—with all the drink pulsating through her veins and with someone as interesting and nonthreatening as the cute little man sitting beside her. It was downright exhilarating. She had to admit that right now this job didn't seem like much of a job at all. She was being paid to drink alcohol, which she seemed to do very well, and talk to strangers, which became easier by the minute. Easier for Erich too.

They were quite a pair, complete opposites, and yet in some ways alike as they filled themselves with drink and talked about nothing important—all the while, knowing where it would end.

Before Emily realized what happened, the delightful warmth from the alcohol was sweeping through her veins. A band had begun to play, couples were already dancing, and suddenly she was desperate to do something with all the energy the drink had given her. She looked at Erich who still reminded her of a bird, yet not so out of place anymore.

"You want to dance?" she asked him.

He gaped at her for a moment, set his drink down, and stood.

"Dancing is not my forte, but I'll give it a whirl."

He followed her onto the dance floor where he stood looking around seeming unsure how to begin. She nodded encouragingly as the tune carried into another song.

The rhythm turned up a notch. And Emily's inhibitions faded even more as passion took her to a place she had never been. Each note of music became like a pounding heartbeat vibrating into her every cell as she moved with the sounds of guitars and drum beats and a horn that wailed like someone in pain. With each chord, and haunting timbre, she felt her old self becoming more like someone new.

Across from her, Erich stood in one spot churning out a jerk while his feet moved in a sort of twist and scratch motion. She was amused by his style and loved his ambitious determination.

"You have an interesting rhythm," she told him as she moved to the beat of drums.

"Thank you," he said. "I've never done this before."

"Me either. Not with a band, at least."

They danced through another song and sat for a drink. She was ready to go back out, but Erich had other plans.

"You ready to go up?" he said boldly.

Everything changed at that moment, the passion and excitement—gone. For the last half hour, she thought they were building a friendship. Now with just a few words, she wondered if this innocent-looking man was as harmless as he seemed. She studied his face in the mirror. And no longer was she able to find warmth in those doleful eyes. She knew it was more about the shock of what she was about to do, and let the moment set in, finished her drink, and stood, wanting to get it over with.

"Let's go."

Why should she care that she was going upstairs with a man that reminded her of a humming bird. Or was it one of those plover stilts she had seen on the way to school. At this point, it made no difference. And to think she had considered herself worthy of someone like Michael.

She grabbed a glass of champagne off a tray as they walked across the room. No, she wasn't staggering, but she was close.

Erich stopped to exchange words at the council. And on the way upstairs, Emily tried to make light of the situation, hoping to convince herself that what was about to happen was not important, just part of life. The others seemed to enjoy themselves, why not her. And even better—this was at least ten steps above what she experienced with Claude. She should be thrilled.

Inside her room, she stepped out of her heels, turned on the lamp with dim lighting, finished her drink and set the glass on the chest. Trying not to look at Erich, she went to the bed, pulling the spread around her shoulders as she sat, and fumbled with a zipper. All the happier he was, the better off she would be.

A motion caught her attention. And when she looked at Erich, he was shirtless and pulling what looked like a whip from a pocket that followed the length of the seam in his pants. She gasped and moved away.

He stretched his arm out. "Go on, take it."

"No!"

"Take it," he said, stepping closer.

She clutched the covers, scooting down some more. "I think you should go."

"Take it. Please. It's what I want."

"Wh… what are you talking about?"

As he stepped closer, she reached over, grabbed the leather, and flung it on the floor. And with a firm yank, she pulled the covers off the bed and flew into the closet, heaving the tail end inside as she closed the door.

"Put your shirt on! And take that thing out of here!"

She waited for a few moments and cracked the door open. "Sorry Erich. It's just that—"

Her bedroom door closed. And she stuck her head out and looked around. When she knew he was gone, she pulled her clothes together, made the bed, and gathered her wits before going back down to finish the night.

Chapter Twenty-Five

In the midst of trials
difficult dealings, and
sometimes impossible *choices,*
whether love is real
or just infatuation,
even the heart may not know
what it longs for....

*E*mily slept until eight o'clock the next day, which didn't seem right, not after getting up between five and six a.m., and sometimes earlier most of her life. When she went down to breakfast, the kitchen was full.

Delilah, Angellee, Ginger, Blossom, and Felice were arguing between themselves about each other butting in on the other's business.

Their voices trailed off when Emily walked in.

"Well...." Delilah said when there was silence. "I think we can all agree on one thing."

She turned to Emily.

"So. We all think you should be the official dancer for *The Palace*.

Right, girls?"

Everyone put their differences aside and agreed wholeheartedly.

Toni had loaded pancakes onto a plate for Emily and she sat across from Delilah, pouring syrup.

"Are you guys serious?"

Delilah took a napkin and dabbed her mouth. "We all dance for the men now and then, but... Not like that. I mean, we don't actually have an official dancer. But I think we should. You put on quite a show last night."

"That's for sure," Felice chimed in. "And from the reaction, it's clear that you'd bring in customers just to see you dance."

"Where have you danced before?" Blossom asked. "You've got some moves I ain't never seen before."

Emily gave it some thought.

"Well, let's see. I've danced in the kitchen and living room, in my bedroom. And the barn a few times."

The girls laughed as if she were joking.

"It's true. But in the kitchen and living room mostly."

Ginger sat next to her with a cup of coffee. "You're really not a professional dancer?"

"No. I'm not. I've thought about it. But...."

She started to say, *not in a place like this*. And decided that even at *The Place*, dancing would be far better than the alternative. So, after breakfast, she went in to talk to Miss Bea.

"Some of the girls mentioned that I should be the official dancer."

"Official dancer? Where?"

"Here. In the lounge."

Miss Bea laughed. "Dance all you want. But if one of the men wants to take you up to your room, you go."

"Whipping too?"

"What?"

"Erich. He had a whip."

"Oh phew. Just a fetish. Have fun with it."

"No!"

Miss Bea came at Emily so fast she stepped back.

"Why do you think you're here!"

"Because you... You *tricked* me."

"Get out!"

"O-out of *The Palace*?"

"You know I should. But no. Out of my office. And do your job!"

Emily left, surprised that Miss Bea let her stay. Oh, how she wished to leave. But, for now, as crazy as it sounded, *The Palace* was her place of refuge. She went to her room and paced the floor, wondering if she could change Miss Bea's mind. Her conclusion was that since the girls believed in her dancing ability, why not Miss Bea.

She would start by working on dance moves then try them out in the lounge. If she was as good as the girls thought she was, something would come of it. Searching for the perfect radio station, she danced for three hours, working on a series of dance steps. It felt good and came natural to her. She had never thought of it in this way before, but it was exciting to realize that when she danced she was interpreting the music through her movements. That would be her goal. She would make the customers experience what she was feeling in her dance.

After finishing a vigorous routine, she sank to the couch to catch her breath. She thought it would take at least a week of hard work and planning to convince Miss Bea that her dancing would bring in customers. And she believed she could do it. She had to. Because thinking about bringing men up to her room made her stomach churn. Miss Bea and Delilah told her she would get used to it, but she didn't want to get used to it. She had been through enough with Claude. While she was preparing to leave the farm, getting away from that part of her life had been what drove her, and now here she was.

She closed her eyes, resting her head on the armrest, wondering if Samuel would have helped her if he was still alive. Maybe she wouldn't even be here if that was the case. She felt guilty for even considering that, thinking about his poor mother, and how she had practically hung up on her. To have one's child die had to be the worst thing that could happened to anyone. And it was clear that Mrs. Dimsmoore deserved an apology from her.

Satisfied with her dancing progress and feeling good that she decided to settle up with Samuel's mother, Emily went to the kitchen to find Toni.

"Hey, Toni, is there a phone I can use?"

"Well...yes. There's one in the maid's quarters."

She reached into her pocket for a key. "Here. It's just out the door down the hall to your right. The phone is on the counter in the entryway."

Emily opened the door to the maid's courters and found a room as lovely as hers. There was a nook to the right with a telephone sitting on top of a phone book. She looked up the number and dialed.

"Hello," came a voice at the other end.

"Hi. Um... I'm Emily. I called awhile back asking about... About your son... Samuel. I... I felt bad for cutting you off when you told me what happened, that––"

"Don't worry, dear. I felt bad for breaking down. I know how much that bothers others. But you see... I'm moving to my daughter's apartment, and there isn't enough room but for a few of my son's things. It's going to be difficult for me to get rid of...of...."

"I'm not meaning to upset you again, Ma'am."

There was a sniffing sound on the other end. "You didn't upset me. I... I break down at least twice a day whether I talk to anyone or not. In fact, your call was appreciated. Just hearing someone say Samuel's name does my heart good."

"Ooh, that's great. That sure is good to know."

"I'm just having a hard time giving up so many of my son's possessions. His bike, his games. He loved his games. And especially his books and his saxophone."

"I understand. I lost my mother when I was born. And though I didn't know her, it was hard for me to leave those few things that were once hers. Especially her books."

"Well, if you want books, Samuel left plenty behind. He loved to read."

"I do too. I love to read. What kind of books did he read?"

"You name it. Although his favorite books were by William Faulkner, Mark Twain, F. Scott Fitzgerald—"

"You said. Mark Twain?"

"Yes. He loved *The Adventures of Tom Sawyer* and *Huckleberry Finn, Tom Sawyer Abroad.* The whole series."

"That's *wonderful,* Mrs. Dimsmoore. I can't believe this. I have Mark Twain's first book and have wished so much to have the others. I'd be glad to pay you for them."

"I'll take no money. But I'd be happy to give them to you. To have someone enjoy them like Samuel did would please me very much. Give me your address and I'll send them to you."

"Oh, well. I... Can you hold on? I just moved here and—"

"I'll wait. Got nothing better to do...besides pack."

Emily rushed back to the kitchen hoping Miss Bea wasn't there. Not that receiving books would hurt her, but just to be ornery she would make a big deal out of it.

"Toni, I have a lady on the phone who wants to send me some books that belonged to... Well... Would you mind if I use your name as the receiver so Miss Bea won't make a fuss?"

"Certainly. Need the address?"

"Yes, please."

Toni opened a drawer, took out a pad, and scribbled down the information. "There you are."

Emily thanked Toni and hurried back to the phone.

"I've got the address Mrs. Dimsmoore."

"I'm ready."

Emily rattled off the address and asked her to send it to *Toni Haddow, in care of Miss Beatrice Rush.*

"Got it. I'll have these out to you real soon."

"Thank you. I promise I'll take care of Samuel's books and read them many, many times. And I'm sorry for...for what you've had to go through."

"Thank you, dear. I appreciate that."

After Emily hung up, she headed to her room feeling as if she didn't have a care in the world. That she brought the woman even a moment of relief from her suffering gave her more pleasure than she deserved. And to think she would receive all the Tom Sawyer and Huckleberry Finn series was beyond what she could have imagined.

Haven't you forgotten something? the voice of the tormenter came from out of the blue. *Remember Claude? Remember how you stabbed him through the heart. How about the police? You realize they could come for you at any moment.*

It was true, she hadn't thought about Claude for a while. Now to have the weight of what happened dropped on her again was more than she could handle. Especially after feeling such pure joy.

When she opened her bedroom door, Ricky Nelson was singing *Poor Little Fool*. She went to the chest, turned down the radio, and lay across the bed, bawling until her eyes puffed so much that she couldn't possibly make it to the lounge.

Emily heard some of the girls come up the stairs from their days excursion. And she knew what she had to do. Checking the hallway, she ran downstairs to catch Toni before she left.

"What happened to *you*?"

"I'd rather not talk about it right now. But can you please tell Miss Bea that I'm sick."

"Yes, I'll do that. Although you have to remember. Miss Bea won't fall for this again for a long while.

She's been distracted by something of late. And she may not notice if you don't show. But I'll make sure to let her know. So, go on up. I'll bring you something to eat before I leave."

"Thank you. Thank you, Toni. And I promise it won't happen again."

Emily gave Toni a quick hug then barreled upstairs before anyone saw her. Her spirits were lifted again. To have the whole night to herself, reading and dancing or doing whatever she pleased, with Toni's blessing, gave her hope again.

*T*he next night when Emily entered the lounge, a number of the girls were waiting on the *strip* for the night to begin. She exchanged hellos with them. But Layla, like usual, had a chip on her shoulder.

When Emily continued towards her favorite spot at the bar, Felice called to her.

"Wait up."

Emily picked a drink off a tray and kept walking as Felice came up beside her.

"Listen. Tonight's a big night for gambling. Big tippers. You know, if Miss Bea sees that we're bringing others into the game, we're rewarded, big time. Actually, she wanted me to fill you in. Interested?"

Emily stopped and looked back at the group. "Oh, really. Well, I'm not much of a card player. To tell you the truth, I've never played at all."

"You don't really have to play."

"Maybe some other time."

"Sure. Just let me know when."

Felice returned to the group and Emily headed to the bar. She noticed two men sitting at a table against the wall. The one on the left, caught her attention.

She took her usual seat and ordered a vodka sour. No more than five minutes later, one of the men from the table came over—the big one. She heard the other man call him Moose. She guessed that with his sparkling sea-blue eyes, chiseled face, and wavy hair the color of sweet marmalade, most would consider him handsome. For her taste, he looked too much like Claude.

He sat, swishing the ice in his cocktail as he glanced at her.

"My friends call me Moose."

"Mine call me Emily."

She knew he was watching her in the mirror as he took a drink.

He set his glass down and turned to her. "When I saw you on the dance floor the other night, I just knew it was meant to be."

Something about the tone in his voice took her aback. She didn't want to answer him, but she felt cornered.

"What was meant to be?"

"Us," he said. He pointed a finger at her then tapped it over his heart. "Us. I knew it the moment I saw you."

She smiled politely, picked up her drink, and finished it off.

Moose signaled for a round. "Hey Abe. Make them doubles."

He turned his stool so that he faced Emily and held her gaze. "I haven't felt a spark like this in a long time. You know what it feels like to... To be *bewitched* by someone?"

Something told her that Moose didn't really care about her feelings, or if she had ever been bewitched. But until she could figure a way out of this, she thought it was best to go along.

Abe came over with their cocktails, and she grabbed hers and took down half. When she set her

---

glass down, Moose turned her chair towards him and placed his hands on her thighs.

"I have this image of us together."

His voice was lower now and softer as if to convince her that they could share something great together.

"Would you like me to fill you in?"

"Okay." She swallowed. "If you like."

"Maybe we should go up to your room so we can discuss it in private."

No! Not ever. Not with him. No matter how gently he speaks to me. There was so much of him that reminded her of Claude that it was frightening.

"Another time. Tonight, well, I've got this problem."

The problem being…she didn't want to go up with him. This had worked with Claude several times.

Moose moved a hand to her chin, lifting her head so that she faced him directly.

"You promise."

This was not a request. And as sick as it made her, she nodded that she did.

"I'll hold you to it," he said, dropping his hand. He winked, squeezed her thigh, and sat back.

She swung her chair back to the counter.

He turned as well, took a drink and thought for a moment.

"Say… Your little *problem* won't keep you from giving Shayne and me a dance, will it?"

So…his friend's name is Shayne. He seemed so gentlemanly sitting over there quietly sipping his drink.

"I'll go check you out so you can dance your heart out. Make it official."

"Make what official?"

"I'll sign you out so you can dance all night if you want. But remember. You owe me."

Emily knew that at some point he would remind her. But for now, she was thrilled when Moose headed across the room, and even more so when Angellee latch onto him.

Smoke Gets In Your Eyes began to play on the jukebox. It made her think of Michael. She couldn't understand why she still yearned for him when he had taken her heart and crushed it like a bug.

"Abe, I'll have another, please."

She sipped her drink as she watched couples meander onto the dance floor. The room was filled with laughter and pleasant conversation. She noticed customers go to the council and leave with a girl, or other times they would take their chosen to the restaurant, the poker room, or sometimes to the dance floor. It seemed most everyone knew each other. Several men approached her. But she apologized saying that she was waiting for someone.

The man from the council took a walk around the room. His barrel chest and arms, the size of two men, reminded everyone why he was there. He patted several backs, strolled through the bar and back to the dining area for a meal. The council, along with a lot of other things, made sense to her now. If one of the customers wanted a girl kept in good standing, have her attention for an hour, or all night long, he would put up money. It seemed that for many, companionship was just as important as anything else.

By the time, Emily finished her drink and ordered another, the alcohol had done its job. Things were looking up. Moose had disappeared with Angellee, and he no longer existed as far as she was concerned.

She turned her barstool around and watched couples doing—what she knew was the *boogie-woogie* to *In the Mood*. There was an article or two and some photos she had seen, but they didn't compare to witnessing it in person. It was time to put her plan into action. And she got up and let the music lead her.

A number of the girls who lived outside *The Palace* had come in and danced on their own until they were joined by customers. One song after another, old and new, put everyone in high spirits. Emily danced with several men and made promises she hoped would be forgotten before returning to her seat to enjoy the music and broaden her knowledge of dance from the sidelines. The drinks kept coming, and it became impossible for her to sit still as a delightful burn began to sizzle through her veins like a wildfire.

When she couldn't hold back any longer, she slid off the stool again, letting the beat work its way into the grains of her flesh and take her where it pleased. She couldn't help but notice Shayne as she danced. When their eyes met, a stirring filled her with such pleasure that it was as if a bolt of lightning shot through her.

His smile was warm, and his deep brown eyes said *trust me* as he stood and walked towards her looking winsome with his dark hair slicked back and a silver chain clipped to his black velvet vest. She knew something beautiful was about to happen as he approached. He took her hand, pulled her close and begun to sway with her. They were like silhouettes in the moonlight, alone in their own world.

When the song ended, *Rockin' Good Way* began to play. And to her delight, Shayne kissed her full on the lips and stood back against a poll.

"Dance for me, darling, dance."

She danced for him as he looked on, his kiss lingering like the touch of a velvety rose petal. Her hips swayed, and her feet moved to the rhythm, with each glance saying, I want to know you more.

When the song finished, a slower melody began to play. He reached for her and pulled her into his arms. They moved further onto the dance floor. And she rested her head against his shoulder feeling safe for the first time in a long while.

"You dance with such passion," he said. "Where does that come from?"

She looked up at him. "The music." She smiled. "The drink. Both."

"What's your name?"

"Emily."

"I'm Shayne."

"I know."

He brushed a wisp of hair from her face. "Has anyone ever told you how very lovely you are?"

The sound of his voice and his breath against her cheek melted away every last drop of fear. They moved together as if they had danced before, gliding across the floor in perfect step. She was happy, oh so happy. Then for no reason, she felt sad to think this would end. For a moment, she imagined it was Michael's arms around her.

Shayne lifted her chin and wiped a tear away. Their eyes met and he bent to kiss her. The urgency in her need for him surprised her. She knew it was in part the drink, but she did...she did need him.

When the music stopped, he took her hand and swept her down the marble *strip,* stopping for a moment at the council. He slipped an arm around her shoulders, and they went up to her room.

Shayne loved her that night. She felt it in every fiber of her being that it was true—that he loved her. Because of that, nothing else mattered.

Chapter Twenty-Six

*B*efore Emily opened her eyes the next morning, Shayne was on her mind. She sat up and searched the room for him. He was gone. She noticed a pile of bills that he left on the nightstand. The money was a reminder that whatever happened between them, whatever feelings she had for him didn't matter. Shayne hadn't come to *The Palace* to find love.

She wanted to throw the covers over her head and sob, but she forced herself up and to the shower. When she returned to the room, she placed the bills in her pouch.

Even though she wasn't hungry, she cleaned her room, dressed, and went down to the kitchen, planning on a hearty breakfast. Toni had scolded her several times for not eating and she didn't want another reprimand from her. In truth, Toni's attention pleased her.

The woman gave her a good looking over when she walked in with several ta-tas before turning back to the stove.

"I'll bet you've lost five pounds since you got here, Emily. Soon you won't have the energy to climb the stairs."

Emily chuckled. "I've got plenty of energy, Toni. Haven't you heard?"

Toni raised an eyebrow. "You've given into the wilds, have yah?"

"Dancing, Toni... Dancing. I'd far rather dance than climb those stairs."

She picked up a plate letting Toni fill it with eggs, bacon, and toast.

"Sure, looks good."

"Good enough to clean your plate, I hope."

Emily took her breakfast up to her room, but when she picked up the fork, she had to force down every bite. When she took in all she could, she wrapped up the leftovers and hid them at the bottom of the garbage, putting the tray aside to take down later.

Her intention was to lay across the bed and enjoy a good read. But her mind kept wandering back to Shayne and all that had brought her to *The Palace*. The *what ifs* and *if onlys* kept coming until it became so painful she had to force herself out of her dark mood.

She closed her eyes and thought of a cool glass of drink waiting for her down in the lounge. Her mouth watered, imagining the potent mix of vodka, fruit, and sour sliding across her tongue, down her throat, and into her veins, where it would saturate every cell of her body and make her forget the calamities of her life. She pushed back the nudging of her aunt's words about the pitfalls of alcohol—because *surely* they didn't pertain to her.

That night she didn't make it to the bar area. Instead, she joined Delilah and Felice's party. The drinks came one after the other. Soon her troubles disappeared into a blur of frolic and laughter.

A number of men asked her to dance with them— and sometimes for them—which brought her tips that she stuffed inside her undergarments. As the night progressed, with the alcohol steaming inside her, each request for a trip to her room became an easily won contest as she beguiled her way out of having to go up with any of them.

When Miss Bea walked in, as she usually did at the end of the night, Emily made sure to satisfy any doubt that could arise about her productivity. And at just the right moment, with another fib and a promise, she found the perfect man who would take her up to her room and say goodnight outside her door. His name was Noah. He was a nice young man who came in with his friend, Walter.

Emily and Noah stood outside her room, whispering and giggling about the fun they had while she interjected apologies and excuses why he couldn't come inside. She watched him walk to the stairs, thinking what a sweet guy he was and wondering when her luck would run out.

*T*he next afternoon Emily was in the kitchen having a snack with Delilah when Miss Bea walked in. Instead of taking coffee to her office she came and sat with them.

"Well, Emily. Looks like you may've had a point about the dancing."

"That's good. Right?"

"Maybe. Maybe not. But… I've given it some thought. There've been several customers who've come to me. They think we should have a dancer at *The Palace* and insist that it be you. I've decided to give it a try.

"Not like those joints up town, though. I know that's what men like. But I refuse to lower *The Palace* to their standards. I've been thinking more along the line of the Geishas in Japan—only with an American twist. Of course, there'll be an extra cover charge on those nights. Even more for private dances. That's where I'll bring in professionals. The attic will be a good spot for that. It'll take time to schedule everything and, at the same time, scout for additional dancers. I know because I've considered doing this for a while and even checked around for the right girls. I think this is the right time.

"So… What do you think, Emily? Do you have what it takes to be our first official dancer?"

"Yes. I think I do."

"Okay. I'll tell you what. To start with, you can dance three nights a week. But those other two nights, it's business as usual. You hear?"

"Yes, Miss Bea."

"That means you dance Tuesday through Thursday until half an hour before closing. Then you sit with the customers until they leave. Make friends for Friday and Saturday nights."

Emily nodded, excited about those three nights. And at the same time, dreading Friday and Saturday nights.

"You'll start this Tuesday," Miss Bea continued. "We'll go into town on Monday and pick up a few more outfits. Since you'll be on stage, I'd like you to have a variety of clothes that will suit your title. I've already talked to a shop who's working on this as we speak. Also, I'm having someone build a stage. I'll put one of the waiters in charge of the music."

"I don't know what to say Miss Bea—"

"We'll see how it goes. I'll try you out for a few months."

When Miss Bea and Delilah left, Emily brought the dishes to the sink, put an arm around Toni and gave her a squeeze.

"I really do appreciate you...you know?"

"I do."

With another squeeze, she left to prepare for the evening.

*E*mily stood at the mirror in her closet, pulled her hair up and clipped it into place. It made her look older and sophisticated. Miss Bea had said she wanted to keep the place classy.

It was Saturday night. That meant this was her last night of empty promises and frivolous conversation before she became the first official dancer at *The Palace*. She wondered if Shayne would come in.

When she went downstairs, word had gotten around that she had a new role. She didn't make it back to the bar again and instead sat with Ginger and James.

"Emily, have you met James?"

"Yes. My first night here."

James reached over and placed a hand over hers. "I just heard the news. I think it'll be good for *The Palace*. Congratulations."

James was professional. He was light-hearted and levelheaded. It seemed that if Emily needed someone to count on, it would be him.

Just when things were looking up for her, Noah and Walter walked in.

"Nice to see you," Noah said as the two men sat. He motioned for a waiter and turned back to Emily.

"Ready for another?"

She pushed her empty glass aside. "Sure. Thank you."

Like James, Noah was a gentleman. Emily liked him, but she had no desire to take him to her room. Even as attracted to Shayne as she was, without the drink, she doubted she would have even gone up with him so willingly. As it was, she was afraid it was time to resign herself to her duties. She picked up her vodka knowing she would put Noah off for as long as possible. It took some ingenuity. And eventually, he started a dice game with Walter, and Charrette, who was a girl from outside *The Palace*.

When Shayne walk in, a burst of joy nearly had Emily running to greet him until Moose strolled in right behind him. She felt like a sitting duck but Angellee and Layla saved the night and slipped over to join the men.

The four walked by the table, and Shayne looked down at Emily and smiled. To her relief, Moose was busy talking and didn't notice her as the group took a seat near the bar.

When Noah set the dice aside and moved closer to Emily, her desire for Shayne made it even more difficult.

"I-I was just thinking that I, um... I need to practice my dance moves."

By a miracle—twice over—Noah graciously took her out on the floor. She realized that he loved to dance which made it easier on her. When there was a song change James asked her to dance. As they walked back to their seats, he asked for a private meeting—his way of asking to go up to her room.

"Oh... Uh.... I-I would love to. But...you see." She nodded at Noah, who was dancing with Charrette. "He and I are...well, you know."

"Sure. I understand. I'll just have to make a point to find you first next time, won't I."

"Don't forget. Starting on Tuesday, I'll be dancing three nights a week."

"And what a pleasure that will be."

She felt bad for lying to him. But if excuses counted for something, she would plead that it was for her well-being. If that wasn't in place, she wouldn't be of any good even to Miss Bea.

Emily had been forcing herself not to look at the table where Shayne sat—partly because she was afraid of what she would see. And also because she feared inadvertently catching Moose looking at her. Eventually she gave in and was shocked to see they were all gone. It bothered her that Shayne chose Layla over her. Who knows how long they would be gone. She turned in hopes of grabbing a waiter for another drink. That's when Shayne walked up.

"Hello, Darling," he said as he approached.

"Shayne."

"My, young lady, you look…*gorgeous*. Would you like to dance?"

He didn't wait for a reply. Instead, he took her hand and led her to the dance floor, pulling her into his arms.

"I missed you," he whispered, kissing her on the cheek.

"Me too. I thought you left."

"Never. Not without seeing you first. We went to the game room. Moose and Angellee are addicted to poker. It seems to be a big thing around here."

"Did he notice me?"

"You mean, Moose?"

"Yeah."

"I don't think so. You know, Angellee is crazy about him."

"I had no idea."

The song ended, and Shayne took her to the table where she first saw him and signaled for drinks. She decided that from now on, this would be their table.

He placed an arm around her and took her hand. "I couldn't stop thinking about you."

"Same here.

"Oh, by the way. Did you hear the news? I'm going to be *The Palace* dancer every Tuesday, Wednesday, and Thursday nights. See over there. They're already building a stage."

"No kidding. Huh. I shouldn't be surprised, though. I've seen you dance." He smiled and gave her shoulder a squeeze.

When their drinks came, they caught up on the last few nights. She noticed he seemed reserved about his personal life. But he began to question her about her future plans.

"What I'm getting at is… How long do you intend to work here?"

"My thoughts are that if I stick around for a year or so, that I'll be able to pay for college. I'd like to be a teacher one day."

"Wow. I'm even more impressed by you. Although I hope you won't have to stay that long."

"Me too."

He gazed at her in thought.

"Soo… Are you ready to go up?"

She glanced at the table where she left Ginger, James, Noah, and the others. When she saw that everyone was gone, she nodded. "I'm ready."

He took her hand as they left, stopping for a moment at the council before going upstairs.

She turned on the soothing lamp, switched on music, and found a song they could slow dance to. He went to her, took her in his arms, and they danced for some time. He kissed her and told her how much he enjoyed being with her. Although he never asked for more. That surprised her. He was so different from Moose.

"Emily. I know we just met. But I care about you. A lot."

He pulled her closer and they danced a while longer then lay across the bed, listened to music, and talked. Emily longed to tell him about Claude, but she knew this wasn't the time. She told him a little about living on the farm, about Haity, and even a little about Daniel, and some about her mother, and her grandmother too. She managed to skirt around everything else.

He went on to tell her that he had probably been far too spoiled when he was younger, chased by girls and later on by women. And that he had made some wrong decisions in his life but coming here and meeting her was a pleasant surprise.

The Palace customers were supposed to be out by two-thirty in the morning. But before Emily knew it, she awoke Sunday morning lying next to Shayne. He was up on an elbow watching her sleep. When she opened her eyes, he tenderly brushed back her hair.

"Good morning."

"Morning."

"I apologize for staring. I couldn't help myself."

"You and my grandmother."

He laughed. "I'm in good company then."

"Hope I didn't snore."

"Nope...you purred like a kitten."

"Did you get some sleep?"

"I did. But I've been awake for a while, thinking."

"Thinking...about what?"

"Mostly about how much I care about you."

She rolled onto her side and ran her fingers across his chin. "I'm glad. And thank you for last night...for talking. I needed that."

"No need to thank me.

"You know, Emily. While you were sleeping I came up with a plan."

"What exactly does that mean?"

"Ok...so... I've decided that I'll be here at opening on Friday and Saturday and make sure you're free for those nights."

"Both nights? But that's *ten* hours. Shayne, that'll cost you—"

"Don't worry. I'll manage.

You realize that they make most of their money on the gambling, don't you? The girls are important too, but they're also a hook."

"I never thought about that. Still... Are you sure?"

"Yes. I'm positive. I've thought it through."

"I don't know what to say. I... Thank you."

He nodded towards the window. "I noticed the sun is rising. I'd better get going."

"Make sure to go out the side door and through the south exit. And don't forget to come back."

"Never."

He kissed her and slipped out of her bed, stepped into his shoes, and left.

Chapter Twenty-Seven

*O*n Monday morning, Miss Bea took Emily shopping for dancing clothes that turned out to be more like costumes. There was one with fringe, one made of blue satin, a flapper dress from the 1920s, and another with tassels. But Emily's favorite was a gold dress with sparkling sequin.

As she tried them on, and waited for some adjustments, it would have seemed by the conversations she had with Miss Bea, that the two were good friends. She had felt this with some of the others as well, but always came to her senses before saying too much. It was hard to hold in the feelings she had for Shayne. But she had learned to trust her inner voice—the good one, at least.

After returning to *The Palace*, Emily was walking upstairs when something came over her. It was time to visit the attic. She stopped at the landing and looked back down before taking the stairs to the third floor. At the top was the door leading to the outside. To the left was a short hallway and entryway. She let herself in and gazed upon a luxurious open space.

There was a vaulted ceiling and three skylights, hardwood flooring, and a rock fireplace across the room. The seating and surrounding paraphernalia was more casual than the lounge, but it was beautiful. There was a dance area to the left. Beyond that was a bar, and further down, an elaborate music center with a jukebox. There were a number of exits that were obviously private areas for customers.

Closing the door, she walked to the jukebox, picked up a handful of coins that sat to the side, and inserted them into a slot. When *Jailhouse Rock* began to play, she slipped off her shoes, and on that shiny hardwood

275

floor, with sunshine filtering through the skylights, she danced her heart out.

When she needed a rest, she took a soda from the bar, went to the back window, and looked out over the immaculate yard that was a pleasure to behold.

As grand as the lounge was, there was something about the additional space in the loft, with sunlight bursting through the roof, that made her feel safe and gave her a feeling of freedom.

As long as she came up in the mornings, or early afternoons, it was unlikely she would run into anyone. This would be her personal space for preparing her dances, enjoying the view out the back window as she contemplated her future and tried to put her past on hold. That wasn't always possible, and there were still times when she became overwhelmed with guilt over what happened with Claude. But those moments were becoming less frequent and short-lived.

She wanted to believe that with time things would work out. And she saw hope beyond *The Palace.* Maybe not the next day or week, or even months from then—if things didn't work out with Shayne—but at some point, she believed there was a good life waiting for her and that *The Palace,* with all of its flaws, was but a stop on her way to somewhere else.

*T*uesday was her first night as an official dancer. Even though she was excited, it was intimidating to have the spotlight put on her.

Wearing the gold dress didn't take away her nerves, but it helped. And as she wandered back to the bar and took a seat, she realized that showing up early helped too.

Abe was waiting for her. "Big night."

"Yep. Need a tall one."

He laughed, setting a glass in front of her. "I figured that when I saw you come over."

Abe went back to preparation, and she took four good drinks, enough to feel the excitement spin through her. Until that moment, she didn't realize just how much she depended on that lift.

One of the waiters went to the jukebox. And it was time to take stage. When *Great Balls of Fire* began to play, Emily slid off her stool and ran onto the stage. Closing her eyes, she waited for the beat to work its way in. She envisioned herself, as a child, tapping her feet on the kitchen floor, swinging her shoulders and hips while her grandmother cheered her on. Only then did she begin her first dance.

She expected that with the infectious beat, most would dance or go about their business with extra vigor, but nobody moved. Instead, they stood or sat where they were. When the song ended, there was a standing ovation. She was taken aback by the hoopla. Although she had to admit it gave her confidence.

Shayne wasn't supposed to be there until Friday, but halfway through her second dance, she saw him sitting at their table. She was in awe of how everything had come together far better than she could have imagined. How could she have known, as she danced for her grandmother so long ago, that one day something that came naturally and unintentionally to her, would be a blessing in disguise.

Later, she walked out into the backyard with Shayne.

"You're quite a dancer, Emily. You're really good."

"Thank you. I sure was surprised to see you."

"I wanted to be here for your first night. And also, to reassure you that I'd be here on Friday and Saturday."

"I still can't believe what you're doing for me."

"Well…it's for me too."

"For you?"

"Yes, for you and me.

"You see... I've never felt this way before. Not ever. And I...um. I've come to realize that I'm falling in love with you."

Emily stopped and looked up at him wondering if the excitement of an older man, at least in his late twenties, was what drew her to him? No one could deny that Shayne was exceptionally handsome. He was kind and considerate, which was a must for her. Maybe her feelings for him were also because she had never known anyone like him, someone who, in the most innocent of ways, was irresistibly suave with a swag that turned heads.

She wondered if this was it—that this is how falling in love happens—even with something as outlandish as a man coming into a brothel on a whim and finding a desperate young woman who makes him feel something he has never felt before.

"Wait right here."

She walked to the door and looked back.

"Don't move," she said, and disappeared inside.

When she returned with blankets, Shayne chuckled.

"What's this?"

"Follow me."

He slipped an arm around her shoulders and they took a shortcut across the lawn to a tree just beyond the fountain. She handed him one of the blankets, and he spread it on the grass while she set the other aside for cover. He sat, pulling her into his arms as he lay back, kissing the top of her head.

"I meant what I said. I'm falling in love with you."

"I think I'm falling for you too. But...."

Even though she was nervous, she had to tell him about Claude. If her confession caused her to lose him, she would rather it be sooner than later after she had fallen in love with him. Besides, she couldn't keep the horrible secret to herself any longer. If she didn't talk to someone about it, she would end up rattling the details off to the wrong person. She had already come close.

"I have to tell you something."

He looked surprise. "Of course.

"It sounds serious."

"It is. I mean... You may walk away."

"Oh, I doubt that."

She sat up and pulled the extra blanket around her. He rose up on an elbow and took her hand as she told him the story of Claude. She stopped at times to take a breath and wipe away tears. Shayne sat up at one point, took her in his arms and let her cry, telling her that everything would be okay.

"To see Claude lying there was a nightmare. I didn't realize at the time that I was in shock.

"One day I'll turn myself in, but.... I panicked. And I left. I just left."

"Of course, you had to leave! After what you'd already been through? You know...you could've fallen apart and just let things happen. But you took a stand for yourself. I think you were brave for doing that. And I'm telling you, Emily. I don't think you should turn yourself in. You did nothing wrong. That horrible man dragged you up to the loft to rape you. He threw you on the floor and kicked you. And he threatened to kill you. See? You're not the criminal. He was. Do you understand what I'm saying?"

"Yes."

"Put it out of your mind. If Claude were alive, he would be the one in jail."

"But... Shouldn't I go... Shouldn't I at least tell the police what happened?"

"No. Why would you put yourself through that? You've already been through enough. If you go to the police, even if they believe you're innocent, they'll be forced to arrest you. And this is the worst part. There'll be some jerk lawyer who will try to turn everything around and make it your fault. You could spend years in jail out of a lie."

"Oh."

"No one in their right mind would expect you to turn yourself in so that you can be abused again."

Shayne's reasoning as to why she shouldn't turn herself in made sense. It was all true. And it felt right to put her trust in him.

*E*mily put on the blue satin dress with heels that matched—heels she would probably kick off once she started to dance. She checked her makeup, put her hair into a ponytail with tendrils hanging on each side, and walked downstairs. Miss Bea's office door was open and she called Emily in.

"I see you've been using the attic."

"Yes. To practice my routines. I hope that's okay."

"It's probably a good idea. I was just thinking that it might do you good to fly down to Los Angeles at some point and see some real dancers, take some lessons. And learn a few tricks."

"Of course."

"I'm flying down later today and interviewing several seasoned dancers. Oh, and Emily. Find a way to properly get off stage and do a slow dance with at least one customer at the end of each night. I see you've done some fast dances, but you need to love it up a bit."

"Sure. I can do that."

"Well. I'd hope so.

"Just to let you know. Someone brought me a new release yesterday called *Poetry in Motion*. I want you to begin each night with that song. Also, it'll be used as your closing number. I had someone put a record in each of the jukeboxes."

When Emily walked into the lounge, there were more customers than usual for this time of the evening. She greeted a few of them as she headed back. When she saw Erich sitting with Charrette in the alcove area down from the restaurant, she hesitated for a moment before finding her step again. She waved and continued on, relieved when he nodded and smiled back.

"Hi, Abe," she said as she slipped onto a bar stool and watched him fix her drink.

"Hey...how's it going?"

"So far, better than I expected."

"You know, you've become quite the attraction around here," he said, setting her drink on the bar counter and nodding at a table next to the stage.

She glanced back. "A couple of men."

"Three. They're here to see you."

"Thanks for putting on the pressure," she teased.

A waiter came for a tray of champagne and Abe turned away. Emily sipped her drink already feeling the heat beneath her collar. She sensed someone beside her and looked in the mirror. Moose was standing next to her. A chill rippled across her shoulders as she watched him sit.

"Well...well... Here we are at last."

"Hi Moose."

"So... You've been one busy girl."

"You know how I love to dance."

"Yes, I do."

Abe walked over and Moose signaled for the usual.

"When you finish dancing tonight, I think it's time we head up to your room."

"I... I can't. I mean. I'm off at two and that's it. I'm done for the night."

Abe brought Moose his drink. He chugged a good portion and turned to her.

"You haven't forgotten your promise, have you?"

"No. No I haven't. But you see... Shayne and I are... Well... We're together."

"You and Shayne. *Together.*"

"Mhmm. It just...happened, out of the blue."

"But you're still here. *Working.*"

Moose laughed. "Shayne, the impulsive dreamer. Shayne, the fickle, yellow belly."

He laughed again, finished his cocktail and set the glass aside.

"You still owe me."

He *had* paid *The Palace* in order for her to dance one whole night. She wondered if she should offer to pay back the money, but she knew that money was no object to him.

She was about to ask him anyway when she noticed Angellee heading over. With everything she was made of, she hoped that would make him happy.

"Hey, Moose," Angellee said, coming up beside him.

"Ready to go?"

She put an arm around him and leaned over. "Hi, Emily. Another night of dance, hey?"

"Yep."

Emily expected Moose to balk and insist on disrupting the good she had begun. Instead, he stood, finished his drink and turned to her.

"Well... Good luck."

He set his glass aside, put an arm around Angellee, and left.

Emily watched them disappear around the corner. She was in shock and so relieved she couldn't help but to laugh.

Miss Bea was talking to the council, probably setting rules before her trip. As upsetting as she could be, it was clear that her strong hand and well-structured business made sure the men treated the girls with respect. Apparently even Moose.

The waiter who took care of the music, put coins in the jukebox. When *Poetry in Motion* began to play, Emily slid off the stool and bolted up the steps. All it took was a slow walk across the stage for her to get the rhythm of the new song.

Later, she was doing her routine to a song called *Lollipop* when she noticed Erich and Charrette leave. She wondered if it was a fluke that he had even gone up with her that night. Charrette was smaller than Erich. This made Emily feel better. It gave him a fighting chance.

As she contemplated what was about to take place upstairs, she messed up. And the lollipop she used for a prop became stuck to her hair. She kept dancing while wrestling with the sucker as if it were part of the act. It ended with laughter and someone giving her a ten-dollar bill for the lollipop.

*E*ach time Emily went up to the loft, she followed the same routine. When she finished dancing, she would take a cool drink to the back window.

Everything seemed to be going well between her and Shayne, but she was still troubled by the comments that Moose made when he said Shayne was fickle and that he was a dreamer. She wondered what he meant by yellow belly.

Even before Moose's outburst, it had crossed her mind that if Shayne was able to pay two full nights a week for her services, why wouldn't he at least suggest a plan to get her a place of her own. Not that she was even sure she should leave at the moment. It was just that if he had really fallen in love with her, that would seem the natural thing to do. As much as she cared about and appreciated him, something didn't seem right. She hoped she hadn't made a mistake by telling him about Claude.

Emily thought about the bad decisions she made in her life. And now trying to get it right, she decided it would be best that once she was free of *The Palace*—and if things didn't work out with Shayne—she should be careful not to jump into another relationship. After falling for Michael so fast, she wondered how it was possible that she was having such strong feelings towards Shayne. Maybe she was the fickle one.

That night, Moose walked in while Emily danced on stage. *The Palace* had been closed for two days, and she shouldn't have been surprised to see him. Maybe it was just that she was disappointed. It wouldn't have bothered her so much if he hadn't sat in front along the strip. She tried to ignore him, but her gaze kept drifting to where he sat.

Thinking about talking to Moose filled her with dread. But she wanted to ask him what he meant when he said Shayne was fickle. If he meant she couldn't trust Shayne's feelings, that worried her. Being a yellow-belly didn't sound too good either. The dreamer part could mean a lot of things.

Needing answers, she had already geared herself up to have a chat with him when she noticed he was gone. Twice now, he had walked away. Maybe it was true, and he had given up on her.

<><><>

*E*mily gave in and took the bus to a movie with Ginger and Felice to see *The Apartment*, a movie with Jack Lemmon and Shirley MacLaine about a man so determined to move up the ladder at his place of employment, he allows his bosses to use his apartment for their selfish philandering's. Both Jack and Shirley, in their parts as Bud and Fran, allow others to control their lives until they fall for each other.

It was refreshing to become lost in someone else's troubles for a while. After how unraveled Bud and Fran's lives had been, Emily was elated by the ending and how they escaped their misery and found something remarkable in each other.

After the movie, the girls went to Fishermen's Wharf, ate seafood and went to several shops. As they looked around and bought a few things here and there, Ginger and Felice never talked about their personal lives, never asked Emily about hers, and seemed completely satisfied to be working at *The Palace*.

Emily wondered if that's the way they saw her too. And she found herself, like other times before, longing for something more. The scary part was that if they had dug into her past she may have told them things she would have wished to take back.

On the way home, she sat on the bus thinking about Haity and missing her more than she had in a long time. For whatever reason, she wanted to tell the girls about her best friend. But she knew their reaction could, and likely would, minimize the beauty of their friendship.

*S*hayne surprised Emily again and showed up on an off night. He looked handsome walking up the strip with a swagger and grin that threatened to melt her heart. But she had to be strong and think about her future and not how endearing and handsome he was. She had to ask the questions that had been eating at her.

At the end of the evening, although she was supposed to spend the last half hour talking to customers, she took Shayne up to her room. She kept her distance, wanting him to know that something was troubling her. When he sat on the couch, she took a seat at the furthest end.

"Shayne. I need to ask you something."

"I figured that."

She wasn't even sure where it came from. It was just something she needed to know.

"What exactly is your relationship with Moose?"

"W-well.... He... He's my brother in-law."

"So. He's married to your sister."

"No... He and I are married to sisters."

".... You're *married*!"

"Yes. But we're getting a divorce. I-I'm living with my parents for the time being... Until everything's settled. And I...."

Emily got up and walked to the window, seeing his car parked in his favorite spot next to the cypress tree.

"Is that why you came to *The Palace*? To get away from...her?"

She turned and walked to where he sat. "How long have you been coming here, anyway?"

"Since that first night you saw me. I came because Moose brought me. I had no plans of doing anything or even returning. Until I met you."

"But you're... *Married*!"

"A lot of men that come in are married."

She paced in front of the couch, stopping to face him again. "I don't know what to think. After everything I've told you about myself. I was so sure I could trust you. And I told you some very personal things. But you didn't even bother to tell me you're *married*!"

He bolted off the couch and slipped his hands on her shoulders. She took both of his hands and placed them at his side.

"I was just thinking the other day that you say you're falling in love me. But why wouldn't you use that money your spending on the week-ends to help me out of here?"

"I...um... Well... You see... It's more complicated than it looks. And you seem happy to be here. I thought you wanted to stay for a while and dance. You're so good. And you love it."

"That's not the point. Why didn't you tell me you were married? After *everything* I confessed to you!"

Looking at him, she didn't feel anything but anger.

"I know, I know. I should've told you. I'm sorry."

"There are white lies and there is deception against those you're supposed to love."

She raised two fingers. "Two different things. You deceived me."

He looked dumfounded...and guilty.

"You may as well leave."

"Are you serious? I admit I haven't been upfront with you. But...."

He looked at her, shook his head, seeming to choke back tears. And his eyes welled as he turned and walked out.

She started after him but let him go.

Lowering to a chair, she moaned and laid her head on the table. It happened so fast and she had reacted with shock and anger. She wasn't even sure she had done the right thing. She sat up and looked out the window as his car drove away. *Well...it's over now and that's that.* What bothered her almost as much as him not telling her he was married was that he had walked out without trying to defend himself.

<><><>

*T*hursday morning, Emily knew she had made a mistake. She missed Shayne and didn't know why his being married had upset her so much. He would be divorced soon. Not only that, but her burst of anger because he hadn't offered to help her get a place of her own was uncalled for. It's not as if they hadn't talked about her leaving. And if he had money to help her get away from *The Palace*, he wouldn't be living with his parents. He was probably spending his last dime on her as it was.

If losing Shayne wasn't bad enough, she had to figure out how she would get through Friday and Saturday nights fighting off those who were waiting to collect on her promises. It looked as though her time was up.

Feeling discouraged, she went down to the kitchen in hopes of talking to Toni.

"What're you up to today, young lady?"

"Oh, just practicing routines in the attic."

Emily poured coffee and took a cookie off a tray.

"It's working out well for you. And I hear Miss Bea is already arranging to bring on more dancers."

"It'll take the pressure off me."

"From what I hear. You shouldn't worry."

"Tell that to Miss Bea."

"She on your case again?"

"Mm. A little."

"Just ignore her and keep up what you're doing. It'll work out in the end.

"Uh. Hang on a minute, Emily. I got something that may just brighten your day."

Toni left and returned with a box, setting it on the table.

"Oh, Toni, it's my books. I can't believe it. Thank you."

"I thought you could use a lift. You okay?"

"I'll be fine. It's just that... I told you about Shayne. I probably said some things to him that I shouldn't have."

"The way I see it. If he cares about you, a few reckless words won't keep him away for long."

"I told him to leave. That it was over."

"I see. Well, just remember. If something is meant to be it'll happen. If not, you're better off."

Emily took the box up to her closet, pried it open, and pulled out the second book in the Mark Twain series, *The Adventures of Huckleberry Finn*. Her first inclination was to immediately devour it. But duty called and she set the book on the nightstand and went up to the attic to work on a routine for the new song.

*O*n any other night, Thursday would be a lift for Emily because she knew the next two nights would have been spent with Shayne. She went down to the lounge trying to think positive. Dancing brought her joy. She couldn't deny that. It's what would come after her last dance each Thursday night that troubled her—Friday and Saturday nights without Shayne. She missed him. And she had no idea what would happen to her once Miss Bea found out that she hadn't been doing her job and had also been lying to the customers.

Delilah was at the bar looking at some photos strewn across the counter. Emily nodded at Gabe and he started on her drink.

"You oughta see these," Delilah said, waving her over.

Emily looked down at photos of herself on stage.

"Where'd you get these?"

"I took them," Gabe said coming with her drink. He set her glass on a coaster and picked up two of the photos.

"Thought I'd put them up here." He found a spot on a shelf with mirrors as backdrop.

"Nice. Don't you think?"

"Yeah, I do."

In all of the years since her grandmother died, except for a school photo, which she never got, this was the first time she had seen a photo of herself over six-years old.

"Hey Gabe? Mind if I have one?"

"Not at all. Take a couple."

"Here." She handed him two photos. "Save these for me, please."

Emily heard coins drop in the jukebox. She took two gulps of her drink and ran up on stage as *Poetry in Motion* started to play. She began a new routine by facing the wall, head back resting in her hands. Just at the right moment she moved across the stage swaying to the beat.

Most everyone took to the floor as the next song played. Some stood next to their seats to join in. Even Gabe was moving to *The Twist*. When the song ended, he brought Emily a fancy towel and a drink. She wiped her forehead and placed the towel with her props. Lifting the glass to Gabe, she took an invigorating drink and waited for that spark of electricity.

The night would end soon and it was time for her to dance with a customer. A song called *All in the Game* began to play. She walked back across the stage and set her gaze out for the right man to slow dance with as the song began....

Many a tear has to fall
but it's all in the game
all in the wonderful game
that we know as love.
You have words with him
and your future's looking dim
but these things
your hearts can rise above...

Her gaze dropped to the table where she first met Shayne. He stood and walked towards her. She took the steps down from the stage as he approached and placed a rose in her hair before taking her in his arms....

Soon he'll be there at your side
with a sweet bouquet.
And he'll kiss your lips,
and caress your waiting finger tips,
and your hearts will fly away....

As the song ended, he laid her back and kissed her. She was on her feet before she could catch her breath. And he disappeared into the crowd. She pranced back on stage, stood facing the wall still feeling the fire of his lips—head back resting on her hands the way she always began *Poetry in Motion....*

When I see my baby
what do I see, poetry
poetry in motion.
Poetry in motion
walking by my side
her lovely locomotion....

Hips swaying, arms reaching, fingers caressing the flower in her hair, strong legs striding across the stage bending to give her hand to a customer. When he wouldn't let go, she used her other hand to lift his...twisting her legs and hips as she stood straight, swaying again to the beat.

◇◇◇

*W*hen the song ended, all she could think about was that she needed to find Shayne. She had fallen in love with him. How could she not. He had been there for her when she needed someone—even on the nights he hadn't planned to come in.

She took the steps off the stage, moving swiftly across the dance floor, and down the *strip*, accepting money from customers, thanking them for their compliments.

Most everyone was down from the upstairs and poker room by now and it was a challenge getting through. Her hope was to get out before someone asked her to sit and have a drink. She zipped past Miss Bea. And if looks could kill, she would be dead, but there was no time to chat. Shayne was waiting for her.

She rushed out the door, up the hallway, glancing into the gathering room as she started up the steps. When she heard a tap at the window, she looked around the banister and saw Shayne smiling up at her. She hurried down as he opened the door.

"I can't believe you're here. What's going on?"

He took her hand and pulled her outside.

"Something good," he said closing the door behind her. "At least I hope you think so."

He put an arm around her, kissing her as they headed up the sidewalk.

"An hour ago, I was feeling downright lost without you. And I made a decision."

At the fountain, with the water cascading over the rocks and into the pond, he pulled her around so that she faced him.

"Emily," he said, brushing a wisp of her hair aside.

"Something came over me. And I knew I had to come."

He moved his arms from around her shoulders, took her hands in his, and got on one knee.

"I never expected to find love like this. But I did... That first night I saw you. Remember?"

Emily nodded, tears streaming down her cheeks.

"When the time was right, I had planned to take you to a fancy dinner…out of town, somewhere romantic and private. But you woke me up the other night. And, no, you shouldn't have to live in a place like this."

He looked around. "It's absolutely gorgeous, better than most, if not all the others. But it's not for you. You deserve better.

"I'll get you an apartment as soon as I can. Until then, you can stay with my parents. I'd take you there tonight. But…I need to talk to them first. You do understand, don't you?"

Emily nodded. "Yes, of course."

"So…get your stuff packed. Have Miss Bea write you out a check. And I'll pick you up tomorrow, at three.

"Listen Emily… What I'm trying to say is that I want you to stop working here. I want you to be my wife.

"Will you marry me?"

She opened her mouth, but nothing came out.

"I know… I know it's on the spur. And I still have to take care of... Well—"

"Yes. I will. I'll marry you."

"I don't have a ring yet." He stood, still holding her hands. "We'll shop for one together so you can have exactly what you want."

She wondered if this was how her grandparents felt when they first fell in love only miles from here.

"Emily. My darling. My fiancé. I love you."

He bent to kiss her, then lifted her into his arms and carried her to the tree where the light from the fountain lit the area just enough to make a romantic setting. There was a blanket on the ground and a basket.

"Just some stuff I picked up at the market on the way over." He chuckled. "The blanket is off my parent's car seat."

"Oh, Shayne. This is so... I don't know. So, you... So *rustically romantic.*"

He kissed her as he placed her feet on the ground. She sank to the blanket and watched him kneel and unpack the basket of snacks.

Emily realized that *The Palace* may not be the ideal place for her to become betrothed. But nothing in her life had been ideal—for heaven's sake, she had shoveled manicure, and helped butcher pigs. And she may not have a father to walk her up the aisle. But Shayne was a good man. He was decent and kind, thoughtful and loving. What more could a woman want out of life.

So, this is why she came to San Francisco. For Shayne. To become Mrs. Shayne La Cauve.

About the author

Kathleen lives in Washington State. She began her writing career some thirty years ago when she learned guitar, just enough, to play the songs she wrote to help her get through the long winter nights in North Dakota.

Book III of the September Wind series will be out in 2024. Poems of Glass is a collection of thirty-five years of her poetry and prose. Knapsack Journey Home is a book she wrote about the loss of her middle son. Scrooge and the Romance Effect is a book of short stories that will tickle your funny bone and take you back to your first love. She has several stories and books in the works.

Website:
https://kathleenjanzanderson.com

Songs used at *The Palace* by permission ~

It's All in the Game: Artist Tommy Edwards (1958)
Lyrics by Carl Sigman
Music by Charles Gates Dawes
Reprinted by Permission of Hal Leonard LLC

Poetry in Motion: Artist Johnny Tilloston (1960)
Lyric and Music by Paul Kaufman and Mike Anthony
Reprinted by Permission of Hal Leonard LCC

www.ingramcontent.com/pod-product-compliance
Lightning Source LLC
Chambersburg PA
CBHW061943170626
46813CB00006B/2521